I knew they were coming, but the question was what to do about it…

"I'm not going anywhere until you bring me the winged woman," the suit demanded.

Forks dropped all around the table as the elders stared at him in shock.

"Winged woman?" some of the men asked each other as if they'd never heard of such a thing.

"Do you mean that you're searching for a woman—" My grandfather paused to chuckle. "—with *wings*?"

Roars of laughter erupted throughout the room.

"And you think *we* know of such a…an anomaly? Such an absurdity?" Grandfather laughed again. "We are not Christians here. We don't even believe in such things."

"How absurd!" Red Elk managed to say between fits of very convincing staged laughter.

The man in the suit turned bright red and started to shake. I could not tell if it was in anger or embarrassment. He stomped out of the house and gathered his soldiers from my yard.

"They are denying her existence," he informed them. "They won't give her up, so we will wait for her."

"How long?" one of the armed men asked.

"For as long as it takes. My orders are to bring her in for testing. I was told that if we take out the woman with wings, we shall encounter no problems with this tribe in the future."

"What are you talking about?"

The suit shook his head. "I've said too much already. You all don't have the clearances that I have."

My vision of the future faded away to nothing, so I opened my eyes and scanned the room.

The year is 2071, and the Hopi angel, Hope White Eagle, is dying after childbirth. She begs Deema, her vampire husband, to change her into a vampire so that she can continue her mission of saving her tribe from the white men invaders. The elders aren't happy about it, but they understand Hope had no choice. However, Dmitrius—the male angel who shows up, claiming to be Hope's eternal soulmate—disagrees. He tries to take her away from her family and change her into *his* type of immortal form, instead of letting her remain a vampire. Hope fears she'll lose her love for and connection to her family, so she refuses again and again. She battles her remembered feelings for Dmitrius and is wracked with guilt over the inevitable choice she'll have to make—her husband and her immortal children, or the angel with whom she's spent nearly all of time immemorial. He helps her regain her ancient memories, thus giving her what she needs to defeat their enemies...or so they think.

KUDOS for *Our New Hope*

In *Our New Hope* by Janelle Samara, Hope is now married to her vampire husband, Deema, and having her seventh child. But something goes wrong during the child's birth and Hope is seriously injured. In order to keep her from dying, Deema must change her into a vampire. Hope's tribal elders are not happy about it, but it is the only way that Hope can accomplish her mission to save her people. Or is it? A male angel comes to visit the tribe, telling Hope that he can change her into a real angel and restore her ancient memories. But he has a price. He wants to take her away from her husband and family, which he calls an abomination. Hope doesn't want to lose the love and connection she feels for her husband and children, so she is torn. What can she do? As in the first book, *Our Only Hope*, Samara's affection for Native Americans and her sympathy and indignation at their oppression by the government comes through loud and clear. A great read! ~ *Taylor Jones, The Review Team of Taylor Jones & Regan Murphy*

Our New Hope by Janelle Samara is the story of an ordinary girl who discovers that she is more than she thought she could be. When Hopi native Hope grows wings and learns to fly, her tribe believes that she is the angel that has been prophesied to save them from the white men who are planning to invade and take what little the Hopi have left. The story takes place some sixty years in the future, and it seems the government hasn't learned a thing. Native Americans are still being oppressed and persecuted. And that is something that Hope and her tribe are determined to defend against. With the magic in her tribe—winged women and male shifters—they prepare to defend their lands. But Hope has other problems as well. A serious injury during the birth of her last child has left her no choice but to become a vampire. And her tribal elders are not happy about that. Neither is the male angel who appears before the tribe, claiming to be Hope's eternal soulmate. He claims she is now an abomination and begs her to let him turn into a true angel. But she has no memory of him and doesn't want to lose the close ties she has with her family and tribe, so she refuses. But without the help the angel can give her, can she defeat the invaders who are coming? Samara tells a complex and intriguing tale of Native American traditions and culture, and fantasy though it may be, it is still very believable. I especially like the closeness between the members of the tribe and the way that they all watch each other's backs—a "them against us" story with a paranormal twist. I heartily recommend it. ~ *Regan Murphy, The Review Team of Taylor Jones & Regan Murphy*

ACKNOWLEDGMENTS

First and foremost, I want to thank my publisher, Black Opal Books, and everyone there who has been so wonderful. Lauri, Faith, Jack—I couldn't have done this without you. Your sharp eyes and attention to detail have been the best part about working with all of you.

I want to thank Otep for giving me permission to quote her song, "Stay." It is beyond my ability to concisely explain the depths of my gratitude and appreciation for you. Not just for your generosity and kindness to your fans, or for your strength, your words, your opinions, your art, your attitude, your articulation of the deprivation that we suffered under twisted justification…But, you. Everything. The whole package. Thank you for being you and for letting me quote your work within my own. It means the world to me.

I'd like to thank all of my friends, family, and coworkers who have listened to me talk about my characters like they're real people for the last three years. You know I'd list names, but I don't want to forget someone, so now none of you get mentioned. You know who you are…Without your questions, and without your allowance of me using you as a sounding board, I might not have caught some plot holes. And without your weirdness, I definitely would not have had many of the ideas that have inspired future stories. You guys rock.

I also want to thank my husband for all of his patience with the amount of time I spend attached to my keyboard. I couldn't have done all of this without your support and your belief in me. *Shukran, zwji. Ana ahbk.*

And last but not least, I want to thank everyone who has told me how much they loved my first book. I hope that you like this one even better than the last, and the next one even more.

Author's note

If you read my first book, *Our Only Hope*, you might recall my brief disclaimer about how all of the mythologies were made up by me. I wanted to reiterate that and add to it for this book. Any rituals, traditions, prophesies, names, and really everything else that appears in this novel is *pure fiction*. Since so many have questioned my motives with this trilogy, I've decided to just lay it all out in plain language while still attempting to be concise.

I was raised to respect Native Americans and their varied cultures even more than my own. Throughout my early childhood, my family used to go watch their public pow wows and admire the beauty of their music and dancing. My father and his Sioux friend taught me Native American sign language when I was little and used to take us to feed small apples to a buffalo herd. I was taught that it is especially wrong to steal from or hurt Native Americans, as they've already had far too much stolen from them, as it is. So I refused to steal traditions from the Hopi people for this trilogy. I could not appropriate their language, their histories, their prophecies, or even the names of their people and their towns. All I've used is the tribal name.

I made up a tribe entirely, using a placeholder name all the way through until the first novel was almost completed. I hodge-podged together remembered bits of this tribe or that and filled in the gaps with things that I needed to make the story work. I could not and would not take the serious beliefs of any one tribe, craft a tale entirely around them, and make a profit from them. But I also couldn't write a book about just another Caucasian heroine. I needed Hope to be special, and to be oppressed—to have a worthwhile mission in saving her people because they truly deserved to be saved.

The decision to use the name of the Hopi people was a multi-faceted one. Yes, how delightful that it is so close to Hope's name, and her name is also a play on words. But still people want to know why. Honestly, I just admire them. It was supposed to be my nod of respect by saying that if anyone is ever going to save us from ourselves, it is the Hopi. And how could I not pay them that tribute? I deeply regret the contrary perspective of those who choose to see it as an insult to name a fictional tribe after a real one.

I felt that making up a name entirely was out of the question. That would have been an affront to all of the tribes that ever did and that still do exist. I also could not bring myself to use the name of a tribe that was wiped out by Europeans because that would be disrespectful to their memory to pretend that they were still around. My desire and my intent was never to slight anyone. I merely needed a semi-familiar vehicle for a story that I wanted to tell, while also trying to show my respect for the many varied cultures among the indigenous tribes of the Americas.

Showing my desire that Native Americans cease to be oppressed was also one of my many reasons for making Hope who she is in this trilogy. I find it repugnant that after so many years of abuse, they are still being mistreated, pushed around, and neglected. That's why I set this trilogy in the future—as my own beacon of hope that the mistreatment of Native Americans, along with indigenous tribes all over the world, will come to an end in this century—even if it takes angels interfering to stop the government's oppression of them in their own homelands.

Thank you for understanding, and I'm sorry if you don't.

OUR NEW HOPE

Janelle Samara

A Black Opal Books Publication

GENRE: PARANORMAL ROMANCE/SUPERNATURAL THRILLER

OUR NEW HOPE
Copyright © 2017 by Janelle Samara
Cover Design by Jackson Cover Designs
All cover art copyright © 2017
All Rights Reserved
Print ISBN: 978-1-626947-09-2

First Publication: JULY 2017

Published by Black Opal Books **http://www.blackopalbooks.com**

DEDICATION

for Otep Shamaya
you are my heroin(e)
my addiction (and my savior)

CHAPTER 1

The three Russian vampires stood over me while I bled out onto the patio. I could feel the grit of the concrete pressing into my palms and heels as I writhed in pain. The pool of sticky blood reached my wings and soaked into my feathers, making them heavier than usual. Or maybe it was merely the loss of blood that made them feel heavy. Some distant part of my brain wondered if the vampires would find it easier to clean up my blood with their tongues, instead of soap and water.

My son, Aleksander, covered his face with his hands and knelt near my head. "She's going to die," he whispered.

"No, she won't, Aleks. I promise I will not let her die," Deema assured him. He checked me again to see if I was healing yet. My husband growled in anger when he saw what I could already feel—I was still bleeding all over the pavement.

"What do we do?" my daughter, Aleksandra, cried. She also fell to her knees beside me.

Part of me almost found it amusing that my son's twin mirrored his pose on the other side of my torso. It seemed like they were always doing similar things without even realizing it.

"It's not working! Our blood isn't healing her," she sobbed, in her tearless way, while her hands fluttered uselessly over my broken body.

"I've consumed too much of your blood too many times," I muttered. I felt myself weakening more and more with every moment that passed. My wings had started to grow numb as they lay sprawled out awkwardly beneath me. I sighed. "She was so strong because I've grown stronger."

Yes, my seventh and final angel/vampire hybrid child was by far the strongest of them all. She'd broken my spine, shattered my pelvis, and crushed my tailbone while I'd pushed her out, still encased in the amniotic sack.

The three vampires—my family from a previous incarnation—stared at me in shock for a moment while I gathered the rest of my strength to speak my last words as a mortal.

"It's time, Deema. You must change me or I'll die." My eyes slid closed, and I heard him heave a despondent sigh. He'd been dreading this day and knew that my tribal elders would be upset with him for changing me into a blood drinker.

He tore open his wrist and proceeded to wipe his blood on the wounds I had received from giving birth. I felt the change start to happen almost instantly. It was shockingly easy and caused me no additional pain. It was actually quite soothing when I felt the agony subside. My broken bones went numb for several moments before they started to knit together.

But while I was in the middle of changing from a mortal angel into an angel who would drink blood and live forever, I was also gripped by a powerful vision. It was terrifying because it was unlike any prophecy I'd ever seen before.

Instead of seeing myself from an outside, disembodied

perspective, I was actually experiencing the vision through my own eyes...

I gazed out over the wheat field that was being trampled by a sea of soldiers coming to invade my people's land. I was stunned that this was happening right now. I, along with the other women who stood before them, held up my hands and spread my wings while we all commanded them to stop. It was then that I saw my skin becoming clear like glass. I gaped at my arms for a moment while the procession of men ground to a halt. They, too, gawked at my glassy skin and all of my visible muscles beneath it. I was, after all, the only angel along the fence line who had transparent skin.

The rest of the vision started to play out as it had before whenever I'd dreamed it. They asked me what I was and I told them, "I am Hope, the first Hopi angel. I am tasked with protecting this tribe from you."

Only this time, many of them raised their guns and aimed right at me. That had never happened before in previous visions of the coming invasion.

I was suddenly jolted out of the prophetic sight, not by waking up, but by the completion of my change. After nearly twenty minutes of lying on the ground in my screened-in patio, it was suddenly over and I was back in my body. Sandra helped me up and I glanced around in the darkness with my new, vampire eyes.

Everything was so crisp! I'd thought things were vivid and clear when I'd first drank vampire blood, but now my vision was many thousands of times better than that. I could focus on dust in the air a thousand yards away. I could discern the twitches of the plants and grasses as they grew. My attention to detail was so great that even over the vastness of my yard and the neighboring field, my brain could pick out the movements in the plants not caused by wind.

Deema appeared at my side with our newest child in his arms. She had his obsidian eyes and my high cheekbones. "How do you feel, Hope?" he asked me.

"I feel…awesome!" I said after a moment. "Oh my god. My voice," I squealed. My hands flew to my throat. "I sound like—well, I don't sound like me."

I peered down and realized I'd already been cleaned up and redressed. I gave Sandra a curious glance and she answered me with a smile. Yes, she had dressed me in my favorite hunting clothes while I'd had my last vision as a mortal. It felt like she'd also brushed out my calf-length hair and left it down. I grinned for a moment while I felt it swirling around with my skirt.

Deema smiled, passing me our unnamed newborn daughter. "You sound beautiful."

"You look beautiful, too," Taniya, my best friend and pseudo-sister, chimed in as she walked outside holding her son and my actual nephew, Dancing Bronco. "I wonder if your wings will change later on." She ran her fingers over my sparkling, opalescent feathers.

I turned and examined my left wing for a moment before I plucked out a few non-essential feathers. They grew back right before my eyes and they were still the same glittering white. "I guess they won't be changing."

"We need to call your elders," Deema said in a hushed tone.

"It can wait until the morning," I chirped before I walked into my house.

I went upstairs to the refrigerator, where we kept bags of blood for the children, and pulled one out to feed my new baby. As soon as she punctured the bag, the scent of blood filled my nostrils and a burning thirst rose in my throat. I made a noise that shocked me—it was like a hiss mixed with a growl. It took every bit of my self-control to not snatch the blood away from my child and devour it myself. Deema was next to me in a second and asked me what was wrong.

"I need to feed," I growled. I cursed myself for not thinking of how things were different now. I couldn't just feed my babies like I always had before. I almost loosed a sob. I'd never have any more babies now that I was a vampire.

He took the child from my arms and encouraged me to go feed with the twins. I crashed through the window beside us and I was back on the ground just outside the patio in barely a second. The broken glass showered down around me, sparkling in the moonlight.

"I must feed now," I told the vampire twins when they stared at me with wonder and surprise.

Sandra threw open the back door and stepped outside. "Then let's go."

We took off into the sky and I sped toward Las Vegas. The twins quickly fell behind and pushed their thoughts to me, saying that I needed to slow down. Poor kids. They could only fly about 200 miles per hour. But bless their hearts for always wanting to try to keep up with my over 600 miles per hour.

'*I can't,*' I replied mentally. '*I cannot escape this thirst.*'

'*But we need to talk about your vision,*' Sandra thought toward me. '*It was different. Where were the shapeshifters? Why weren't the vampires there? Why did the soldiers point their guns at you once you'd said your name? In all of the other times that you dreamed that vision, it was only because more winged women and warriors were joining you. Why is it different now? Why will the soldiers fight you and not join you?*'

'*My sweet, wonderful daughter,*' I said inside my mind, pumping my wings with every bit of my new strength. '*Can't you see? It's because of my skin. It's because I'm a vampire now. That's what has changed. Because, now, they will certainly want to exterminate me. This change may have put my whole tribe in danger rather than saving them, as is my duty. Because I've loved your father in two lifetimes now, I may have spelled the end for all of my people.'*

CHAPTER 2

Pushing my wings to their limits, I reached Las Vegas in less than thirty minutes. I landed in an alley that we often hunted out of and waited on edge for a worthy victim to come my way.

After several minutes of waiting, a racist walked past the alley. He was guilty of numerous hate crimes, including murder. I had no patience for any of the ploys we usually used. I simply jumped out of the shadows, grabbed him, and dragged him back into the cover of darkness. I drained him of his sweet, evil blood before I emptied his pockets and threw him with ease into a nearby dumpster. Even though I knew what to expect from my new strength, it still surprised me how easily I was able to throw around the full grown man.

What I hadn't expected was the connection I had to him while he died. Reading his mind was one thing and rooting around in it was another. But the blood connection was a whole new world. It was kind of like watching his life flash before his eyes right along with him, only I could *feel* it. I felt his love, his hate, his lust, his greed, and his resentment. I was forced to witness that sick bastard's "cherished" memories of killing minorities.

It was the most terrifying, disgusting, and intimate thing that had ever happened to me.

But my bloodlust was not eased. I still felt the burning thirst throughout my core. Before I could even wipe the blood off of my face, another man walked into the alley. I read from his mind that he'd seen me pull the first man off the sidewalk. It was a friend of his that he'd spotted a few blocks back. He was trying to catch up to him to see if he wanted to party. Lucky for me, the man had also been a partner in crime with the still warm corpse that lay in the dumpster beside me.

"What the hell?" he mumbled when he noticed my massive, opalescent angel wings. I turned to face him head on and he saw the blood that stained my mouth. He stumbled backward, stuttering incoherently.

Faster than he could comprehend, I pounced on him and latched onto his neck. He tried to scream, but I easily snapped his spine so that I could feed undetected. Even though he was dead, his brain continued to live on the residual oxygen so I still had the connection to his memories. I shuddered in disgust at the feelings he poured into my mind as I sucked his delicious blood into my body.

After I'd finished and tossed him into the dumpster with his friend, I noticed that my thirst was somewhat sated, but still not fully satisfied. While I waited for my next victim to find me, the twins landed in the alley.

"You should have waited," Aleks scolded. "We've hunted in this part of town far too often lately. We need to relocate."

My shoulders slumped and my wings sagged. "Oh. Okay," I muttered.

We pushed off into the sky and flew a few blocks west. We found a gang conspiring about a casino robbery they planned to commit in a few hours, and we landed in their midst. Several of the men dropped to their knees, made the sign of the cross, and started muttering prayers when they saw my wings and flowing white dress. The rest of the men drew their weapons and aimed them at the twins.

"What's the meaning of this?" the largest, most heavily tattooed man demanded as he turned his gun on me.

I spread my wings wide. "I flew down from the sky on sparkling wings of white while you are plotting a crime that will surely kill a number of people. What do *you* think is the meaning of this?"

The smell of their blood—their sweet, sick, twisted, evil blood—was about to drive me mad. It took all of my restraint to keep from pouncing on them and ripping them to shreds. I wondered if it would always feel like this. The last thing I needed was to be filled with a longing to feed from my family or my tribe members. It wasn't until later, once I'd spent some time around my mortal loved ones, that I knew their blood would never draw my desire for it.

"Are you going to kill us?" whispered one of the men who'd fallen to his knees.

"We are here to judge you and dole out punishment accordingly," I informed him in the stern voice of my hunting persona. A few of the men started to rise in an effort to run away. "Don't bother trying to run," I said as the twins grabbed the men so quickly that their movements could not be seen by mere mortals. "There will be no escaping me or my children."

The volume of the prayers increased from the men who still cowered on their knees.

I pointed to the large, tattooed man. "Randall, you have taken many lives and you have destroyed many more by orphaning the children of those you have killed. You are certainly the leader here, and you are certainly the most evil man in this gang. You will die a painful death at the hands of my daughter."

Sandra grinned, handed off her captive to her brother,

and pounced on the man. I quickly sent her the thought that I could not contain myself once I smelled flowing blood, so she held him roughly by the nap of his neck while I judged the others.

"You," I said, pointing to a man on his knees at my feet. "You have never killed another human being, but you have damaged and ruined countless lives through your theft and deceit. Therefore, I will grant you a quick death." I snatched him up, broke his neck, and tore open his jugular. I was careful not to let any of his blood get on my white dress. I drank deeply while the minds of the men around me swam with confusion and my mind filled with his most vivid memories. I shuddered when the flow of both blood and memories ended.

Sandra's captive tried to wriggle out of her grasp, so she moved her grip to the front of his throat and slowly choked him. I emptied my victim's pockets and threw him into a dumpster at the far end of the alley with a flick of my wrist.

"Now, you three," I said, pointing to three more men on their knees. "You've never killed, raped, or robbed anyone. All of the stories that you told to get into this gang were lies. The guns you carry were even bought legally with money you earned in an honest way," I said with a disapproving stare. "So, you will be spared. For now. But know this, if you tell anyone of what you've seen here tonight, or if you ever return to lives of crime, I will not hesitate to return for you."

They looked at each other and wondered if that meant that they were free to leave. I gave them a curt nod. "If you want to continue living, you should go immediately." The three men scrambled to their feet and ran from the alley as fast as their wobbly legs would carry them.

I turned to the last two men who remained on their knees. "And you," I sighed. "You have not killed as many as this piece of shit," I said while I jabbed my thumb at the man Sandra held. "But you have still taken lives. Darren, you killed your own cousin—over, what? A few hundred dollars? That is so petty. Allen, you have killed family members as well. For your punishment, my son will *slowly* take your lives."

Aleks grabbed a fistful of hair in each hand and pulled the men to their feet. They both let out shocked screams before my son ripped out their throats and drank their blood one after the other.

I turned around to face the last three men who awaited my judgment. I frowned when I read the evil things from their minds. "You know what you have done. You know you will die, so I suggest that you face it like men," I told them in a steely voice.

I grabbed the closest one and sank my teeth into his neck. I greedily drained him dry before I killed another murderer. When I was down to one man left to kill, I paused for a fraction of a second to see how my thirst felt. It was definitely more tolerable, but certainly still there, too. I shrugged to myself before I grabbed the last man and tore open his neck.

The flow of memories was also easier to control and ignore as my thirst was eased. By the time I finished with the last man, there was a significant difference in intensity. I was considerably relieved by that fact. The horrible things I'd seen in those men had shaken me to my core. I'd known people could have terrible thoughts—dark and evil minds—but the depths of their wickedness had left me feeling cold and bitter in the aftermath of their vile recollections.

We emptied the pockets of all the men we'd killed, threw the bodies into a dumpster, and left them to rot with the garbage.

"How is your thirst?" Sandra asked once we were air-borne.

I hesitated for a brief moment of reflection. "I think it will be manageable. How is your thirst?"

"We're fine," Aleks replied. "We don't need to feed as much or as often since we are so much older. But don't worry—the thirst will get easier to control as you age. The first few weeks will be the hardest."

"Good," I breathed. "I was worried about that. But I'm sure you heard that in my mind."

CHAPTER 3

The sky was starting to lighten by the time we reached Native Lands and, when we touched down in my yard in southern Colorado, the sun was rising over the eastern horizon. I stayed in the backyard to marvel at my newly paled skin for a few moments. It faded to translucence just like the other vampires, and I couldn't help but smile while I walked into my house.

White Buffalo stood in the large kitchen. She was cooking breakfast for everyone in the house who still ate food. She turned around and beamed at me. She gracefully flitted across the room and gave me a hug. "Greetings, Mama. How was your first blood?" she inquired as she spun around and returned to the bacon sizzling in the pan.

"It was...interesting, I guess," I replied. I followed her into the kitchen and studied her with my new eyes. There were bulges on her back that were indicative of growing wings. "When did those bumps appear on your back?" I asked as I ran my hands over them.

"They were not there yesterday, but they were there this morning," she said sheepishly, a grin spreading across her face. "I'm really growing wings, aren't I?"

"Yes, love. You are. Let me see," I said before I lifted the back of her shirt. "Taniya!" I called over my shoulder.

She walked down the stairs with my baby in her arms and her son following behind her. "What's up?" she asked. "How many days growth does this seem like to you?" I asked her. I gently ran my fingers over the large protrusions on my daughter's back.

"Oh!" Taniya exclaimed. "They look like they'll burst through any day now, so…what? A few weeks?"

"They've been growing for less than a day." I poked one of them. "Oh!" I cried as the bump I'd just touched burst open and a tiny, featherless, chicken-sized wing pushed out of her back. "I'm sorry! I didn't think I was being rough," I apologized in a rush. I was petrified with fear that I'd caused pain to my own child.

A few seconds later, the other bump burst open to reveal a mirror image of her first wing.

"What's wrong?" White Buffalo demanded while she twisted around in a futile attempt to see her own back. "What's happening?"

"Can't you feel it?" Taniya asked in quiet shock.

My eldest shook her head no as she reached her hand behind herself and felt the blood running down her back.

"Your wings have emerged. I guess they will be growing with super speed just like you did," I postulated. I noticed that her blood did not bring out my bloodlust, but instead it smelled like honey, which I no longer found appetizing. Just to test myself, I steeled my nerves and swiped my finger through the path of blood. I tasted it and gagged. Despite its pleasant smell, it was the bitterest thing I'd ever tasted. I felt a heavy relief that my children would not be at risk of death by my hands.

A few moments later, the rest of my children came down the stairs. I carefully hugged and kissed them each in turn before they all took their seats at the large, twenty-seat dining room table. Taniya handed me my newborn and retreated to the kitchen to help White Buffalo finish putting the food on platters and carrying them into the dining room.

Even though I had no need for human food anymore, I decided to sit at the table with them anyway while they all ate. During the meal, Deema walked through the front door with my brothers following closely behind him. They all took seats at the table and my brothers dug into the piles of meat and eggs that remained on the platters.

"So, you're really a vampire now, huh? Thanks for bothering to tell us," Brian grunted, dishing out a plateful of food for himself. Being such a tall and muscular guy, I wasn't too surprised that he filled his plate to capacity.

"Yep. I killed six men last night. Or was it seven?" I mused. I decided to ignore his attitude since it would just cause a fight. He'd get over it eventually.

Sandra snorted a quick laugh from the backyard where she was tending the garden. "Six!" she called out.

"Okay, six."

Brian rolled his eyes while Will tried not to gag on his eggs.

"Look, I won't have to feed as much as I get, um, older, I guess, even though I won't be aging anymore," I said with an irrepressible grin. "But for the time being, I need to feed a lot and often so that the bloodlust doesn't consume me. I would never want to do anything to risk the life of anyone on this reservation."

"When were you planning on calling us? When were you going to tell the elders what happened?" Brian asked in a disgruntled tone. He folded a piece of toast in half and shoved most of it into his mouth.

"Well, I haven't been home from hunting for even thirty minutes yet. I wanted to sit down with my family and be with my rapidly growing children for a while before I disturbed the sleeping old men," I shot back at him in a sudden burst of anger. *God! Can't he just be happy for me since I don't have to worry about dying anymore?*

"We should have been here last night. This is the third time you have not called the elders to be here during your labor," he replied after he swallowed his toast.

"Yes, and this is also the third time I've given birth in the middle of the night, if you hadn't noticed. Besides, Taniya was here to sing the birth song, and you know as well as I do that it's acceptable for the midwife to sing it. It does not *have* to be the elders," I retorted.

His square jaw tightened and his eyes narrowed before he composed himself. "All right," he conceded. "And what about your wings? If you are a vampire now, why are your wings still white? Aren't they supposed to turn black?"

I heaved a heavy sigh that bordered on a growl. "I am not evil just because I drink blood. My wings will remain white. I mean, for God's sake—how could we be evil if only the blood of criminals is appealing to us? I just tasted the blood from White Buffalo's wings popping through, and it was disgusting. If we were evil, wouldn't we want the blood of innocents or something?"

"That's a great point, but how do you know that about your wings?" Will chimed in, his tone genuinely curious. "What about when your feathers fall out naturally? Maybe they'll turn dark so you can blend in better with the night."

I plucked out a large feather in a conspicuous spot on my left wing and dropped it on the table. Everyone stopped eating and watched in awe when my feather grew back instantly. Just like the night before, it came back as the same sparkling white that the rest of my feathers were.

"Oh," was all my little brother could say.

"So what's on today's agenda?" Jumping Wolf, my first son, asked when he had finished eating.

I turned to Deema and wondered if he had contacted the elders yet, or if he'd just called my brothers.

"The elders will be here in an hour," he told our son after he met my gaze for a moment. "If past experience serves as a guide, they will sing the healthy child song and then we will all go with them to the Hall to name our final daughter," he said with the tiniest hint of sadness. I took his hand under the table and gave it a gentle squeeze. He leaned over and kissed me softly on my cheek.

"And until then, it's time for pictures." The oldest children nodded as they gathered up the youngest two to pick out various outfits for them. Jumping Wolf and Long Falcon remained downstairs to help the twins clear the table and do the dishes.

"Make sure the date is turned off on the camera," Deema instructed. "The last time I took the memory card in to get them developed, they noticed that it appeared to be the same children growing rapidly over the course of a few months," he gently scolded me. "Luckily, I was able to convince them otherwise."

"Sorry, lover," I said as I ducked my head.

I followed the group of children upstairs and proceeded to take photographs of my rapidly aging offspring. The hour seemed brief and while I was dressing my youngest daughter for the third time, I heard several vehicles pull into my driveway. I noticed that I could even hear the old men speaking to each other in hushed voices.

"Do you think this is truly the final time? Do you honestly believe that she will now return to her mission of training to protect the tribe?" Tall Grass asked.

"I do," my grandfather replied. "The vampire said that there are several surprises waiting for us here today. I assume that he was forced to turn her. After all, we knew it was only a matter of time."

"He better not be drawing us here to our deaths," one of the middle aged men grumbled under his breath.

I chose that moment to dive out of the third floor

window and glide down to meet the men who were still climbing out of the vans.

"Welcome, Elders," I greeted them while they stared in open shock at my translucent skin.

"Hope!" the chief exclaimed. "What happened to you?"

"I nearly died while I was giving birth," I replied gently. "So, I am a vampire now."

The men gasped and took a collective step back. They'd never been around a newly turned vampire before.

"Worry not, my friends," I assured them. "I have no desire to harm any of you since your blood is not evil, and therefore not appetizing to me."

They relaxed slightly and followed me when I bid them to come inside.

"Why have your wings remained white?" the chief inquired once he was seated at the head of the table in my dining room.

I sighed so loudly it bordered on a groan, and Deema stifled a chuckle.

"We are not evil creatures," I replied, using great effort to keep my voice even. "My wings will remain white." I pulled out what I hoped would be the last feather for demonstrative purposes. All of the elders watched intently while my feather grew back right before their eyes. Of course, it was the same sparkling white that my feathers had always been.

"Speaking of wings," Tall Grass said. "Taniya, how goes the development of yours?"

"Fine, Uncle. I flap every day to build my muscles, but they are not quite fully grown yet, so I have not attempted to fly," she replied. She spread her wings to illustrate that they were still smaller than mine.

"Excuse me, Elders?" White Buffalo said before she handed me my unnamed child and turned her back to the group. She lifted her hair to expose her back and the wings she was growing. They'd begun to grow feathers now, but they were a very dark, chocolate brown. "Perhaps the prophets of old saw *my* wings and thought them to be black. I also have her hair and her eyes. Maybe they just thought I was her with lighter skin," she postulated.

"When did this start?" the chief asked calmly.

"This morning," I replied. "I think she started to grow her wings either once I gave birth or once I was changed into an immortal. She was asleep when they started to grow, so we cannot be sure."

"And what of the other girls? Are they growing wings?" Tangled Tree wondered aloud. "The boys have animal names as well. Could they possibly change into their animals? Or did the spirits name them as such simply because they are warriors?" he speculated to no one in particular.

"Hmmm…I suppose only time will tell," the chief replied quietly.

"Even though she appears twenty-five, we have to keep in mind that White Buffalo is only a year old," I chimed in. "Perhaps the other girls will grow wings when *they* turn a year old, and maybe the boys will become their animals when they are old enough."

The old men nodded and mumbled their agreements while the younger elders remained quiet in their thoughts.

After a few moments of quiet contemplation, the chief stood and the rest of the elders followed suit. "Well, shall we get this show on the road?" he asked me and my immortal family.

They all gathered in a circle around me while I held my new baby. The elders' voices joined together in a beautiful and haunting harmony and they sang the ancient song of our people that welcomed my child into the tribe. She grew still in my arms, frozen as she drank in the music of their intonations. I found myself captivated as well, since it was the first time I got to listen to it with such precise hearing.

When they were finished, my grandfather gave me a gentle hug, careful not to press against my newborn. "I know you'll do me proud," he breathed in my ear. None of the other elders could have heard him.

"You wish to name her today, too?" the chief asked once my grandfather had released me from his embrace.

"Yes, Chief. We will meet you at the hall shortly. Those of us who can fly, will fly. My children can run while my mortal family rides to the Hall with my brothers," I said as I looked around at my family and tribal elders. The chief nodded in agreement before he turned toward the front door and exited my house.

CHAPTER 4

When Deema and I got to the Hall with our daughter, they were all waiting for us outside the back door. I was fairly surprised by someone else walking through the door behind me once we were ready to begin. I'd been certain that everyone who needed to be there *was* there. My eyes swept the area to verify this as I turned to see who had interrupted our naming of my last daughter.

I sprang back a few feet when I saw the wings. They were fully developed and attached to—to a *man!* He wore no shirt or shoes, but had fine linen pants that seemed to be hand-made. His skin was the same shade that mine used to be and he appeared to be racially ambiguous, like he was mixed from every race of mankind. His dark brown hair flowed past his shoulders in silken waves that stopped just above his nipples. He was also stunningly handsome. I'd never before laid eyes on a man so unbelievably attractive.

"What?" I was so shocked, that was all I managed to get out.

He stopped, turned to face me, and clasped his hands loosely together in front of himself. "I have returned as a reminder," he told me with a small, respectful nod. I merely raised my eyebrows in question—words were still beyond me. "You do not remember who you are any-more."

"Of course she does," Sandra said after a few beats of silence.

"Does she?" he replied without ever turning away from my eyes.

I, on the other hand, could not take my eyes off his wings—wings that were identical to mine. None of the others had nor would have wings exactly like mine, but this *man* did. How? Men were not supposed to have wings—only women could be angels. At least, that's what I'd been taught. It made me wonder what else I'd always been wrong about.

"But who are you?" I finally managed to whisper.

"That she does not know me is proof that she has for-gotten who she is," he said to my immortal daughter, again without even glancing away from me. "I am a different kind of immortal from you, and yet we are the same. But you have changed as no other like us has before you. You are an...original." He said the word with thinly veiled disgust. "These strange new creations you've made with the blood drinker...we do not even know what to think of all of this. I turned away for only a year and some months—just a blink of the eye—and this happens? Do you even know what an abomination you've become? Can you even see how wrong you are? How wrong this is?"

"There is a calm center," I replied, even though I didn't really understand what he was asking me.

"No!" He moved so quickly that my eyes could not even follow him. *My* eyes! My beyond-perfect vi-sion—my vampire vision—could not track his movement. "There is no *knowledge* in your center! You may have calmness at times, but you have lost so much of your *hearing* that you have become nearly worthless at your job! You remember nothing of before this life. You no longer know anything of the time spent between lives!" He was right in my face, yelling at me. His breath was not hot like my children's, nor was it cooled like the vampires. It was actually the same temperature as the rest of the air around us, but it smelled of flowers. Gardenia, lilac, lavender, jasmine, roses, and iris were just some of the scents I could discern.

"No one does," I snapped back when he paused for a breath.

"All who are like us remember their time between bodies if they choose to. You should have regained your memory after your wings finished developing. Why did you not accept those memories?" He had calmed down some and seemed genuinely curious about why I could not remember.

I had also calmed down a bit since he was backing up to give me space. "How were they to come? I mean, how am or was I supposed to accept them?"

"In dreams or flashes and floods of memories when you are awake." He shrugged. "Sometimes, one of us will simply wake up one day and be filled with all of our eternal knowledge."

"I wonder what happened," Deema mused. His tone was casual, but there seemed to be a viscous glint to his eyes.

"You happened," the winged man snarled. He finally spun away from me and turned on Deema. "You did this to her!" he bellowed as he took a step toward the powerful immortal.

"I met him after I started flying," I interjected. My anger started to rise again when I sensed the threat to my husband's life. "I'd already flown to New York on my own before I'd ever met him. He did not stop me from accepting anything that has or hasn't come to me. Other things were distracting me when my wings grew. Like the fact that I was keeping it a secret. I was worried about my sister." I gestured to Taniya and he turned his head to examine her full-on for the first time.

His eyebrow raised just a bit as he studied her. "Your wings are not like the others of our kind," he commented, seeming somewhat satisfied in that assessment. "None of the other women here will have wings quite like her, because none of them *are* like her. None of you have an immortal soul," he told Taniya and my daughters as he gazed at each one of them.

"What do you mean by that?" Taniya interjected. "I've always heard people say things about mortal souls. I've never heard anyone say that someone's *immortal* soul was in danger."

The angel scoffed. "That is because only *mortal* souls are ever at risk for temptation to the other side. Immortal souls are different. Our sides were chosen eons ago at the time of the Fall. Hope is on our side—she is on my side. She just does not remember that because she remembers none of her time as an unincarnated angel."

"Explain that," Deema demanded.

"I owe you nothing. You deserve no explanation, vampire!"

I put my hands on my hips and glared at him. "If I must know, then so should he. We've been joined. We are—for all intents and purposes—married."

"Irrelevant. I owe him nothing. I owe you everything." His face crumpled in pain for a brief second before he covered it with his hands. An instant later, he scrubbed his face with his fingers before he dropped his arms to his sides. He had a blank expression again that I was beginning to think was what he wore when he was all business.

"Please," he said evenly, staring into my eyes. "I wish to speak with you alone."

"Will you be around for long? We kind of need to finish

naming my child," I said with a touch of harshness.

He planted his feet and clasped his hands before himself again. "I will wait until you are done."

My brother actually seemed a little bit relieved. "And I suppose you intend on waiting right there for her?"

"I do." The angel closed his eyes. It seemed as if he was trying to be as nonintrusive as he could, despite remaining.

Curious, I tried to enter his mind, but I hit a wall and couldn't get inside. His eyes snapped open and he gave me a look I had trouble deciphering. There was a hint of a smile, a bit of mischievousness in his eyes, but there was a familiarity about it, too—like he'd known me his whole life. Once I thought that, his eyes took on a bit of tenderness, as if in reply.

"All right then. Hope? The child?" my grandfather asked as he gestured for me to hand her over to them.

After the elders sang another welcoming song for my final daughter, they made the preparations to name her as well. Shortly before noon, the drumming escalated and the elders exited the sweat lodge.

"Do you agree?" the chief asked Tangled Tree, the first man to exit the hut.

"We agree," he replied breathlessly. He sat on a rock for a moment while he caught his breath before he turned to me. "White Eagle, the name that the spirits have placed on your daughter is Silver Panther." He stared helplessly at the chief and the other old men sitting around the drum. "Naming a woman who can fly after a bird is one thing, but this is unheard of. The spirits have never named a woman after a cat. Large cats are strictly shifting warriors."

"They name our people as they see fit," my grandfather replied with a reassuring smile. "We are not meant to understand these things just yet."

Tangled Tree shook his head lightly in confusion and

turned to walk inside the Hall of the Elders.

Suddenly, my newly named child started squirming in my arms as my fully grown boys began vibrating and moaning behind me. Silver Panther let out a pained scream that quickly turned into a growl. I turned to my grandfather in shock, and he stood halfway out of his chair to see what was going on. I heard a horse snort and stomp behind me and felt my baby change shape in my arms. Glancing down again, I saw that she had transformed into a panther cub with sparkling gray fur that rivaled the beauty of my wings. I looked behind me and saw that my boys had transformed into a wolf and a horse.

I searched the group of elders with panic in my heart, but none of them had any idea of what they could say to comfort me. The tiny panther in my arms yawned widely before she nuzzled into me and fell fast asleep.

"Is she going to stay like this?" I whispered to no one in particular.

"We've never seen or heard of a woman *or* an infant shape shifting before," was the only answer I was offered.

CHAPTER 5

I could feel the bloody tears streaming down my face as I took off into the sky and flew toward my valley to be alone with my daughter and my thoughts.

'*Should we follow you?*' I heard Sandra ask in my head.

'*No,*' I replied simply. Even the voice in my mind trembled with emotion.

I landed softly, crawled into the tent to lie down on the pallet, and I wrapped my wings around us both to shade her from the bright summer sun. She stirred for a moment, but fell back asleep without any fussing. Once my bloody tears ran dry, I sobbed in silence for hours while I rocked my panther infant. I was terrified that she would remain like this. I had no idea how to care for her or help her. It was much simpler when she was just like my previous six children—feed her blood and watch her grow.

But what would I do with a baby that wasn't a baby? I had enough problems mounting without having more wrenches thrown in to mess things up. I felt that I had failed her somehow, that it was my fault she'd turned at such a young age. Did she not feel safe enough with me to even remain in her human form? Was I, as a newly changed vampire, so dangerous in the infant's eyes, that the only way she felt safe was as a panther? On some level,

I knew she wouldn't be sleeping if she didn't feel safe with me. But it still nagged at me enough to keep me crying, to keep me feeling like my old doubtful and insecure self. Of course I'd try my best, just as I did with anything that matters, but that didn't necessarily mean that I'd be capable of succeeding.

She awoke with a yawn around sunset, but she remained in panther form. She peered at me curiously for a few moments before she started to lick her paws like a common house cat.

I remembered what the elders had said when I brought the twins back from Russia. Tribe members in animal form still had human thoughts. As Silver Panther crawled away from me and shook off the clothes she still wore, I searched her mind for some sign of humanity. I got the feeling that she was hungry, but I had no clue as to what I was supposed to feed her. I followed her out of the tent while I contemplated my next move.

The wind shifted direction and a plethora of scents hit me like a wall. I quickly spun around and saw my vampires flanked by my children. They all stood 150 yards north of me in the valley. The male angel stood higher up on the mountain, watching us, but clearly trying to avoid interacting with us.

"I'm sorry, love," Deema said softly as he rushed toward me. "We didn't want to disturb you until you were ready to be around others. I know you need your alone time every now and then."

I collapsed into his arms. "I'm just so scared," I sobbed. "She hasn't changed back and it's been hours. Now she's hungry, and I don't know what I'm supposed to feed her. I mean, do I go catch a squirrel for her to tear apart? Or should someone fetch a bag of blood? Does she need milk since she's still a...a kitten?" I babbled through my wracking, dry sobs.

He stroked my hair to soothe me and he held me against his chest. "It's all right, Hope. Everything will be okay," he assured me.

"And how do you know? Now that I'm immortal—now that I don't sleep—I can't dream the future anymore."

A smile slowly spread across his face as he watched over my shoulder. "Look."

He jerked his head toward the south and I spun around. Silver Panther was vibrating and the air around her became hazy.

After a few moments, the air cleared and she was a normal "human" baby again. The most relieved sigh I'd ever uttered escaped my lips as I ran to her and scooped her up. She gazed up at me and rubbed the side of my neck like White Buffalo used to do when she wanted some blood.

"She thirsts," I told my family while they watched me clutch her to my chest.

Deema handed me clothes that would fit her. "And you?"

"Yes, I thirst as well," I said pensively while I dressed her.

"Shall we go to Vegas?" Aleks asked.

"What about everyone else? Four of us can fly, but seven of us cannot," I replied.

Deema smiled at me. "I can carry one on my back and one in my arms, and so can the twins. And since you still fly with wings, you can carry one of our children, too. But that's fine, isn't it? Everyone can catch a ride that way."

"Oh, of course," I said. I felt like if I could still blush, my cheeks would've been blazing red with embarrassment. "Well, shall we go?" I asked my immortal family.

They all smiled and gave me a nod before the children climbed onto the vampires. In a few moments, we were all airborne and flying west.

"Mama!" White Buffalo called from her father's back. I turned to look at her. "Fly crazy for her."

I grinned back at her before I started dipping and diving like I used to do when she was small enough to fly with me. Silver Panther's eyes grew wide and she started to shake with fear. I ceased my erratic flying and watched her carefully. I was afraid she'd change back into a panther cub and be unable to feed. She soon calmed down and I breathed a sigh of relief as she snuggled against my chest.

After two hours of chasing the sunset, we touched down in Las Vegas on the roof of a brothel. The dark finished spreading in the sky while we waited for the scum of the earth to crawl out of their daytime hiding places. After a short wait, Deema spotted two men a couple of blocks away dragging an intoxicated gambler into an alley. He told me to take Silver Panther with me and I was off in a flash.

Unfortunately, I was too late to save the drunken man's life. They had bashed him over the head so hard that his skull was crushed in that spot. His breathing was labored, and by the time I had drained the two thieves, his breathing had ceased all together. I listened carefully for his heartbeat, but found none. *Waste not, want not,* I decided. I emptied the pockets of the three dead men.

After a moment of thought, I decided to not waste the blood in the beaten man, either. I propped him up against the wall of the alley and crouched down next to him. I scratched his neck with my fingernail and made a cut over his jugular. I held my daughter next to him and encouraged her to feed. She didn't enjoy it, but she was too thirsty to not drink. Once she refused to drink any more, I finished draining him. Since it was dying blood, it wasn't very pleasant, but it was not as bitter as I'd expected. He must have been evil in his own right to have blood that was that level of sweetness. It was a bit of a relief to not have to hear his memories, though. I threw the drained bodies into a dumpster before I picked up my daughter and flew back to the brothel roof.

Just before I landed, I caught a strong, sudden thought from someone on the ground. I'd been seen! He watched me land on the roof before he ran into the whorehouse. I listened intently while he rushed past the brothel's madam and searched for a way to access the roof.

CHAPTER 6

W e need to leave," Deema growled as he started to gather our children.

"Not yet," I hissed. "Don't you feel it? He has a sense of 'otherness' about him. He's not like normal people. A normal person would have told themselves they'd imagined seeing me, or that they just saw a large bird flying low. Normal people don't study the night sky anymore," I said so quickly that it would've sounded like a low humming to a mere human.

The twins stood by, listening attentively to his thoughts, but also ready to attack or flee at any moment. The stranger found his way to the roof in less than a minute. He burst through a trap door of sorts and leapt onto the rooftop with a smooth jump. I had just passed the baby to Sandra so I could step between the newcomer and my family. I drew my sword and held it at the ready in front of me.

"What—Whoa!" he said as he held up his hands to show he meant no harm. "I just—I saw an angel and I had to—please, don't hurt me," he pleaded, taking a few steps back from me.

I slowly dropped the sword to my side and studied his face while I dug through his mind. "Why did you leave your tribe, Silverwolf?" I asked him after a moment. I saw the answer in his head, even though he avoided saying it aloud.

"My name is Jonathan," he said.

"That may be the name your parents gave you, but your Cherokee elders named you Silverwolf. How long has it been since you have shifted?" Again, I saw the answer in his thoughts, even though he dodged my question.

"Are you really an angel?" he asked as his feet pulled him toward me against his will.

"I am," I replied simply.

His shuffling feet stopped. "Are you an angel of death?"

I smiled and stepped toward him. "You could say that."

"Please—" he began.

I laid my hand on his shoulder. "Don't. I will not harm you. I'm sorry for what happened to you, but you must understand that it wasn't your fault. Now, if you would like to, I can ask my elders if you may join our tribe. About twenty percent of our men are shapeshifters, and we could always use some more. A war is coming, and we are the only ones prophesized to last through the coming battles."

I heard a couple of pained groans behind me and turned my head to watch my son become a wolf. I faced Silverwolf again and gave him a big grin. "We have several angels living among my tribe, and even the rarest shape shifter of all. My youngest daughter is a panther. Will you join us?"

"A female shifter? That's impossible!" he gasped as he stumbled backward out of my grasp.

I could understand his disbelief. I was still just as stunned over that man with wings. Part of me wondered where he was at that moment. Was he hiding somewhere, watching all of this? Or was he so thoroughly disgusted with me for being a vampire that he could not bring himself to watch me feed?

Sandra stepped forward with Silver Panther. "She shifted for the first time only moments after the naming ceremony. She was not yet a day old the first time she turned. See for yourself. Smell her."

He glanced at me for approval and I gave him a curt nod. "But be warned," I growled, raising my sword as I moved to Sandra's side too fast for his mortal eyes to see. "I will not hesitate to kill you if you lay a hand on my child."

A flash of disbelief mixed with fear flitted across his face before his mind gave me assurance that he would never harm a child. I stood down, but remained close. I could feel that someone in close proximity had ill intentions, but it was not this man.

He leaned over my daughter and inhaled deeply before he stumbled backward. "Blood drinker!" he cried out in shock as he stared at Sandra.

"Yes," I said quietly. "We are all blood drinkers here. And we are all immortals, tasked with protecting the Hopi tribe until our days come to an end. But you see now, don't you? The child *is* a panther, yes?" I knew that some of the things I was telling him weren't exactly straight facts, but I wanted to keep it simple for the moment. He could learn how it all really was once he was a tribe member.

"Yes," he muttered.

Suddenly, the trap door that he had burst through swung open again. Three men filed out of it. Two were armed with baseball bats and the other one had two lengths of large-link chains.

"Get off my roof," the largest of them boomed. His deep voice echoed off of the building across the street and some people passing by stopped to listen to the confrontation.

The two with the bats came at me first, and I was stunned at the thoughts that poured from their minds into mine. They were both hell-bent on, not only beating me and raping me, but any other woman they found on the roof, too. I was shocked that they already had a plan in place for women who wouldn't be missed. Half of their "staff" were basically sex slaves.

Before I entirely realized what I was doing, I crouched, bared my teeth, and hissed at them. Then I charged. In one graceful sweep, I cut off the heads of the two men. My sword sliced through them like a hot knife through butter.

The third man stumbled back a few steps until he tripped over the edge of the door and fell. He landed ass-first in the small opening and found himself wedged. Once he realized he could not free himself, he swung one of his chains at me. I just scowled at him.

"My skin is impenetrable. I am an immortal and an angel of death. Do you really think you can do me harm?" I sauntered over to him, my sword dripping with fresh blood. I glanced back at my half-breed children and jerked my head toward the headless bodies, indicating that they should feed before the corpses lost any more blood.

The man ignored my warnings and tried to swing his chain at me while my head was turned. I grabbed the chain before it struck me and ripped it from his hand.

"I warned you," I growled before I threw it to the floor and pulled him to his feet. I sank my teeth into his neck and relished the flavor of his blood. His thoughts and memories flooded my mind as I fed—he was by far the most evil man I'd killed so far. He was a rapist, an abusive pimp, a murderer, a thief, and now he ran a brothel illegally. He actually *knew* that most of his ladies were infected with some form of STD. In fact, two of them had the fatal AUTO virus and they were infecting unwitting clients. I was so filled with rage that I crushed his body while I drained him.

I dropped the bloodless body and turned back to my

family with a smile on my lips. "That was fantastic! He was more evil than any other man I've ever fed from."

Silverwolf stared at me in shock. "How can you be an angel if you are a blood drinker?" he whispered.

"We are not evil creatures." I wiped the blood off of my sword on the dead man's shirt. "But we help rid the world of evil. You see, the blood of a good man does not taste good at all. But the blood of an evil man…mmm!" I licked my lips and re-sheathed my sword. My whole family murmured in agreement behind me.

I scrutinized the shocked Cherokee and dug through his mind for a moment before I started to answer the questions that were swimming through his head. "No, we are the only blood drinkers in our tribe of 10,000. We come here to Sin City every few days so that we can hunt evil men, since it is against our ways to kill any Natives. Your safety will be assured if you join our tribe and our elders can teach you how to control your shifting so that you don't hurt anyone else by mistake ever again."

"Can you still remote view?" Deema asked me after a few moments of silence.

"Hmm…I don't know. I haven't tried since I was turned. But I guess there's no time better than the present."

I closed my eyes and searched for my brother with my mind. I had just found him, when Aleks shook me and pulled me from my trance. I heard sirens and knew right away that the pedestrians on the street had called the authorities after they'd listened to the struggle on the roof.

"We've got to go," Deema growled quietly as he peered over the edge of the building. He snatched up White Buffalo and Jumping Wolf before he flew in the opposite direction of the blaring sirens. Aleks scooped up Singing Sparrow and Black Horse and took off after his father. Sandra handed me Silver Panther, pulled Silverwolf into her arms as Long Falcon climbed onto her back, and followed her brother. I held Silver Panther in one arm and scooped up Tall Filly in the other before I flew after my family. I was less than a block away when I heard the police cars stop in front of the brothel.

"We're going to have to find another city to hunt in after tonight," Deema grumbled when I'd caught up to them.

"I'm sorry," I mumbled. I was ashamed of myself that I hadn't cleaned up my mess.

"No, Mama," Sandra assured me. "It's not just that. We have hunted too much in this city for the last year and rumors are starting to spread outside of the police department of vigilante killers who are draining blood from wanted criminals. Not all of the bodies we leave in dumpsters make it to the landfill undetected."

"We could try Phoenix, and maybe Denver," I suggested.

"We'll see," Deema said thoughtfully. "But the rest of us still need to feed tonight."

"And soon," Aleks mumbled.

We touched down a few minutes later in one of the seedier parts of town. Silverwolf stood with his back to us while we fed and wondered what he'd gotten himself into. After we'd all finished feeding, we gathered up those who could not fly and took off for the reservation.

Once we were away from the city lights, I heard Brian's voice in my head. *'Did you call me? Am I wrong to assume that it is about the strange man who is flying back with you?'*

'Yes. I'm sorry I could not hold the connection to explain, but we had to flee. I didn't realize I'd woken you up or I would have looked in on you again. He's a Cherokee and a wolf. I'd like to ask the elders if he can join our tribe since he was kicked out of his for killing his parents the first time he shifted. He was not taught about his gift and

he was frightened. It was a mistake—one that he deeply regrets,' I replied.

'Bring him to my house. I will talk to him tonight and we will meet with the elders in the morning.'

'Okay. We'll see you in a bit.' I broke off the connection and turned to Sandra, who was carrying Silverwolf on her back.

"I heard," she said when I opened my mouth to explain to her what had just happened in my head.

I smiled at her for a second before I sped up to catch up with Deema. "Lover?" I said softly. He turned his head slightly to look at me while he sped through the night. "We're dropping off Silverwolf with Brian. He will take him to the elders in the morning and they will discuss him joining our tribe," I informed him.

"Do you think they'll let him join?"

"I don't see why they wouldn't. He's a shifter without a tribe, and we need all the magic we can get infused into *our* tribe."

"Hmm…I guess we'll know within a day, huh?"

"Yep."

We flew the rest of the way home in silence. I landed in Brian's yard along with Sandra while most of the rest of our family went on to our house. I introduced the two wolves before I bid them goodnight and flew away.

When I got home, I changed the clothes my two growing children wore and put them to bed. I wandered back downstairs, and found Deema sitting alone in the living room.

I sat on his lap and stretched my wings toward the ceiling. "What should we do tonight?" I asked him.

"I have a few ideas." He smiled mischievously, wrapped me in his arms, and pulled me closer to him. "We could go to your valley for some privacy, and we could come back in the morning when the kids get up."

"Oh? And what would we do in the valley?" I asked him while he kissed my neck.

He moved his lips up my neck and across my jawline. "What would you like to do?"

"Well, I think I know what *you'd* like to do." I giggled and pulled away to stand up. He tightened his hold around my waist, pulling me back to him. "I thought you wanted to leave," I teased while I tried to stand up again.

He grinned back at me before he released me and gave me a small, mock bow. I stood up and turned to dart out to the patio. Before I could take my first step, he scooped me up in his arms and ran out the back door.

As he lifted into the night sky, he started to kiss me with a severe ferocity. By the time we landed in the valley less than a minute later, I was ready to maul him. We touched down next to the tent, and I ripped his shirt off with one hand while I shredded his pants with the other hand.

He took more care in removing my clothes, but I understood why—one of us still needed to be able to go back to the house without being nude in front of our children. Once we were both naked, I pounced on him and we made passionate love for hours until the sun rose in the eastern sky.

CHAPTER 7

After the children ate breakfast and we took pictures of the youngest two, I went to the Hall of the Elders to meet with them concerning the man I'd brought back from Vegas the night before. Deema was more than willing to join me, but I encouraged him to remain behind to help the twins till some more fields and plant crops for the tribe. The twins worked tirelessly to help grow food for our people, but I felt like Deema needed to try harder to do more for them.

"Greetings, Chief, Grandfather, Elders. I see you have met my new friend," I said on my way to my seat.

"Indeed, we have," the chief replied. "May I ask what made you decide to bring him here? How did you come across him?"

"I was going in for a rooftop landing and he saw me. He ran through the building and up to the roof before anyone could stop him. He found me up there with my husband and all of our children. I dug through his mind and saw who and what he was and, well…after that, I felt like the decision to bring him back here was already made for me."

"Would you care to enlighten us as to what you have learned of this man?" Red Oak asked me.

The other angel walked in at that moment. I tried my

best to ignore him as I had been for the last day. I knew he still wanted to take me away somewhere and yell at me some more. I also knew that I wasn't feeling it. I kept hearing the whispering when he was around, and it had always freaked me out ever since the first time I'd heard it when my wings had started growing. A few of the elders met the angel's eyes and gave him small nods, but no one spoke to him so I answered Red Oak's question.

"His name is Jonathan Silverwolf. For the last seven years, he has been wandering the country, doing odd jobs to feed himself and killing wild animals in his wolf form when he could not buy human food. He is a Cherokee who was expelled from his tribe after he lost control the first time he shifted. No one in his family had shifted for many generations, so he and his parents had no knowledge of the tribe's waning magic.

"He was terrified of what was happening to him and he accidentally killed his parents when he tried to get out of the house and run away. He shifted back to a man when he saw what he'd done and became overcome with grief. His elders kicked him out instead of killing him because they understood that it was an accident and he was not completely at fault."

I peered around the room and made eye contact with every elder who would meet my gaze. "I think that he felt drawn to my presence. That is why he was scanning the sky when I flew overhead and that is why he ran up to the roof to find me. I believe it was the right thing to do to bring him here. And, didn't you say last summer that we could use more magic infused into our tribe? Well, he is clearly magical." I looked over at Silverwolf, who only stared at me in shock.

"How do you know so much about me? I didn't answer any of your questions last night," he whispered.

"I am more than just an angel and a killer of killers. I can read minds, remote view, and when I was mortal, I could dream the future."

The male angel scoffed. "Parlor tricks," he muttered under his breath. I ignored him and no one else's ears were sensitive enough to have heard him.

"Can you still see the future?" one of the old men asked.

"Well, I haven't tried yet. But I did successfully remote view last night before Aleks pulled me out of it. My mind reading has improved a hundredfold since I was turned, which is actually unexpected." I paused and thought that over for a moment. The other vampires hadn't gained their ability to read minds until they were two hundred years old. I shrugged it off and chalked it up to just another one of those things I'd never understand about myself and my unusual gifts. "I will try to focus on it later and see if I can still see the future."

"It would be a shame if you no longer can tell us what to expect," the chief said while a frown deepened all of his wrinkles.

I wasn't sure what to say, so I just bobbed my head in understanding. We all sat in silence for a few moments while the elders silently deliberated on what to do next. I opened my mind to the thoughts of those around me and smiled when it seemed as though they would accept the Cherokee outcast.

A few moments later, the chief stood and walked over to the man who stood beside my chair. "We have decided to allow you to stay. Silent Wolf will teach you how to control your shifting so that you no longer shift against your will when you become angry or scared. Welcome to our tribe, son. You are Hopi now." He smiled at him and extended his hand.

Silverwolf eyed at him curiously for a split second

before he accepted the old man's offer and they shook hands.

"Fantastic. I will inform my family," I said as I stood. "Welcome to the tribe, Silverwolf." I gave him a slight bow and turned to take my leave.

"Sister," Brian said as I was walking through the door. I turned back around to face him. "Yes?"

"Lunch?"

"Sure, Brother. I'll see you then and we can discuss the future." I offered him a small smile before I sped from the building and flew off into the sky.

Our worries of non-natives on our reservation were far less than they had been a year ago. Once every scattered tribal member had returned home, they reclaimed their properties and the population on our reservation was entirely Hopi now. Of course, others still frequented our casino, but that was at the far edge of our lands, and they never strayed to my side of town. I flew freely now during the day as well as at night. I felt a little bit less free with the strange angel following me, though.

I landed in my backyard and wandered into the garden where White Buffalo was teaching Tall Filly about the different plants. I walked up behind my daughter and inspected her still growing wings. They were nearly the size of Taniya's and they were completely covered in beautiful, chocolate colored feathers. I ran my fingers over them and discovered that they felt like satin.

She smiled over her shoulder. "I will fly soon, won't I?"

I beamed back at her. "Indeed, you will. By my math, if your wings grow as fast as you did, they should be a year and a half along by five and a half days. Although, it looks like they will be a year along within a matter of hours, so perhaps you will be flying by…tomorrow night?" I postulated.

"Yay!" she cheered, throwing her arms around my neck. I returned her joyful embrace for a moment before I heard footsteps behind me. I swung around to find Deema approaching me with a paintball gun.

"One of the neighbors gave this to me to help you practice," he said. He held up the gun along with several bags of paintballs.

"Sweet! Let me go get changed first." I flitted off into the house and ran upstairs to my bedroom. I changed into some cut-off jeans and a stretchy, low-backed, spaghetti strap top that I could step into before I flung myself out the window to fly toward the valley. Every time I dove out of a window, I was grateful that the builder, Black Panther, had had the foresight to have every window in the house made large enough for me to fly out of them.

When I reached the valley, Deema was already there with the gun loaded and aimed at me. The winged man was also there, waiting for me, and circling high above the valley floor. Again, he made no attempt at talking to me. He merely watched from afar.

"Wait!" I cried as I dodged the first one. "I shouldn't be ruining my sword with paint like this. I should do this with my bokken."

"Good point," he conceded. He was off in a flash and returned a minute later, bokken in hand. He threw it at me once he landed and I caught it with ease.

"Has anyone ever shot at you with a real gun?" I asked him as he fired five quick shots at me and I dodged them all effortlessly.

"Yes." He fired again.

"And do real bullets harm you?" I dove closer to the ground to slash at him with my wooden sword.

"No, love. We are bulletproof." His grin widened as he shot some more paintballs at me.

"Then would you mind telling me why I should need to

dodge bullets?" I asked when I turned to make another pass over him.

"We don't know if your wings are bulletproof."

"Oh," was all I could come up with.

We practiced until he ran out of ammunition for the silly weapon and then we sped home. "I forgot—my brother's coming to lunch today. I'm supposed to see if I can still see the future," I told Deema on our trip back to the house.

"It's almost noon," he observed. "I hope the kids are already making lunch," he said when we landed in the back yard.

CHAPTER 8

I sat down in my hammock and tried to focus my mind. I had no idea how I was supposed to see the future while I was awake, since I'd never tried before. But I had to do whatever I could to save my tribe, so I was more than willing to give it a shot. I started to think about the last vision I'd had when I was mortal, but nothing new happened.

I remembered how I used to see the future change when people changed their paths, so I made an effort to focus on that. I pictured in my mind the vision I'd had while I was changing and shuddered when they all pointed their guns at me. I made a choice to change what would happen, and the vision snapped into a crisper clarity.

"Wait," I told them in a commanding voice. Some of them hesitated in pointing their weapons at me. "What day is it?"

I stood on the fencepost, my skin glass-like in the sun. Taniya stood on a fencepost to my right, her off-white wings spread wide so she could keep her balance. White Buffalo stood on a post to my left, her skin sparkling slightly and her chocolaty wings folded gracefully behind her. I held my sword at the ready, while Taniya held her hand on the handle of her sword, ready to draw it if needed. I could see others beyond each of them, but could not seem to focus on who they were. The other angels who stood with me were still a mystery.

No one had answered me yet.

I scanned the crowd and saw a flash of green eyes, flecked with blue, and filled with menace. Surprise jolted through me—both in the vision and in real life. I tried to find the eyes again, but they were gone. He knew. He knew and he was hiding now.

I gritted my teeth and pointed at a man who was just outside of what they thought was striking distance. Silly humans. "You," I demanded. "Tell me what day it is." He gawked at me before he informed me that it was June 29, 2072.

I was snapped out of my vision by the sound of the back door slamming shut. I jumped up from the hammock and spun around as I drew my sword.

"Whoa!" Brian exclaimed while he held up his hands defensively. "Sorry. I forgot how easily the door slides shut. I didn't mean to slam it."

I re-sheathed my sword. "It's cool. I guess I shouldn't go into trances unless I've got someone watching over me, anyway," I said with shrug.

"I was watching over you," the male angel whispered.

He stood at the outside corner of my patio. His eyes were intense. I almost couldn't look away. I managed to force myself to focus on my brother instead of the stranger who was trying to intrude on my private life and drive a wedge between me and my family.

"So, did you see the future?" Brian asked, his eyebrows raised hopefully.

"Yes. The white men will invade on June twenty-ninth of next year," I informed him.

"Will we be ready? Can you stop them?" he asked with a hint of worry in his voice.

"I don't know yet." I frowned while I ran over the vision in my mind so he could see it for himself. "So, lunch?" I asked before I turned to go into the house. He followed me inside and we sat down at the table with the rest of my family.

All seven of my children were already seated, along with Taniya, her son, and Silverwolf. Deema took his seat next to me while the twins carried in platters full of meat, bread, and various vegetables.

"I have some announcements to share with you all," I said while they passed around the massive plates of food. "The elders have given Silverwolf permission to stay here and he is now a member of our tribe." I paused for a few moments while everyone welcomed him and gave him congratulations. "Also, I can still see the future, but I'm still figuring out just how to do it."

"What did you see?" Taniya asked with great interest.

I recounted my vision to everyone and they all listened with intense fascination.

CHAPTER 9

S o, we've got about a year?" White Buffalo asked pensively.

"Yep. But that should give us plenty of time to ensure that everyone is capable of fighting, and everyone's wings should be fully grown by then as well. It also gives us one more year to grow and stock up on food for the tribe."

"Now that we're done having children, perhaps we should go somewhere else for a month or so to hunt and raise money for the tribe," Deema suggested. "We still need to build a warehouse to store food and a few silos for grain wouldn't hurt, either."

"Where should we go?" I was afraid to ask what we'd do about our new hanger-on who was lurking around the yard while my family ate. I was certain that the other vampires could also hear his soft, pacing footsteps in the garden. But they seemed to be following my cue of ignoring him when he was around.

"How about New Orleans," Taniya suggested. "I saw on the news the other night that it has been rated the most dangerous city in America. They've had the number one murder rate for over a decade, and they rank pretty high in assault, rape, and robbery as well."

"Saint Louis has a really high murder rate, too, if you all are wanting to kill killers," Silverwolf chimed in.

"So does Washington DC," Brian commented. "I read a few weeks ago that for every 100,000 people, 257 get murdered every year. Plus, there's bountiful thieves there, as well."

"Oh, yeah! We could take out a bunch of crooked politicians and lobbyists!" I cried out in joy. "I bet they taste amazing. Because they don't just ruin one life at a time, they ruin thousands or millions of lives at a time. I wonder if we could get more money off of them," I mused.

"When should we go?" White Buffalo asked.

"How about after the next tribal meeting? It's only a week away and you should be flying by then. Also, Silver Panther will be walking and talking by then, so she can make her own kills." I smiled down at my baby who was sitting in a high chair next to me.

"How is that possible?" Silverwolf asked politely.

"See, all of my kids, except the twins, are half-breeds. Deema impregnated me when I was still mortal, so they are all half angel and half vampire. That is why they can eat food *or* drink blood to sustain themselves. They age rapidly, but by the time my children reach an age of about three months old, they appear to be twenty-five, and they stop aging entirely. Only time will tell if they are just as immortal as we are, but if they start to age again, we'll just turn them all into full vampires so they can live with us forever," I informed him.

"And what of the twins? They look like teenagers," he said after a moment of thought.

"I am a reincarnation of Deema's wife from over 500 years ago. When I was alive then, I gave birth to them and he turned them into vampires when they'd turned sixteen."

"Huh," he said. He sank into thought and returned to eating his lunch.

I heard the angel in the yard snort derisively before he pumped his wings and flew away. Good. One less problem to deal with that day.

Everyone finished their lunch and after we'd all pitched in to clear the table, we went out to the back porch to enjoy the rest of the afternoon. It was surprisingly mild weather, and a pleasant breeze blew through the screened in porch. I pulled out my rolling tray and rolled up several joints to share with my family and friends. Smoking cannabis didn't alter my mind or the way I felt anymore, but I loved the taste of it, so I continued to smoke it. Since it was genetically altered, it tasted like food. I enjoyed being reminded of the tastes of cinnamon rolls, chocolate cake, and blueberry muffins.

"So, can you change at will now?" I asked Silverwolf as I passed him one of the joints.

"Not really," he grunted. "The last time I shifted, I was starving and I saw a deer. I shifted when I ran toward it," he said for the benefit of the others. He knew that I already knew what had happened the last time he'd turned into a wolf. He turned to face Brian. "What do you do to shift? And how do you stop the change when you feel it coming on and don't want to shift?" he asked my older brother.

"I just think angry or calming thoughts, depending on what the situation calls for," he replied as he lit a second joint.

"Why don't you give it a try?" Deema suggested, settling into the hammock with me.

"Here? Now?" Silverwolf asked in disbelief.

"Sure," Brian said. "No time better than the present. You never know when you might need to shift, even if you've been smoking. If you used it right and meditated on it instead of thinking of it as a time to party, it might even help you clear your mind so that you can shift easier. Plus, it wouldn't hurt to get some practice in with fighting.

We've got a year left to get everyone ready for battle and that includes all the shapeshifters."

"Who would I practice fighting with?" Silverwolf asked after he took another hit off the joint.

"I'll practice with you," Deema volunteered.

"But what if I hurt you?" Silverwolf was shocked that my husband would risk getting mauled.

Deema laughed for a few seconds before he was able to answer him. "My skin is impenetrable. The only thing that can draw my blood is a vampire's teeth, and even then, I heal very quickly and it leaves no scar. Fire also harms me, but my flesh repairs just as quickly," he explained.

Silverwolf studied him for a few, silent moments.

Deema stood and walked out to the backyard. "So, let's go."

Silverwolf followed him into the yard and stood still for a few moments, a row of previously harvested lettuce between them.

"Think angry thoughts," Deema instructed him.

Silverwolf bobbed his head and started to focus. He wasn't coming up with anything that helped him change, so I pushed some thoughts into his head. I made him see a sea of soldiers marching toward our lands, hell-bent on our destruction so that they could steal our food and shelters. The air started to vibrate around him when the change into a wolf began. It took him nearly a full minute before he was an animal, and he was still wearing his clothes.

White Buffalo giggled at him. He cocked his head to the side, giving the impression that he was curious. She pointed to his clothes and he let out his own little wolfy chuckle. She stood up and walked over to him. He stepped out of his shoes while she removed his shirt and then she took off his pants. He pulled his lips back over his teeth, let his tongue loll out the side of his mouth, and gave her a wink.

Deema grimaced momentarily before he announced that it was time to fight. I could tell that he was trying to be gentle with the wolf, but he appeared to be having a hard time of it.

I raised my eyebrows at Sandra. *'What's wrong with your dad?'* I asked her with my mind.

She stifled a giggle. *'Silverwolf has a crush on White Buffalo,'* she thought back. *'Dad's not too happy with that.'*

"Oh, right," I said aloud with a giggle of my own.

Deema whipped around and turned his focus to me. "Oh, what?" he growled.

Silverwolf took his distraction as a chance to attack and jumped onto Deema's back. The wolf tried to sink his teeth into the vampire's neck, but he just slid off. He fell onto his back, but quickly regained his feet while Deema swung back around and held up his hand.

"Just give me a minute here," he said with more than a touch of irritation. "Just what is so damned funny?" he demanded, turning his attention back to me and Sandra.

"We can talk about it later," I told him gently. "There's no need to embarrass anyone."

He stomped toward me. "You'll tell me right now," he growled.

"You can't be angry at him for thinking she's beautiful," I whispered as quietly and quickly as I could. I knew he could hear me, no matter how soft I spoke. "She *is* all grown up, even if she is only a year old. She's going to find a mate someday anyway, and we can't stop her."

"I can stop anything I want to!" he boomed when he stopped in front of me.

Everyone turned to stare at him in shock.

I stood and laid my hands on his shoulders. "Calm down, lover," I said gently.

He took a couple of deep breaths, but he was still fuming.

"Do you want me to try and see if I can see what's going to happen?" I asked.

He gave me a curt nod, so I sat back down in the hammock and closed my eyes. I kept a hold on one of his hands, though, and pulled him down to sit beside me.

CHAPTER 10

I focused my mind on White Buffalo and Silverwolf. At first, I just saw them as they were that day, but my vision twisted, grew hazy, and then shifted to something else entirely. I saw them sleeping in a bed, in a room I'd never seen. She mumbled and grimaced in her sleep. He held her tighter and murmured comforting words to her. She fluttered her wings and fell back asleep after she cuddled closer to him.

My vision twisted and grew hazy again before it re-cleared. This time, I saw her in labor. He held her hand and gazed at her lovingly while she pushed out his child—a boy. I saw several more brief flashes, and in them I watched him grow up. He seemed to grow at a normal rate, because I watched his father age as well while his mother remained the same.

I started to worry about her being out of commission for the invasion, so I turned my mind back to June twenty-ninth. When I pictured the vision I'd had before lunch, I realized that nothing would change there—she would still be able to stand at my side.

I pulled myself out of my vision and squeezed Deema's hand. "Worry not," I assured him. "All will be well." I stood and faced my immortal lover. I laid my hands on his shoulders again and stared into his sparkling eyes. "So, don't try to stop this," I said sternly.

He growled deep in his throat before he stood and took a few paces away from me. I kept my hands on him and took the steps with him.

"Don't," he warned me.

"No," I growled back. "*You* don't! And don't you think for a moment that I won't stop you if you try to hurt him." I took my right hand off of him and drew my sword in a blur of movement.

His eyes softened a bit. "You wouldn't dare," he said in disbelief.

"Just try me," I snarled. I was pretty sure the ra-zor-sharp sword wouldn't even cut him, but the threat of harm coming from me was enough of a shock. I could hear whispers behind me. Everyone was wondering what was going on between us and the twins were quietly trying to explain. "Shut up!" I demanded without turning toward them. The murmuring became silence and I continued to stare Deema down. "This is going to happen, and it *must* happen. My tribe needs new magic, and I will not stop any one of my children from finding a mate. *And neither will you!*" I screamed in his face.

"Fine," he grumbled. "But someone else needs to practice with him. I can't do this anymore or I'll kill him," he snarled. He took off straight up into the sky and flew away as fast as he could.

Aleks made a move to go after him, but I put my hand up. "Let him go. He'll come back when he's made peace with this," I said bitterly.

"What is going on?" White Buffalo demanded.

"Your father is upset because he saw in the wolf's mind that he finds you attractive," I told her.

"He's also upset because he saw your visions of the future through my mind," Brian told me.

"Oh." I felt a blush spread to my face that no one could see. I hadn't considered the consequences of having so many mind readers in the same place while I was doing my whole precognition thing. "Maybe I *should* go after him," I said pensively.

"No," Brian said gently. "Just leave him be. He'll come back later. Don't worry."

"Okay." I turned around and faced the wolf. "I'm sorry about this drama. You must think we're all insane."

He chuckled in his wolfy way and shook his head back and forth.

"Aleks?" I called over my shoulder.

He appeared at my side instantly.

"Would you mind training with Silverwolf? I'm going to spy on your dad."

My sixteen-forever-son smiled widely at me before he took a fighting stance. I walked back to the patio and I was instantly bombarded with questions from my children.

"Will you tell me what you've seen?" White Buffalo asked me desperately.

"When will Papa come home?" Black Horse wanted to know.

"Mama, can I have some blood?" Tall Filly begged me.

"Me, too," Silver Panther demanded.

"Enough!" I shouted.

They all gawked at me with utterly stunned expressions. I'd never raised my voice to my children before that day.

"I'm sorry," I said after I took a deep breath. "Sandra, will you take the girls upstairs to feed?"

She scooped up the girls before she zipped through the house and up to the top floor.

"I don't know when he'll come back," I said sadly as I turned to my youngest son. "I have to search the future before I find out. And as for your question," I said after I turned to my first born. "I will take you aside in a little while and tell you. I don't feel comfortable telling everyone every single thing I see about the future."

She reluctantly accepted my promise, so I took my seat in the hammock and tried to relax.

I focused on Deema and sought him with my mind's eye. I saw him while he flew through the sky. He still had anger rippling off of him. He flew as if he was mad at the wind and the clouds. I watched him for at least ten minutes, but I saw nothing that gave me any clue as to where he was or where he was going. I broke from the vision after another five minutes.

I stood up and turned to White Buffalo. "The girls should be done feeding by now, so it is safe for me to go upstairs."

She watched me curiously.

"We should go to your room and discuss my visions of your future," I elaborated.

Silverwolf stopped his advance on Aleks between rows of squash and trotted over to me. He let out a small whimper, so I took a peek inside of his mind. He wanted to hear my visions, too, since he was sure they had to do with him as well. I thought for a moment before I answered him.

"Okay. I suppose you can also hear this, but you might want to stay in wolf form."

The question of '*why?*' rolled off of him in waves.

"You have trouble changing quickly, for one thing. And for another, you can't speak or blush when you're a wolf. You may find this embarrassing."

He ducked his head and glanced over at White Buffalo.

They followed me inside and we went up to the second floor to White Buffalo's bedroom. She sat on her bed while I stood across from her. Silverwolf sat at her feet and she absentmindedly began to pet him like a dog.

"So?" she asked anxiously.

"Well, I've seen your future together. I don't think that my telling you this will change the future, but—I guess I don't really know."

"Just spit it out!" White Buffalo ordered.

I pressed my lips together in a tight line of disapproval before I started to speak again. "I saw you give birth to a son. I saw you two sleeping in a bed in a room that I've never seen before. I saw your child age at a normal rate. I also saw him shift into a wolf, as well as a hawk. As far as I know, no one has ever been able to shift into more than one animal. *That* is why I won't let Deema stop any of our children from finding mates. And yes, it is fairly awkward for me since you're only a year old and already looking at a man in such a way, but—" I sucked in a deep breath and sighed. "But you are the size of and have the mind of an adult. So there is nothing that we can or should do to stop you or any of the others from reproducing. *Someday.* The elders will agree with me because they want fresh magic infused into this tribe just as much as I do. Perhaps even more so."

Silverwolf started to vibrate under White Buffalo's hand and I knew he was turning back into a man. I turned around and grabbed a long bathrobe from her closet. I tossed it to him and he quickly put it on once he was human again. He stayed on his knees and turned toward my daughter.

"Are you really only a year old?" he asked cautiously.

She blushed. "I am. But that certainly does not mean that I have the mindset of a child so young."

"She's right," I chimed in. "She has always had a mind beyond the age of her appearance."

He thought for a moment before he turned back to her. He took her hand in his and gazed at her with love in his eyes.

"What do you think of all of this? What do you think of me?" he whispered.

"I think you're very handsome," she admitted. "And I trust my mother's visions. If she says that we end up together—that we stay together—then I believe her."

"Will you…Would you like to build a house, a life, and a family with me?" he asked hopefully.

She peered at me curiously and I gave her a small nod of approval. She gave him a timid smile, her blush deepening. "I would like to stay with my family until we are sure that the tribe is safe," she told him while she stroked the back of his hand. "But you are welcome here—"

"Well," I interrupted. "We better make sure that your father has calmed down and accepts this before you go making promises to him about his staying here."

"Of course. I'm sorry."

I smiled at her. "No worries, love. I will talk some sense into him when he returns."

"Any idea yet when that will be?" she asked hopefully.

I sat down next to her on the bed and closed my eyes. I searched for Deema with my mind and found that he was still airborne. He was flying over the ocean. I decided that he must be on his way to Russia. I tried to search his future, but all I saw was him running in the woods. He tore up trees by their roots and threw them with all his might. I also saw no clue as to when he might return, so I pulled myself out of the disturbing vision.

"He's going home to Russia, I think. He's going to tear up the forest to release some of his anger. And since he has not yet made a decision about when he'll return, I cannot *see* when he will return," I said sadly. "It takes a day to fly there, and a day to fly back, so he will be gone for at least several days." A sob broke in my chest and White Buffalo hugged me to try to comfort me. "We've never been apart for so long ever since the day we met," I cried through my tearless sobs.

Silverwolf stood up and slipped out of the room to give us some privacy. Or, maybe he was just uncomfortable around crying women. I didn't care to peek into his mind to see. I was far too upset over being separated from my husband.

"Would it make you feel better if we went hunting?" she asked me gently after several minutes.

I thought about it for a moment while I tried to get my emotions under control. The thought of fresh, evil blood caused the burning thirst to rise in my core, so I told her yes.

We went back downstairs and found everyone still sitting on the back patio. "Who wants to go hunting?" I asked when we emerged from the house. A chorus of yeses came at me from all sides.

"But how can we all go?" Singing Sparrow asked me.

"And where will we go?" Long Falcon chimed.

I examined White Buffalo and jerked my head toward her wings. "Why don't you give those a try and see if you can fly yet," I suggested.

"Will you show me how to take off?" she asked with a hint of fear, or perhaps nervousness, in her voice. I bent to the correct angle I used for a standing take-off and slowly started to flap my wings so she could observe the angle of them. I bent my knees and pushed off as I flapped faster. I took to the sky for a few moments and I circled around the house before I came back in for a landing.

She gave me a nod and tried it herself. I corrected her stance only once before she launched successfully. Once she was airborne, I joined her in the sky.

"How do you feel?" I asked her while we circled the neighborhood. "Do you think you could fly several hundred miles while carrying someone else?"

She beamed at me. "Yep. I feel like I could do this all day. It's so easy!"

"Awesome. Now, let's try a landing," I said before I dove toward the ground. My landing was smooth, as usual, while my daughter's was decidedly less than graceful. She grinned at me with a touch of shame, and I instructed her to try again. Her second landing was better, and her third was perfect.

We loaded up all of my children, and the ten of us flew away around two in the afternoon. "Where should we go?" Sandra asked once we were airborne and heading east.

"Hmmm…" I pondered. "Let's try DC."

"Fantastic," Aleks exclaimed. "We'll surely find plenty of evil men there."

CHAPTER 11

We flew for over nine hours before we finally arrived at our destination. It was after one o'clock in the morning—perfect for finding evil men. We landed near a government building and waited for someone worthy of death to cross our paths. I instructed the twins to open their minds with me and comb the surrounding streets for those who had committed heinous crimes. It didn't take long for us to find a gang rape occurring five blocks to the north. I handed Silver Panther to Sandra and the four of us who could fly took to the sky while the rest ran through the streets to follow us.

I landed near the end of the alley to block any escape, but my arrival went unnoticed. They were too wrapped up in their crime. The others landed behind me while those on foot halted behind them.

"Stop!" I commanded in a voice that shook them all to the core.

Seven men turned their glares on me while their victim curled into a ball on the filthy pavement and continued to weep. Their mouths fell open and they stared at me in shock while I took several steps in their direction.

"You are all evil men with souls that rival the moonless night with their darkness," I snarled as I approached and stopped a few feet away from them. "You will be punished for your crimes tonight."

One of the men lifted his handgun and fired a single shot at me. The woman on the ground flinched and whimpered, gripping her arms tighter around her head to hide her face. I gleaned from his mind that he wasn't worried about a single discharge drawing attention. People around there didn't call the cops unless there were numerous gunshots. I sneered bitterly when the bullet disintegrated against my skin and left me unscathed. A few shocked cries erupted from the men.

"Your pitiful weapons are of no use against me, and you've got nowhere to run," I said in a disgusted tone. I pointed to the man who'd tried to shoot me. "Sergio, come here."

"H—how do you know my name?" he stammered, taking a few steps backward.

"I said *here*," I snarled, taking four lightning-fast steps toward him. I grabbed him by the throat and held him a foot off the ground while I spoke to him again. "I know many things about you. Do you really think God would make an angel who could not see your sins?" I scoffed. "I know that you used to rape your own cousin when you two were children, and now she is so scarred from it, she has become a prostitute. I know that you pimp her out to your friends and sometimes you even watch through a hole in the wall. For your crimes against children, you will die at the hands of a child."

Sandra was suddenly at my side with my youngest in her arms.

"I will eat your soul," Silver Panther said in her tiny, wind chime voice as she reached for his neck. It wasn't hard for me to not laugh at her because even killing horrible people wasn't funny. But the humor of her fib wasn't lost on her siblings. They, too, remembered watching some old movie the day before in which that was a comedic line. I heard their mental giggles even though they were strong enough to not voice them.

His eyes grew wide and he tried to struggle out of my grasp, but I would not release him. The harder he struggled, the more I tightened my grip around his thick, muscled neck. My youngest child sank her perfect, razor-sharp teeth into his flesh and drank his blood as if she was dying of thirst.

The other six men stared at me in horror for a moment before they noticed the others standing behind me. They tripped over each other—and the woman who was still crying on the pavement—in their efforts to escape their punishment.

"You all know your crimes," I announced. "And your efforts to flee are useless. You will all be punished tonight, so I suggest you make your peace with that and die like a man—not a whimpering, crying, pitiful version of a man."

I glanced over my shoulder at my children and jerked my head toward the terrified evil-doers. Faster than mortal eyes could see, my half-breed offspring were on them in a split second. When Silver Panther could drink no more, I gladly finished off the blood of the man who'd shot at me.

After all the rapists were dead and thrown into a dumpster, I approached the cowering woman on the ground. "Lexanna," I said gently as I laid my hand on her shoulder.

She jerked away from me and whimpered in a pitiful way.

"It's all right, love. We came here to save you. I'm so sorry we didn't get here sooner," I said quietly in my most soothing voice.

She peeked out from under her arm that was covering her face.

"Are you really an angel?" she squeaked between sobs.

"Yes, dear, I am," I assured her. '*Aleks, give me your shirt,*' I told my son with my mind. He quickly removed it and tossed it to me. I helped the terrified girl stand up and I gently put the shirt over her head to cover her nudity. They had ripped her clothes into useless scraps that would cover nothing of her frail, broken body. Luckily, he was taller than her, so his shirt hung on her petite frame like a short dress.

"Now, I cannot take you to a hospital for obvious reasons," I said, rustling my wings. "They would want to catch me and do experiments on me. But one of my daughters can escort you and make sure that you get good treatment. Is that all right?"

She shivered in my arms when a cool breeze blew through the alley. "How did you kill them? How did you find me? Did God send you? Did He answer my prayers?" she asked me, her voice still shaking. I peeked into her mind and saw that she'd been so terrified, she'd kept her face covered the whole time while we drank their blood. I breathed an inaudible sigh of relief.

"None of that matters now," I said. "What matters is that you got away from them, okay?"

She feebly nodded her head.

"Long Falcon," I whispered.

My daughter came to my side and took the terrified woman in her arms.

"You are safe now," she assured her, scooping her up and speeding from the alley.

I stood silently, closed my eyes, and watched with my third eye as the battered woman was whisked off to the hospital. Along the way, Long Falcon explained to her what she needed to tell the doctors and nurses so that we would not be discovered.

"If your thirst is satisfied, I suggest that you return home," I told my children. "I must feed some more, and I will carry Long Falcon back home." They all regarded me with similar expressions of doubt and uncertainty. "I will catch up with you in a few hours," I assured them.

Singing Sparrow and Jumping Wolf climbed onto Aleks while Black Horse and Tall Filly climbed onto Sandra. White Buffalo took Silver Panther in her arms, and they all flew away.

CHAPTER 12

"H ope," a soft, sultry voice said in my ear once I was
alone.
I whipped around and saw the male angel a few
yards away. He stood with his hands clasped behind his
back while he watched me with a stoic expression.

"How'd you do that?" I demanded. "I felt and heard no
movement."

"Do you mean, how did I do this?" Again, I heard his
whisper in my ear, even though his lips didn't move. But
this time I also felt his hand caressing my face.

I stepped back and swatted away the invisible hand.
"Stop that," I said with a gasp.

"When will you give me some time? It is so hard to get
you alone." He spoke normally this time.

I hoped he'd keep it up. "Who says I want you around?"
I snapped.

"Want me or not, you need me. Hope, you have to remember who you are. You must regain your knowledge of
everything that you can do. For the love of God, Hope, you
need to remember your love of God!"

"What if I don't want to remember?"

He sighed and rubbed the bridge of his nose. "Always
so stubborn, are you not? Cannot even remember who you

are, but yet you are still so perpetually obstinate." He shook his head ruefully and cracked a tiny smile before he seemed to remember himself.

"So, you know me?" I couldn't help but wonder.

"Hope," he said tenderly. "We all know each other."

"Oh." I grew a little confused and glanced away from his penetrating gaze.

"Yes," he said as his expression grew soft and sad.

"Yes to what?" I whispered.

He sighed and glanced away for a moment before he swallowed hard. "You should know, Hope. You should not have to ask. You should be in here with me—with us." He tapped his temple. "You should be out there with me. But here you are—an abomination."

"Hey, fuck you, man!"

His lip curled up and his nose wrinkled like he smelled something bad. "Disgusting," he grumbled, shaking his head.

"I thought angels liked sex. You know, hence all the Nephilim and everything?"

"We are all products of our environment," he said while he stared up at the sky.

"What's that supposed to mean?"

"Again, you should already know. I need to figure out how to fix you. I will be around. You should know, but you will not."

"I'm beginning to dislike you."

"You should not," he whispered in my ear as his phantom hand caressed my face again.

I moved away in protest and started to yell at him, but he was already gone.

I was shaken and confused, but I was also still thirsty. I combed the surrounding streets with my mind until I found another worthy victim. He was in his fancy townhouse where he sat in his office and planned his next betrayal of the American public. I searched his mind for his crimes. He was indeed a very evil man whose only concern was his own wealth and success. I took to the sky and flew silently to his home, breaking the lock on his back door with ease, and slipped inside without a sound.

"Andrew," I whispered in a chiding tone while I stood in his doorway.

He peered up slowly, expecting his mistress who was sleeping upstairs. His eyes grew wide when he saw my sparkling, white wings. I stepped into the room and expanded my wings to their fullest.

"You are quite an evil man, Andrew, and there is nowhere left for you to run," I said in a matter-of-fact tone.

"A—are you the angel of d—death? Am—am I dead?" he stammered, clutching his chest. I could hear his rapid pulse and his thoughts that told him he must be having a heart attack, or perhaps a dream.

"This is no dream," I assured him. "And yes, I am an angel. And no, you are not dead. Yet." I strode forward and laid my hands on his desk before I continued. "But I am here to punish you," I said in a voice so cold, it even chilled me to the core.

"Please," he whispered. "Please, don't kill me. I'll give you anything you want." He glanced over to the book shelf and I saw in his mind that he had almost a quarter of a million dollars in his safe that was disguised as books by Mark Twain.

"Oh, please," I scoffed. "Do you really think you can buy your way out of this? Do you really believe that a creature of God cares about wealth?" I walked over to the hidden safe and ripped the door off, exposing the piles of cash.

He gasped in disbelief at my display of strength.

I heard him wonder why I'd come for him and not any of the other congressmen who'd assisted him in passing so many unconstitutional laws. I was by his side in a flash. "Oh, they will all get their turns to die by my hands." I grabbed his hair in my left hand and his shoulder with my right. I pulled his head to the side and I sank my teeth into his neck. The blood squirted into my mouth like a hot fountain of deliciousness and I relished in the wonderful taste of his evil blood.

Once I'd swallowed that first draught, I was deep into his mind and owned all of his memories. I joined him in watching his life flash before his eyes. Parts of it made me sad, but most of his adulthood made me wish I could kill him again and again. I sucked every last drop from his withered, old body before I dropped him to the floor with a thud.

That was when I heard his mistress upstairs. She'd heard the noises and wondered if there was a break-in.

I grabbed his briefcase, dumped its contents onto the floor, and filled it with the cash from his safe. I dove out the window a split second after the young woman ran into the room. I listened to her mind while I flew away, and I knew that she'd seen me.

She was shocked, to say the least, but she was not beyond believing in angels. She knew what she'd seen, and she planned on telling everyone she knew. After she watched me fly into the distance from the window I'd crashed through, she turned and tried to tend to the dead man on the floor.

I decided that there was nothing I could do about it at that point because she wasn't an evil woman. She was just young and dumb. I couldn't very well kill her for being stupid enough to think that sleeping with a congressman would land her a good job in the nation's capital. I also decided that my thirst was not yet satisfied, so I landed on top of the Library of Congress and searched the area for some more killers from which to feed.

CHAPTER 13

I soon found my next victim a few blocks to the south. He was standing in a dark alley, waiting for a woman to pass by that he'd been stalking for several weeks. He'd gotten her routine down pat, and tonight was the night, he thought to himself with a good deal of relish. Tonight, he'd make her his own and she'd never be with another man again. I looked around him with my third eye, and saw that she was only steps away from his path. I left the briefcase on the roof and pushed off toward the dark alley where he was crouched. He sprang from the shadows before I could make it there and dragged her into the alley.

"There's nowhere to run," he whispered into her ear. He pulled her into the shadows, his hand clapped over her mouth to muffle her screams.

"Indeed," I said as I landed between him and the street. "There's nowhere for you to run, either, you sick son of a bitch."

He stared at me in shock while he tried to figure out what to do. He couldn't draw his weapon or attack me, because then his prize would get away.

"She's not your prize, Eddie," I growled at him as he continued to drag her away. "Release her!"

Her teary eyes were wide, staring at me, begging me

with her mind to save her. I took three lightning-fast steps toward him, hissing in anger at his defiance. He finally dropped her and she crawled away to cower next to the brick wall.

I lunged at the dirtbag and quickly sank my teeth into his neck. His blood was not as sweet as the politician's, but it was certainly evil enough to be worthy of death. While I drained him of his blood, I watched his memories of all the women he'd kidnapped, raped, and murdered. Once he was dead, I emptied his pockets and threw his corpse into the dumpster in the back corner of the alley. He'd been caught before and served some time. I'd learned from his memories that he might even have been back under suspicion for crimes he'd recently committed. I figured if the cops found him, they wouldn't be too worried about finding his killer and they could even identify him by his dental records.

"I'm sorry you had to witness that, Lucia," I said gently before I helped her to her shaking feet. She was terrified that I would kill her next. "Don't worry, honey. I came here tonight so that you may continue living. You have helped the lives of many, and I want you to continue living so that you can help others, too. I only ask that you tell no one what you've seen here tonight."

She pressed her back against the wall. "Are you—are you a—You drank his blood. But—but you have wings. Are you an angel? Or are you a vampire?" she stammered.

"I *am* an angel," I assured her as I spread my wings wide.

"But you drank his blood," she said in disbelief.

"Yes, I did. Vampires are not evil creatures," I assured her. "The blood of the innocent tastes very bitter to us. Sort of like bile, I suppose."

She gasped. "So you *are* a vampire."

"Easy, love, easy," I said, taking a step back to give her

some space. "The only way you should ever fear a vampire is if you turn to a life of crime. We only kill evil people. But please, tell no one of what you've seen here tonight. If anyone were to know of my existence, they would stop at nothing to catch me and experiment on me." I sighed. "And it would not be the first time."

She stared at me curiously, so I felt I should explain.

"The AUTO virus is a man-made manipulation of the vampire virus, which was created by God to keep crime in check. The government wanted to create an army of super soldiers who would never die, but they made a mistake and instead created a deadly virus that cannot be controlled or cured. So, please, tell no one of what you've seen," I implored.

She bobbed her head up and down as she started to back out of the alley. "Will I ever see you again?" she whispered.

"Let's hope that you don't," I said with a wink. I pushed off into the sky and flew away while she watched in awe.

I landed on the roof of the library where I'd left the case full of money and tossed in my latest victim's wallet. I crouched on the corner like a gargoyle and scanned the area for evil thoughts.

After a few seconds, I found another group of men who were cornering an innocent woman. I pushed off to the east and found them in time to prevent them from raping her. I folded my wings back and silently dropped from the sky. I landed behind the five men and broke the neck of the one farthest from the defenseless woman. Her eyes grew wide but her tears continued to fall. Her cries for mercy ceased when she watched me drain the man of his blood.

It surprised me a little bit that none of the other men noticed my appearance, but they were too engrossed in their enjoyment of the woman's terror to watch their own backs. They taunted her while I fed, making kissy noises, pinching her, and touching her hair. I dropped the drained corpse at my feet and stepped over him to pluck another from the group.

That time, the man standing next to him noticed when his partner in crime was suddenly dragged backward. He spun around to face me and caught me "red-handed" while I was killing his friend. I sneered at him as I drank and pushed the thought of *'you're next'* into his mind while I hastily sucked out the blood instead of waiting for it to pump into my mouth. In just a couple of seconds, I'd completed my fifth kill of the night. I dropped him at my feet before I snatched up my stammering observer.

Once his babbling ceased, his comrades noticed his absence. The last two men turned their backs to their cornered victim and faced me with mine. I leered at these last two when they drew their weapons and demanded that I drop their friend. I took two more deep draws before his lifeless body hit the pavement.

I licked my bloody lips, raised my hands, and stretched my wings to the sky.

"You wouldn't shoot an unarmed angel, would you?" I said with a frown.

They glanced at each other quickly before they both fired at me. The woman let out a shriek and cringed away as the bullets crumbled against my chest.

My frown deepened and I stepped toward them, clearly unscathed. I wrapped my hands around their necks to keep them silent while I drained them of blood one by one.

When I had finished killing them, I turned to the woman who still cowered in the corner. I gently pulled her hands down from her face and told her that she was safe now. "But tell no one of what you've seen tonight," I warned her as I walked her to the mouth of the alley. "No one would believe you anyway," I assured her.

She regarded me doubtfully, but she agreed to not tell

anyone. Then I saw a flash of her roommate in her mind, along with the thought that she would only tell her.

I stopped in my tracks. "Lucia is your roommate? Yes, I can read your mind," I confirmed before she could ask me. "Well," I said pensively. "I suppose you can tell her since I saved her from a similar fate before I came to your rescue." I stepped back into the shadows to wait for her to leave before I emptied the pockets of her attackers and disposed of their corpses. "But only Lucia," I said sternly. I pushed the thought into her head that she should hurry home, and she didn't hesitate to turn around and run away.

I felt sloshy when I pushed off into the sky and headed back toward the Library of Congress to retrieve the briefcase. I threw the five wallets into the case before I took off and turned west.

My family had had about a two hour head start, so I figured I'd catch up with them in an hour or less. I marveled at how easily I could feel my internal compass since I'd become a vampire. I knew as I soared through the sky that I'd never need a compass again. Every time the wind blew me slightly off course, I'd feel the change and adjust my direction.

I pushed my wings to their limits and, before I knew it, I was soaring past my children. My first thought was that if I kept going, I could get some much needed alone time with Deema.

But my heart dropped as I came to two realizations at once. First of all, Deema was gone and he wouldn't be back for days. Secondly, I'd left my daughter in Washington DC. I was supposed to pick her up after she was done at the hospital, but it had slipped my mind. I quickly turned around and went back to my kids who were flying home. "I have to go back," I said shamefully. "Please, please don't tell Long Falcon that I left her behind. I was so distracted—I will return shortly."

Sandra and White Buffalo giggled when I turned around again and sped back to the capital. I was quite high in the sky, so I felt confident in searching for her briefly with my third eye. I immediately found my daughter and, much to my relief, she was still sitting in the hospital with Lexanna. I pulled myself from the vision before I started to fall too low in the sky.

I made it back to DC in less than an hour and landed on the dome of the capitol building. I clung to the back of the statue at the peak of the roof and I searched for her with my mind again.

She looked up after a second and scanned the room suspiciously after I began watching her. I wondered if she felt my presence, so I pushed my thoughts into her head. '*I am ready to leave whenever you are,*' I whispered in her mind.

She seemed surprised for a second before she closed her eyes and I felt our minds connect. '*I would like to wait until I can escort her home. She has not even seen a doctor yet,*' she explained. '*She is still very shaken up.*'

'*Okay,*' I replied. '*Let me know when you're ready. I'm going to look in on the other women I saved tonight.*' I pulled back from the connection with her since I saw a nurse approaching them as I said my last words to her.

I scanned the minds of those in close proximity to make sure I still hadn't been seen. Once I was satisfied that I'd remained unnoticed, I searched the city for two somewhat familiar mind signatures.

I found the two women whose lives I'd saved only hours before sitting in the living room of the townhouse they shared. They both fully agreed on my description and my insistence that they tell no one of their encounter. I watched them for about forty-five minutes, just to ensure that they would keep their word to me. After a lengthy discussion of their encounters with the "holy blood drinker," they made a pact to never tell anyone else. Even if others came forward and went public with similar stories, they swore that they'd never tell another soul.

I pulled myself from the vision and searched for my daughter once again. The sun was rising and my concern over being seen was growing extreme. It was a city of early risers, and I needed to get out of sight soon. She was walking down the sidewalk with Lexanna. She held her around the waist and supported most of her weight while she limped down the road. Long Falcon kept her head up and watched with intense alertness as they made their way through the streets in the wee hours of the morning. I saw them getting close to her home, so I flew there to meet them.

Once Lexanna was safely in her house with the doors locked, I swooped down from the roof and scooped my daughter up in my arms. We took off into the sky and I pushed my wings to the limit, heading west.

CHAPTER 14

Once everyone was settled in for the night, I took off by myself to practice in the valley with my sword. Aleks had offered to come with me, but Sandra stopped him.

"If she wanted help, she would ask," she whispered to him in Russian.

"Of course," he murmured. "You know where we are if you want some company." He turned back to the garden and began to pull weeds again.

"Thank you. I shouldn't be too long. I'll try to be back before the kids have breakfast." Without another word, I flew west and landed in my valley alone. Or so I'd thought. The angel was waiting for me.

"Hope," he said in a quiet, mournful voice.

"Please, leave me alone."

"You cannot truly mean that. If only you would re-member." He sighed, long and deep. I heard his voice again, but it was just in my head and it wasn't in English. It was the language of the whispers that had been scaring me for over two years.

"Stop that!" I gasped.

"I miss you so much. We all do. Will you not let *us* help you instead of these abominations?"

I narrowed my eyes. "Who is we?"

"Your own kind. We can and will help you, if only you would ask and accept us."

"My own kind are already helping me," I said through tight lips and gritted teeth.

"Those creatures you call your children should not even exist." He turned his back on me and began to walk away. "That bastard whom you call your husband has already killed both of us more times than you know."

"What are you talking about?"

He spun around to face me again with an intense, desperate expression. "Come with me, Hope. Turn away from them and leave with me. Let me help you remember who you are—what you are. Because this—" He gestured to me with a suddenly disgusted countenance. "—is not what you are meant to be."

"I'm not leaving my family for you." My voice was as icy as my skin.

"Please, Hope. I need you. You need me. We belong together. We need to defeat your enemies together."

"I don't know you, therefore I cannot trust you."

He covered his face with his hands and a sob escaped him. I watched with a small amount of sympathy as his shoulders shook and he wept. "I have missed you so much, for so long. My sweet Hope. I have never seen you so cold in so many ways. Please, please, remember."

"I'm not going anywhere with you," I said firmly. "Now, I want you to leave."

Without another word, he disappeared into thin air.

"Asshole," I muttered. "My family is not an abomination. My children are wonderful and beautiful and I'd do anything for them."

'*Then you should remember who you are so that you are powerful enough to save them,*' the angel's voice said in my mind.

"Dick," I grumbled.

'*Potty-mouth,*' he retorted.

I growled in frustration and drew my sword. "If you come back here, I'll fucking cut you!" I screamed into the night.

He suddenly appeared right in front of me. "You could not kill me even if you tried."

Before I could even lift my arm, he was gone again. I felt his spectral hand caressing my face. Despite the futility of my action, I swung my katana. It bounced off of my cheek. Of course, I was unscathed. I growled again in rage.

But somewhere, deep down inside of myself, I still felt my calm center. This serene part of my mind wondered just how much of my temper was the vampire I'd become. I certainly hadn't always been so hostile. This small, muted part of myself desired to grow. Could I let it? Would I allow it to become more of who I was? What if I did let this angel teach me about myself? Was it going to make me stop loving my family if I let him make me what he wanted me to be?

No. I couldn't do that. I wasn't willing to risk losing my kin just to please this creature who could pop in and out of reality at will. I was determined to keep myself as I was. So what if I'd known him before? How much use would my old memories actually be in helping my tribe avoid destruction? I had plenty of powers already. I couldn't imagine anything this angel could offer me that would be worth giving up the love of my husband.

I used my anger to my advantage while I spent the rest of the pre-dawn hours swinging my sword. I still wasn't able to move how I felt I should—like the blade was an extension of my own body. But I did feel like I was showing some improvement.

CHAPTER 15

Three days after Deema's abrupt departure and my trip to Washington with our kids, my husband finally returned home. I was flying around with White Buffalo over the practice valley, teaching her some offensive and defensive flying tactics when he appeared over the western horizon. Much to my relief, his appearance caused the angel who'd been watching us to disappear into the ether again.

"I'm sorry I reacted like that," he said quietly while he floated next to me.

"I think you should be apologizing to your daughter," I said in a neutral tone. I was no longer upset with him, but I wasn't exactly ready to embrace him and welcome him home with the usual passion I had for him, either.

"I *am* sorry, White Buffalo," he said with shame slathering his voice.

"What made you change your mind?" she asked him.

"I—I'm not really sure. Maybe I just..." He sighed deeply and thought for a moment. "I tore up acres and acres of trees," he confessed. "I guess I worked out all of my anger and then I was able to think clearly. Your mother is right. I should not stop you or any of the others from finding mates. I realized eventually that if it was one of the boys—who are even younger than you—if one of them had found a woman they wanted to be with, I would not have thought twice about it. I realized that that was a terrible way to see things. It is backward reasoning and I should not be thinking in such a way. Can you both forgive me?" he asked with desperation in his eyes.

I glanced at my daughter and she gave him a brief nod before she flew into his arms.

"Yes, Papa." She grinned as she embraced him. "Thank you for seeing it my way."

She released him and turned to fly home as fast as her wings would carry her. The others would be anxious to learn of Deema's return.

"I guess I can forgive you, too," I said in a sullen voice while a teasing smile played on my lips.

He turned back to me with a look of shock spread across his face, but once he saw my smile, one of his own took its place. He tackled me to the ground and covered me in kisses.

"I've missed you so much," he whispered fervently. His hands ran over my body and his lips traveled to my neck. I felt my desire for him burning in my loins and I pressed against him. I started to unbutton his shirt. "I see you've missed me, too," he said as he stopped his groping and ran his fingers through the base of my loosely braided hair.

I grinned at him for a split second before I finished removing his shirt and started on his pants. He smiled back at me before he took off my pants and floated up underneath me. We made passionate love until the sun set and I relished every second of our contact.

"We should probably go home," he muttered between kisses in the fading light.

I attacked him again. "Mm…I don't want to."

"Shouldn't we go hunting?"

At the mention of hunting, the thirst rose in my core and

started to spread to the rest of my body. "Okay," I conceded. I stood up and put my clothes back on in a rush
before I flew home.

"What took you so long?" Taniya asked once I landed.
"I thought he got home hours ago."

I looked at her sheepishly and smiled the smile that had
always graced my lips whenever I blushed from embarrassment. Even though the blood could no longer redden
my checks, she recognized my expression well enough to
know what we'd been doing.

"Oh," she said with a giggle. "Gottcha." She continued
to chuckle as she went inside to gather the others. "They're
back!" she called out through the open door. Our children
all rushed down the stairs and out the back door at the
same moment that their father landed in the backyard.

"Who wants to go hunting?" he asked everyone who'd
gathered around him to welcome him home. They all
agreed that a late dinner of blood would be nice.

"Where should we go?" Black Horse wondered aloud.

"I heard they're having a problem with a bear overpopulation in the Rockies," Aleks suggested. He got a
mixed reaction. Some stared at him like he was crazy,
while the rest were thoughtful. "I just figured that we
could stay close to home tonight since we're about to leave
for a whole month soon. It would also be a lot of meat for
us to dry for the tribe," he elaborated.

"Okay," Deema said. "Where?"

"Due west of Castle Rock and just north of Devils
Head."

"Everyone ready?" Deema asked, turning back to the
group. They all nodded their heads before they started to
pile onto those of us who could fly. "What about Silver
Panther and Tall Filly?" he asked after a moment.

"I think they need to be getting to bed. If they need
blood, there's still plenty in the fridge and I don't want

them hunting big game until they're fully grown. But—" I drew a few lines in the dirt absentmindedly with my foot.

"But?" Deema pressed when I didn't continue.

"Well, I was wondering if maybe the wolves would like to come with us." I glanced up as I spoke and saw Deema was about to protest. "It would do them good to hunt something that they can kill," I clarified. "And, since we have five hunters now that can fly, and only four that can't who will be going with us, I just thought it would be nice," I mumbled.

Deema raised his eyebrows at me while I begged him with my eyes.

"I don't know," he said pensively. "What do you guys want to do?" he asked my brother and our daughter's new boyfriend. They were still standing just inside the back door. They both considered for a moment before they shrugged, nodded, and came to join our group.

White Buffalo cheerfully pulled Silverwolf to her and pushed off into the sky. Singing Sparrow climbed down from Sandra's back and jumped into my waiting arms. Silent Wolf mounted the eternal teenager's back and the rest of us took to the sky to join my first born. I did my best not to laugh at my massive brother being carried by the petite vampire.

The trip to the mountains took a little over an hour. We landed in a small clearing and waited for a moment while the three wolves changed shape. Jumping Wolf had announced shortly before we landed that he'd decided to hunt as a wolf with the other two. After the wolves emerged from the trees with their clothes in their muzzles, we vampires smelled the wind, searching for some large game to hunt.

I caught the scent first and took off running toward it. I crashed through the trees and knocked over the ones I didn't have room to dodge. In a matter of seconds, I was on top of the massive bear. I latched onto his neck and sank my razor-sharp teeth into his jugular. It tasted odd to me since I'd never drank blood other than a criminal's, but it was acceptable. It had a sort of woodsy flavor. I drained the bear and stared at him for a moment when I was done. I'd have to remember where I left the carcass so we could haul it back to cook for the tribe later. I scanned the forest and saw Deema perched on a tree limb, smiling at my first wild kill.

"That was...interesting." He grinned, jumped down from the tree, and landed a few inches in front of me. He leaned over and kissed me for a second before he licked the dribbles of blood from my face. "You need to work on getting *all* of the blood into your mouth, though," he teased.

"Come on," I said, rolling my eyes. "I need to drink some more. And it would be nice if you made a kill, too." I turned and ran through the trees.

CHAPTER 16

Running was effortless. I felt like I could run for days on end if I needed to. I sniffed the air while I ran, searching for another bear. I made a sharp turn when I caught the scent and burst through the trees into another small clearing.

I wasn't expecting what I found. There was a mountain lion crouched next to his own fresh kill—the bear I had smelled.

He rose to his feet and growled at me from deep in his throat, the moonlight glinting off of his eyes.

"Easy," I assured him, backing away and rustling my wings. "I mean you no harm."

He stood his ground, but he also stopped growling at me. His head cocked to the side a bit.

"That's no mountain lion," Deema told me from a tree far above my head.

I didn't dare to risk taking my eyes off of the predator to glance at Deema, so I continued to stare into his eyes while I dug through the lion's mind.

"Fierce Lion," I said once I learned a few things about the "cat" who stood before me. "I see you are a Navajo man underneath your furry coat." He jumped back—a bit like a startled house cat—and I felt the confusion rolling off of him in waves. "I am Hopi," I said as I took a step closer. "We live in such close proximity and...well, we had no idea that your tribe contained such magic. We thought that the Hopi were the only ones who could still shapeshift, and even our numbers are dwindling. Only twenty percent of our men can shift." I'd continued to walk toward him while I spoke and stopped just a few feet away from him. The scent of the blood from his kill caused the burning thirst to rise inside of me, but I tamped down the feeling. "I can read your mind, so if you don't want to change back to talk to me, that's okay. Just think your answers," I informed him.

'*You are white,*' he thought. '*You are not Hopi.*'

"Oh, but I am. My name is White Eagle."

'*...wings?*' I only caught the trail end of his thought.

"I grew my wings several years ago. I was the first of the Hopi Angels. But I mated with a vampire and I had to be turned into one after the birth of our seventh child. All of our girls will grow wings like mine, and our boys shift. Also, our last daughter is Silver Panther," I told him gently.

'*Impossible!*' His mind echoed the word a few times before he shook his head in an attempt to clear it.

"Are there many like you? In your tribe?" I asked him while I called my brother with my mind.

'*No. I am the first to change into an animal for many generations. Our elders also thought that the magic was gone from our tribe. They told me I should roam the mountains and try to find others like me to bring back to the tribe, but I have found none. I have been out here, all alone, for almost three years. But I am so curious now. You have shapeshifters that are men and women?*'

"No, not really," I said with a small smile and a shake of my head. "My daughter is the only female shifter."

I heard the wolves crashing through the woods to my

right and the Navajo lion turned to face the oncoming opponents.

"Wolves! Stop! He's one of us," I called out when they got closer to the tree line.

They skidded to a stop and stared at the massive cat, panting heavily after their long, hard run.

"Fierce Lion, I would like you to meet some of my family. The largest is my big brother—Silent Wolf. The smallest is my son—Jumping Wolf. And the gray one is my daughter's boyfriend. He is a Cherokee, whom we very recently welcomed into our tribe, and his name is Jonathan Silverwolf. Guys, this is Fierce Lion. He is Navajo and he is the first to shift in his tribe in many generations. So, be nice," I warned them. "He may be our close ally in the near future."

'We need to speak with him,' my brother informed me. *'Please leave so we can shift.'*

"Of course," I told him before I turned back to the mountain lion. "I will take my hunting elsewhere. My brother would like to speak to you since he is on our Council of Elders and he knows much that I do not. Please, shift into a man because the other two can't read your mind like he and I can." I saw the air start to shimmer with the magic of the change around all four men, so I turned my back to them and ran through the trees.

I caught up with White Buffalo after she finished her second bear. "Where ya been, Mama?" she asked me when I burst through the trees.

I beamed at her. "We found a mountain lion. The wolves shifted back into men, as did the lion, and they're all having a little sit down. He's the first Navajo to shift in many generations."

"Navajo? They border our lands, don't they?"

"Indeed they do. But, since he is their only shifter, he may end up joining our tribe. Actually, I think I'm going to look into that before I finish my hunting. Watch out for me?" I asked her as I leaned up against a tree.

"Of course," she replied gleefully.

I closed my eyes and turned my thoughts to the Navajo lion. I saw him standing in a familiar field, helping my sons harvest wheat. Then I saw him sitting down with the elders and asking permission to marry my second daughter, Singing Sparrow.

I was jerked from my vision by White Buffalo's hands shaking my shoulders. "Mama, we've got to go," she hissed when I opened my eyes.

Without even thinking, I scooped her up in my arms, crouched down, and sprang straight up to land on a tree branch. I crouched and sprang again to reach a higher branch. I needed to see sky before I flew since I didn't know if breaking trees would hurt my daughter or her wings. After my third vertical jump, I saw a break in the trees and I took to the sky.

"What's happening?" I asked her once we were airborne.

"I heard voices that were not anyone we know," she told me. Her voice trembled with adrenalin.

"We need to land somewhere and find out what's happening. Where were they? Can you fly to them if I release you?"

"I think so," she replied.

I let her go and she spun around to head back the way we'd come. She dove down through the trees and landed silently on a branch. I followed her and landed just as noiselessly beside her. She pointed down to the ground below us, and I saw a group of armed men tromping through the forest. I dug inside their minds for a moment and discovered that they were also out hunting bears to try and ease the overpopulation. I couldn't help but wonder what kind of idiots would hunt at night.

I searched the area for the rest of my family and saw that the hunters were about to come across the four naked shapeshifters. I turned to the sky and howled long and loud like a wolf. It was enough to grab my family's attentions and they knew that I was calling them. Brian latched onto my thoughts and understood my warning right away.

"Hunters!" I heard him whisper from two hundred yards in front of me. "Scatter!" he instructed the others before he took off running toward me. As he sped past the stunned hunters, he started to shift. They had no idea what to think. It was quite a shock to find a huge naked man running through the woods in the middle of the night, dozens of miles from the nearest town. Luckily, they didn't see him transform since the change didn't complete until he'd disappeared among the trees. When he reached the elm I was standing in, he howled as he blew past it.

I searched the forest again for the rest of my family and saw that they were all gathering again in a clearing about a mile away. I turned to my daughter and pointed to the sky, then the direction she needed to fly toward. I jumped down from the tree as she took to the sky and I ran to the clearing. I stopped once I was amongst my family and tried to explain what was happening.

"We need to relocate. I think a few miles away should do it," I informed them when they eyeballed at me quizzically.

"There is a group of men who are hunting the bears to decrease their population, just like we are. Only, they are using guns," Deema explained.

"Should we just call it a night?" Black Horse asked no one in particular.

"I haven't fed enough yet," I told him.

'*And the wolves haven't fed at all,*' Brian pushed into my head. '*We've been a little busy talking to the Navajo.*'

"And my brother says the wolves haven't eaten yet,

either," I told them all after Brian finished his thought.

"Are you sure?" Singing Sparrow asked me. "I saw a half-eaten bear about a mile away from here."

"That was mine." The deep, husky voice came from behind me. I quickly turned around to face the man who'd somehow managed to approach us silently. My sword was drawn by the time my turn was complete, but he stood his ground. He was one of the most beautiful men I'd ever seen. His muscles were chiseled to perfection and his russet skin lightly glistened with perspiration. He was completely nude, but he held a large piece of bark in front of him to hide his genitals. I immediately realized that he was Fierce Lion and I re-sheathed my sword.

"We need to go quickly," I urged, turning back to my family.

"Who is that?" Singing Sparrow asked dreamily.

Sandra giggled at her tone and her father clenched his jaw.

"Later," I said before I ran past them all to lead the way to a new place to hunt.

I heard the wolves coming up behind me, so I slowed down and let them take the lead. They made a few twists and turns, but soon came upon a pair of mating bears. I laughed to myself while I took down the male and the wolves tore open the female to feed from her. Fierce Lion quickly joined the wolves and the four of them devoured the bear. The twins ran on to find themselves a couple of other bears to kill, while the rest of the family spread out to hunt some more as well.

Once everyone was done feeding, we gathered again to discuss our next move.

"What do you see happening in the future with this lion?" Deema asked me.

I peered at my lover apologetically. "He needs to return to the rez with us. I've seen him having discussions with our elders." I decided not to tell him about the lion's request for marriage to our half-breed daughter just in case he got angry again.

He studied me as if he knew I was hiding something, but he shrugged and said that we'd better move out before the hunters came upon us again. I looked at the twins and sent my thoughts to them, showing them where all of the bears I'd seen killed had been left.

Sandra peered around at the others. "Does everyone remember where they left their bears? Aleks and I could spend some time today bringing them back to cut up for meat."

Everyone took turns sharing their mental maps with the vampires. We all agreed that the hundreds of pound of meat would be a great addition to our food storage if we could get it all dried.

We swiftly loaded up those who could not fly and took to the sky.

CHAPTER 17

We arrived home shortly before sunrise. After they dropped off the shifters they carried, the twins went back to the mountains to start bringing home bears. I attempted to usher my children off to bed.

"But, Mama," Singing Sparrow protested. "I want to say up and talk to the new guy," she whispered. She glanced over at the man who wore only her father's shirt tied around his waist.

I sighed and rolled my eyes at her before I turned to the rest of my fully grown half-breed children. "Fine. If you all aren't tired, I can't make you go to bed. The rest of the house should be awake soon, so if someone could start making breakfast, I'm sure they'd appreciate it." I walked upstairs to check on my sleeping daughters. Silver Panther's clothes were stretched incredibly tight over her rapidly growing body. I pulled out a much larger outfit for her and proceeded to change her clothes.

"Mama," she yawned. "It's still dark outside," she moaned when she sat up so I could put on her shirt.

"You don't have to get up if you don't want to," I whispered. "But your clothes were way too tight, so I decided to go ahead and change them."

"It's okay," she said with a yawn. "I'm thirsty. Can I have some blood now since you didn't take me hunting?"

"Of course," I said with a smile and I pulled her into my arms.

I leaned out the window to call down to White Buffalo. She flew into the room and saw in my mind that I wanted her to feed her baby sister. She grinned at the little girl before she pulled her from my arms and darted up to the attic level where we kept the refrigerator full of blood. I went into the next room to check on Tall Filly and found her sitting at the edge of her bed, rubbing her eyes.

"I'm thirsty, too," she mumbled as she slid off the bed and staggered over to her chest of drawers. She pulled out a larger set of clothes and dressed herself before she plodded up the stairs to get her own blood.

"Come down for breakfast when you're done," I called up to them. "We've got another addition to the household."

I walked back down to the ground floor and checked to make sure that someone had started cooking breakfast. After I confirmed the smells coming from the kitchen, I drifted out to the back patio.

"The girls should be down shortly," I told Deema and gave him a peck on the cheek.

He pulled me into his arms. "Would you like to go flying later? We could teach White Buffalo how to dodge bullets."

I smiled up at him. "Sure. That sounds nice. But, what about..." I trailed off as I glanced over at Fierce Lion. He was sitting awkwardly on the hammock, trying to keep his nudity covered with the button-up shirt tied around his waist. Deema growled for a split second before I elbowed him in the ribs. I followed his gaze and saw that he was watching Singing Sparrow stare at the beautiful stranger.

"Your brother can take him to the Hall to meet with the elders after breakfast," he told me stiffly. "Come with me,

Lion," Deema said as he released me. "You need to put on some clothes." He glanced back at our daughter who was practically drooling while she gawked at the man's perfectly muscled body.

The Navajo blushed deeply as he stood and followed my husband into the house.

"Sparrow," I said sternly once the men had started up the stairs.

"I'm sorry, Mama. But, I mean—just—just look at him!" she stammered. She turned her eyes to the ground and blushed again. "Do you see anything between us?" she asked after a moment.

I sighed. "Yes. I saw him ask the elders for your hand before you had even laid eyes on him. I guess that means that this is fate. Just don't tell your father I said that," I quietly instructed her. "No need to get him all riled up again so soon after his return."

"Don't bother," Deema's voice boomed from our bedroom window. "You forget I have such powerful hearing."

"Oops," I muttered. I turned to face the third floor window. "Please, love, don't be angry with me."

"It's fine," he grumbled before he slammed the window closed. It was a wonder that it didn't break.

I sighed and offered Singing Sparrow a shrug before I walked inside to roll up a joint. I sat down on my stool and lit it just as the lion was coming down the stairs behind my husband. The cannabis tasted like apple pie and made me miss my grandma.

"I am not angry with you," Deema said, walking over to me. "I just don't want to see these things in the minds of my children. At least you can turn your telepathy off and on at will. I cannot. I hear almost everything everyone is thinking around me all the time." He grimaced. "Imagine how that feels for me. How would you feel if you had to listen to your daughters wonder what sex would be like with a man who is standing right in front of you? How would you feel if at the same moment, that man was undressing your daughter inside his mind and thinking of how he could get her into bed with him? It is quite unnerving," he said with a scowl.

I glanced over his shoulder and saw Fierce Lion turn a deep shade of red. That guy sure was good at blushing.

"I'm sorry," he whispered. "I'll try to keep my thoughts elsewhere from now on."

The vampire seemed doubtful, but accepted his apology anyway.

After breakfast, I took White Buffalo, Deema, and Silverwolf to the practice valley. We practiced flying and dodging paintballs until lunch time. The wolf watched with great interest as his new girlfriend flew with incredible grace and speed.

When we returned to the house for lunch, we had some unexpected visitors. Bob and Nallia were sitting on the back patio, talking to Taniya.

"Good afternoon, Nallia. Bob," I said as I gave them each a nod. "What brings you here today?"

Nallia beamed up at me. "We have some wonderful news. Our wedding will be on the next full moon and your whole family is invited."

"Congratulations."

"Took you long enough to set a date," Deema mumbled under his breath. I nearly elbowed him for his rudeness, but I quickly realized that they had no idea he had even spoken.

"We also got named recently. I am Dark Hawk and Bob is Black Bear." Her grin stretched from ear to ear when she saw my eyes light up.

"So, you will grow wings? Bob, you're a bear?" I screeched in shock and excitement.

Nallia turned around and showed me her wings that

looked like they had emerged earlier that day, or perhaps the night before.

"Holy shit!" I exclaimed, rushing over to her to inspect them. I could see the tiniest indication under the skin on her wings that they would grow off-white or possibly gray feathers.

"I became a bear for the first time right after they named me," Bob said with a sheepish grin. "I was pretty freaked out."

"I bet. I know I was pretty freaked out the first time my kids shifted, 'cause they all did it at the same time and one of my shifters is my youngest daughter *and* she was only about a day old."

The couple stared at me with wide eyes and slack jaws.

I couldn't help but laugh at their expressions. "I know, right? Little kids aren't supposed to shift, and female shifters are just completely unheard of. But, it happened." I shrugged.

"Can we meet her?" Nallia whispered.

"Of course." I closed my eyes and scanned the house for the location of my toddler. A shudder went down my spine and the thirst rose in my core as I opened my eyes. "She's on the top floor with Tall Filly. They are drinking blood right now. They'll be down shortly."

The couple both tried to hide their disgust, but I just laughed at them.

"I know—it's gross. But it's part of who we are. Speaking of which," I said, turning to Deema.

He raised his eyebrows in questioning and I gave him an exasperated eye roll.

"I thirst," I said in a tone that suggested he was blind to have not realized what I meant.

Just as I was about to ask Deema where I should go to hunt, I heard Singing Sparrow scream, "Mama!" from her bedroom.

I ran through the backdoor and up the stairs as fast as I could.

"What's wrong?" I demanded upon entering her room.

"My back," she cried. Tears streamed down her face and she turned her back to me. Blood soaked her shirt, running down her back in streams from where her wings had punched through her skin. "Why is my back covered in blood?"

"Baby, your wings are growing. Can't you feel it? Does it hurt?"

"No, that's what scared me. Shouldn't I feel it if I'm hurt?"

"Deema!" I yelled. He was instantly by my side. "She's not even a year old yet. Why are her wings coming out already?" I asked him helplessly.

"I don't know," he muttered as her stared at the back of her bloody shirt. "Maybe..." He paused in thought. "Maybe the kids are transforming faster because we will be invaded sooner than you think. Or maybe her wings started to grow because her sister's wings are done growing. I guess maybe we'll never know," he said with a shrug.

Fierce Lion burst into the room then, his eyes wide with fear. He rushed to her side and turned to face us, ready to attack if we harmed his crush. He glanced from her bloody back, to me, and then to Deema. I felt the apprehension rolling off of him, so I slipped into his thoughts.

'*Don't worry, Lion,*' I assured him. '*Her blood is not appetizing to us because she is not human or evil. Also, even if it were, I'd never dream of hurting my own child.*'

He relaxed a bit and turned back to Singing Sparrow. He bent over her back, ripped small holes in her shirt, and studied the tiny wings for a few moments. "I can almost *see* them growing," he said, clearly astonished.

"Yes, they'll be fully grown in a matter of days," I informed him. "Come on, honey," I said as I took my daughter by the hand. "Let's get you cleaned up."

I led her out of the room and into the massive bathroom at the end of the hall. Deema had made sure that it was large enough for me to spread my wings to dry them after showering. The shower was also quite large and it had several shower heads so that the water came from three sides, as well as from above. I carefully helped her remove her bloody shirt so that the holes would not tug on her fresh wings. I left the room so she could get cleaned up and I went back out to the backyard.

Nallia seemed surprised to see me exit with the torn and bloody shirt. I unceremoniously threw it into the fire pit where we burned all of our trash that could not be composted or recycled. It was never much, so it generally only got lit once or twice a year.

"What happened? What's going on?" she squeaked.

I sat down in my hammock and started to swing front to back. "Singing Sparrow started to grow her wings. They just broke through. If you don't mind, I'm going to go somewhere else for a while. You can stay for lunch. Some of the kids are cooking it now and, of course, you're always welcome in my home," I said with a smile.

I leaned back and closed my eyes in preparation to search the future. First, I pushed my thoughts toward White Buffalo and asked her to watch over me while I was in my trance. She rushed to my side and beamed at me before I closed my eyes again.

I slipped into my trance and focused my attention on my children. I wanted to see if Long Falcon would grow her wings when Singing Sparrow's were complete. I also wanted to see if Tall Filly would grow wings or become a horse or perhaps be the only one of my offspring to not metamorphose. I saw Long Falcon grow wings identical to White Buffalo's, but I could not determine when they would grow. I shifted my focus to Tall Filly and I was quite surprised with what flashed into my vision. She would grow wings that were multicolored and had the pattern of a red tail hawk. I also saw her shift into a horse that was the most beautiful shade of burnt ocher I'd ever seen.

I was pulled from my vision then by the sound of a cat making a scratchy, weak roar. My eyes opened and I jumped out of the hammock as if I'd been shot from a cannon. White Buffalo laid her hand on my shoulder and told me to calm myself. I peered down to see that Silver Panther had shifted to show off to our guests. She squeaked out another pitiful roar while I reached down to pick her up. I snuggled her close to me and she started to purr while she nuzzled in my arms. After a minute of cuddling, I set her down before I took my place back in the hammock to focus on the future again.

Without even trying to see anything, a vision flashed into my mind. I saw an army Hummer driving through my reservation shortly before sunset. Our police force tried to stop them, but they flashed the officers a piece of paper and continued on their way. They stopped in front of my house. Six soldiers climbed out of the back while a man in a suit climbed down from the passenger seat. They approached my door cautiously and had their weapons drawn. The man in the suit carried himself with confidence while he walked ahead of them and knocked on my front door. The door opened a crack to reveal my older brother.

"What do you want?" he demanded.

"May we come inside?" the suit asked politely.

"No." Brian was obviously irritated.

"May I speak to you out here, then?" His tone hadn't lost even a bit of the sugar he was using to coat his words.

"Who are you looking for? After all, you have no business here on our rez. Whites have no jurisdiction here." Brian's tone and posture were growing even more hostile. His back was rigid, his hands fisted, and his sharp jaw was clenched tight.

The man turned around and nodded to the armed men. They spread out and started to circle my house.

"Lunch is ready!" Sandra called from the back door. Her voice pulled me from my vision.

I bolted to my feet and glared daggers at her.

"Were you searching the future?"

I gave her one curt nod.

"I'm sorry, Mama."

"It's fine," I snapped. "I'll be back in a while. I need to feed and then I need to go see the elders." I hurried upstairs and opened the door of the refrigerator we kept blood in for the growing kids. I drank ten barely palatable pints before I threw myself out the window and headed for the Hall of the Elders.

CHAPTER 18

W e have a problem," I announced as I burst through the door.

"We have more than one," the soft voice of the angel said from the far corner.

"What's going on?" Brian asked, rushing to my side. His huge hand enveloped my shoulder and I peered up into his concerned gaze.

I quickly went through the vision I'd had so he could see it for himself in my head. I pointedly ignored the other angel. I still wasn't sure that I could trust him. Even though, in a way, I felt drawn to him, I could tell that he was quite opposed to Deema being around. And any threat to my husband was also a threat to me.

"Oh," Brian muttered when my vision was complete. He released his grip on me and returned to his seat. "Can you go back to the vision and see what happens next?" he asked after a few moments of thought.

"That's why I came here. Apparently, I can't be at home when I have my visions because there's always so much commotion and interruptions. Also, I know some of the elders can read minds, so I figured that the more opinions I got on this, the better."

The men all nodded in agreement.

I pulled my tall chair out of the corner and sat down. I focused on the vision I'd had a few minutes before while I felt several of the men dig inside of my mind. There was another presence inside my thoughts, too. I decided it must be the other angel. I still couldn't read his mind and it bothered me immensely.

My mental vision cleared and I watched as the armed soldiers walked in a circle around my house. Brian remained behind the front door, which was still only open about six inches.

"Why are you here?" Brian demanded again.

"We have reason to believe that this household is harboring an enemy of the state," the suit replied. He'd dropped the pleasant tone and was starting to show a harsher side of his character.

"Let him in," came the chief's voice from the dining room.

Brian's expression darkened further, but he complied.

My sight shifted to the kitchen and I watched the suit walk into the house.

"Your guns may remain outside, suit," the chief grumbled. "We don't allow weapons on this property."

The man appeared surprised, but he complied and closed the door behind himself.

"Why have you come to my home and interrupted our dinner on this fine summer night?" the chief asked with a touch of irritation.

"This is *your* home?" the suit asked, shocked. "That's not what our records show."

"This was my granddaughter's land. She moved away to New York to live with her childhood friend," my grandfather replied.

"And who lives here now?" the suit inquired suspiciously.

"We do," the chief answered, sweeping his hand around to indicate the elderly men.

"Bullshit," the suit spat.

"How dare you disrespect me in my home? You need to leave now," the chief said with acid in his voice.

"I'm not going anywhere until you bring me the winged woman," the suit demanded.

Forks dropped all around the table as the elders stared at him in shock.

"Winged woman?" some of the men asked each other, as if they'd never heard of such a thing.

"Do you mean that you're searching for a woman—" My grandfather paused to chuckle. "—with *wings*?"

Roars of laughter erupted throughout the room.

"And you think *we* know of such a...an anomaly? Such an absurdity?" Grandfather laughed. "We are not Christians here. We don't even believe in such things."

"How absurd!" Red Elk managed to say between fits of very convincing staged laughter.

The man in the suit turned bright red and started to shake. I could not tell if it was in anger or embarrassment. He stomped out of the house and gathered his soldiers from my yard.

"They are denying her existence," he informed them. "They won't give her up, so we will wait for her."

"How long?" one of the armed men asked.

"For as long as it takes. My orders are to bring her in for testing. I was told that if we take out the woman with wings, we shall encounter no problems with this tribe in the future."

"What are you talking about?"

The suit shook his head. "I've said too much already. You all don't have the clearances that I have."

My vision of the future faded away to nothing, so I opened my eyes and scanned the room.

"So?" I asked cautiously. "What do you think?"

"I think we're in trouble," Brian said in a subdued tone. "And I think they're coming in a few days."

I gawked at him in utter shock. "Why?"

"Because we were planning on having dinner with you after the next tribal meeting," my brother replied. "We scheduled the meeting for noon, and then we were all going to come over for dinner before your family left town for a month. This changes so much. We will have to remove all of your family's clothes from the house. We need to get rid of the refrigerator full of blood in your attic. We must clear every trace of you and your family from that house. The elders will move in and stay there while your family is gone. Taniya must leave with you."

"Nallia, too," Red Elk interjected.

"As will Austyn, Chelsea, and Cassandra," Tall Grass added.

I raised my eyebrows and tilted my head to the left, trying to remember if I knew them.

"They are all of the women who are growing wings right now," he informed me.

"So there are five mortal women who are growing wings?" I asked them. All the men nodded. "So we'll have eleven angels?"

The other angel scoffed and cast me a disparaging glance. "You are this tribe's only angel, if you are even still one yourself."

"Oh, shut up!" I snapped at him.

Sadness softened his features. "Such hostility. And toward one of your own." He sighed and slowly shook his head. "I wish you would come back to us, Hope."

"What's that supposed to mean?" I demanded.

He sighed dejectedly and turned away from me. "If only you could remember, you would know."

The chief cleared his throat before he spoke. "All of

you daughters are growing wings?" he asked me.

"White Buffalo's wings are done growing. Singing Sparrow's started growing today. Long Falcon will grow hers soon. And—" I paused and tried to figure out how to explain what I'd seen. "Tall Filly will grow wings, but she will also start shifting into a horse. I'm not sure if Silver Panther will grow wings someday, but if her sister shifts *and* has wings, I don't see why *she* wouldn't do both as well."

"Interesting," my grandfather mused.

"But we have five who can fly right now—two with wings and three without. White Buffalo and I can each carry one adult or two children, because we still need to be able to move our wings to fly. The vampires usually carry two people each—one on their back and one in their arms. But—I mean, if we have to carry all five women who are growing wings, but cannot yet fly, plus our kids who can't fly yet, plus Silverwolf and Fierce Lion—I just don't see how this is going to work." I pouted. "And what if these other women have kids that must come with us?"

"They can stay with their fathers. Bob will also remain behind, and so will the men who will someday marry your daughters," the chief replied.

"No one's going to be very happy about this. The girls are going to throw a real fit about being whisked away from their new boyfriends," I mumbled.

"If everyone can be transported safely, with no one left behind, then the new men may go with you. Dancing Bronco will remain behind with his father, and none of the other women who are growing wings have kids. Also, if we have four days until the meeting, and thus your departure, won't Singing Sparrow be ready to fly by then? And Taniya's wings are getting quite large. They may not be fully grown yet, but surely they will allow her to fly—even if they just support her own weight and she can't carry another." My grandfather stopped speaking and did a little counting in his head. "That should be just fine. White Buffalo can carry the wolf and one of your daughters. Singing Sparrow can carry the lion and the other small child. The twins can carry the four winged women who cannot fly, while you and your husband carry your other three children." He smiled when he was satisfied that he'd accounted for everyone.

"That's perfect. I will go home and tell the others. We'll start moving our clothes, photos, and such over to Taniya's house tonight after dark." I paused to ask my brother silently if he'd bring his truck over after dinner and he gave me a nod.

"Inform the other three women that they need to be ready to leave for at least a month immediately after the meeting. Nallia is still at my house, so I'll fill her in on what's going on." I smiled confidently at the elders before I left the Hall to fly home. I could feel the other angel still watching me.

'*He's staying here to talk to us,*' Brian told me inside of my mind.

I just growled in response and I sped toward my house.

CHAPTER 19

The twins were clearing the table from lunch when I landed in the back yard.

"I have some news," I announced as I entered the house. "Everyone needs to take a seat." I stood at the head of the nearly empty table. Once everyone was seated and I had their full attention, I began my announcement. "So, the American government knows about me and on the night of the next tribal meeting, they will send armed men to collect me."

Gasps and murmurs of shock and anger arose from the group. I raised my hands to quiet them before I continued.

"I've spoken with the elders, and we've come up with a plan. Taniya," I said as I turned to her. "You need to start flying immediately. Since your wings aren't yet fully grown, we figure that you won't be able to carry anyone else and you won't be able to fly as fast as I could when I was mortal, but you should be able to support your own weight and at least keep up with the twins."

"What if I can't?" She seemed incredibly worried.

"We'll try later in the valley. If your wings cannot support your weight, then we will catch you before you fall," I assured her. "But your son will need to remain be-hind with his father. There are three more women in the tribe who are growing wings and they cannot fly yet, so the twins will have to carry them."

"Who else?" Nallia piped up.

"Austyn, Chelsea, and Cassandra. But I don't know any of them and the elders didn't tell me their last names." Everyone shrugged to imply that none of them knew them either, so I continued with my explanation. "We need to clear the house of all of our clothes, photos, and anything else that would indicate that we live here. Brian will bring his truck at sunset with an extra bed to put in Silver Panther's room, and he will haul away her crib and our boxes of clothes. The elders will fill our drawers and closets with their own clothes the morning of the meeting and they will live here in our absence. Any questions?"

"Um, how do you know all of this?" Nallia squeaked.

"I can see the future when I focus and go into a trance."

"What exactly did you see?" Deema asked me gently.

I explained every detail of the visions I'd had.

"Will we be safe? Where will we go?" Tall Filly asked.

"Can the shifters come with us?" White Buffalo asked hopefully, glancing over at her boyfriend.

"If Taniya can fly on her own, then yes. The lion and the wolf may accompany us. The twins can carry the four women who cannot fly. You two," I said with a nod toward my two eldest daughters, "can carry your own boyfriends along with the youngest two girls. I can carry one of the remaining three, and Deema can carry the other two of our children. I'm not sure where we will go. If the government is aware of my existence, then I'm not sure if we should remain in this country. Perhaps we should go back to Russia, or maybe South America. But wherever we go, we will be safe. I'll see to that," I said with a grin and a few taps to my temple.

"What about raising money to build a warehouse and silos?" Deema asked.

"Oh! I totally forgot about the briefcase." I ran up to the bedroom I had no use for anymore and pulled the congressman's briefcase out from under my king-sized bed. I dashed back down the stairs and dumped its contents onto the dining room table. "If this doesn't cover it, then I think everyone in the tribe can give up $100 or so out of their casino checks to cover the cost of building the silos and warehouse."

"Where did you get all that money?" Nallia gasped.

"Um…Well, I killed a very evil man. He was a thief, a liar, and he'd ruined many lives. The wallets and wads of cash came from a couple groups of rapists I sent into the afterlife."

"That's over $200,000," Deema whispered as he glanced over the pile of cash.

"Yeah. Do you think it'll be enough?"

"It might be."

"So what comes next?" Taniya asked, pulling her son up to sit in her lap.

"Should we go to the valley and see if you can fly?" I asked her.

She sighed nervously and gave me an unsure nod.

"It'll be fine," I smiled.

She stood up, gave her son one more hug, and followed me out the door.

Sandra stood and followed us. "I can carry her to the valley," she suggested.

Taniya accepted her offer and the three of us took to the sky. While we flew, Sandra turned her back to the ground, and I instructed Taniya to spread her wings.

"Do you feel how the wind catches them?" I asked her.

"Yes."

"Now adjust them and feel how they make you want to turn," I told her.

She did what I said and her face lit up. She continued to

practice catching the wind in her wings the whole way to the valley.

"I think I'm ready," she told Sandra. The vampire released her, but stayed right underneath her in case her wings wouldn't support her weight. Taniya glided for a few hundred feet before she started to slow down and had to flap her wings. She was a bit unsteady for the next hundred yards, but she quickly evened out. When she reached the far end of the valley, she made a wide turn and flew back toward the south.

The three of us flew back and forth countless times over the following hours. The male angel stood on top of the western ridge and silently watched us. Once Taniya grew hungry, we returned to the house just in time for dinner.

When we got back home, she was afraid to try landing, so Sandra carried Taniya to the ground. "We can practice landings later," my vampire daughter promised before we rushed into the house.

"Deema, I thirst," I whined as I plopped down next to him at the table.

He rolled his eyes at me. "Well, there are gallons and gallons of blood in the attic. And don't we need to be getting rid of it over the next few days?"

I ducked my head in shame before I gave him a sheepish grin and rose to my feet.

"Mama! Mama!" Silver Panther cried, jumping out of her chair. "I want some, too!" She sprang into my arms and I carried her up the stairs. I opened the fridge and handed her a pint of blood while I pulled out two in each fist for myself.

I hated drinking it cold like that, but it was better than nothing. When I sank my teeth into the first one, I decided that even chilled human blood laced with anti-coagulants was better than warm, herbivore blood. I drank ten pints while my little girl sucked down two.

We went back downstairs and joined the others who still sat at the table.

"You should finish your dinner, little one," I told my youngest daughter once she was seated.

She pouted in response.

"You're growing very rapidly, you know. You require lots of nutrition."

She grimaced but picked up her fork and eventually cleared her plate.

Once dinner was over, we started to pack every suitcase in the house with our clothes. By the time that was completed, my brothers arrived with several piles of boxes and a few rolls of tape. We finished packing the rest of our clothes in less than an hour. We left out only three sets of clothes per person and packed them into a hiking backpack. For the children who were still growing, we packed another entire backpack full of various sizes of clothing. We decided that someone carried by a vampire would have to wear the packs in order to bring them with us.

Deema pulled the crib from the room and jumped out of the window with it while my brothers carried the twin-sized bed up the stairs. We finished loading everything into the truck, and the twins flew on to Taniya's old house while my brothers drove the load of personal items over there. They all came back about an hour later, and we sat down to come up with a more solid plan of action.

CHAPTER 20

W here will you go for the next month?" Brian asked after we sat down around the empty dining room table.

"We haven't quite figured that out yet," Deema replied. "We need to find out how they know about her. If they know where we live, then they know her name," he pointed out.

"What if the government has their own psychics?" Brian postulated. "What if they have their own remote viewers? What if they can see us right now? Perhaps we should not plan on where you will go. Maybe you should just fly randomly out of the country and move to a different place every few days so that they don't catch up with you."

We all gave that some thought for a few minutes.

"Okay," I conceded. "But wouldn't we feel it if someone was watching us? Brian, you always feel it when I'm watching you remotely. And before Taniya even discovered that she could remote view, she could feel me watching her."

"True, but I can also hide my spiritual presence from people," Brian explained. "Remember when you were in New York? I watched you for, what? About half an hour?

And you had no idea that I was there until I pushed my thoughts into your head. If they have someone as powerful as me, they could certainly be watching us, and we'd be none the wiser."

"Okay, but if that's the case, then can't they find us anywhere anyway?" Deema asked him. "Can't they just focus on her and see where she is?"

"All the more reason we need to find out who these people are and what they can do," Brian replied.

"Can we change my vision? Can you make a choice to ask the suit for identification before you let him enter? Because when someone changes their mind or their choices about the future, my visions change. And then, you can focus on him in the here and now. We can find out who he is and what exactly his assignment is. Then maybe we'll have a better idea of what we're dealing with here."

Brian seemed to light up. "That's an excellent idea."

I closed my eyes and slipped into my odd trance. When the haze cleared, I saw the suit knocking on my door again.

"Who are you?" Brian asked immediately upon opening the door just enough to stick his head out.

"May I come in?" the suit asked pleasantly.

"Not until I see some ID," Brian demanded. "Whites don't come here. And they certainly don't come here knocking on our door, interrupting our dinner, and waltzing into our house when we have no idea who they are." His voice was slathered with irritation and anger. He loomed over the little man in a suit—jaw taut, muscles flexed, and brow creased. It should have been enough to make the smaller man balk, but he didn't.

The suit flipped open his wallet to reveal an FBI badge that identified him as Walter Sarkovski. "I'm with the Federal Bureau of Investigation and we have some questions for the lady of the house," he replied politely.

"No women live here," Brian spat back. "This is the home of the elders of our tribe."

"Then may I have a word with them?" He had a smug smirk on his bony little face like he thought he was about to catch my brother in a lie.

Brian turned to the chief and awaited his instructions, while the suit signaled the soldiers to circle the house.

"He may enter," the chief said sourly.

My vision faded then and I assumed that meant that the rest would play out as before. I opened my eyes and turned to my big brother. "Did you get all that?"

He grinned. "Yes, I did. Now it's time for me to look in on this Walter Sarkovski." He leaned back in his chair and closed his eyes. After twenty minutes of impatient silence, he opened his eyes and stared at me in shock.

"What did you learn?" I asked anxiously.

"You fucked up."

My jaw dropped open in astonishment. "What?"

The male angel appeared out of thin air in the corner of the room behind my brother. "Surprise, surprise, surprise," he said in a condescending tone. "Hope made a mistake."

"Shut up!" I snapped at the other angel. Deema remained seated on the couch. I assumed he was just letting me fight off this interloper myself, but I soon figured out that he was mad at me, too.

"You killed a congressman," Brian growled menacingly. "You left a witness behind along with a feather. They have your DNA on file because you donated blood in high school to the Red Cross and they matched it to the DNA in your feather. That's how they know who you are and where you are." He was fuming. I could hear his clenched teeth grinding together. A vein in his temple throbbed with his furious, racing pulse.

I turned to Deema for some comfort, but he was just as angry.

"How could you do something so stupid?" he demanded.

"I'm sorry," I muttered, deeply ashamed. "So, they don't have psychics who found me? No one's watching us?" I asked after a moment.

"No," Brian spat. "But you've brought this on yourself. You've put your entire tribe in danger and drawn unnecessary attention to us by your careless actions."

I couldn't help but notice the other angel's disappointed expression while he watched me from behind my brother. "One way or another, it was bound to happen," he muttered quietly.

"We'll just have to deal with the consequences," Deema said more gently. He stood and took my hand. "This is partially my fault, too."

I gawked at him in surprise.

"If I hadn't left you in anger, then you would not have gone to the capital without me. I would never have permitted you to kill a man in his own home. I would have never allowed you to leave witnesses behind without wiping their minds or at least making them believe it was all a dream."

The angel in the corner wore an expression that said he wanted to contest that point, but he kept his opinion to himself and heaved a soft sigh instead.

CHAPTER 21

So, what happens now?" I asked nervously.

"We will travel to New Orleans," Deema said in a stern tone. "The twins and I can purchase food for the mortals, or if the women are still able to hide their wings, they may go into public themselves. We will rent out a house or break into abandoned properties. We will keep you hidden and you will show yourself to *no one*." He frowned at me to drive home his point. "And you three," he said as he indicated the other women who could fly, "will also stay out of the public eye. Anyone with wings cannot go outside once we arrive. We don't need any reports being filed with the police or on the news."

"How am I going to feed?" I asked skeptically.

"I'll bring you donated blood," he said matter-of-factly.

I felt my face distort in disgust. "I hate donated blood. You can't convince a few criminals to come with you so that I can have some living blood?" I asked hopefully.

"We'll see," he said pensively. "Silent Wolf," he said, turning to my brother. "Are you able to push thoughts into people's heads so that they think they are their own? Can you make people believe they have seen something that they haven't?"

"What are you thinking, vampire?" my brother asked, sounding genuinely curious.

"Could you make them believe that she is no longer living? Could you show this Sarkovski an empty patch of the backyard and make him believe that her body is laid out on a pyre? Then he will return to his people in Washington and tell them that she is dead," he suggested.

"I could try, but he's going to want to take her body with him, or at the very least, take photographs and another feather to prove that it is her. Making *him* believe could be simple, but convincing others could be impossible."

"Damn," Deema muttered in defeat. "How can we get them to leave?" he wondered aloud.

"The Natives are restless," I murmured teasingly.

"What did you say?" my little brother asked as his eyes lit up.

I felt the corners of my mouth turn up in a sheepish grin. "I said that the Natives are restless."

"That's it!" Will jumped up from his seat and started to pace while he spoke. "We'll tell the tribe at the meeting that the whites will come soon, and that they must gather the next day to drive them away. Screaming about our rights, our sovereign lands, stuff like that. We won't be another Standing Rock. We won't let them walk all over us like they did to the Osage in the 1920s. They can't push us around again like they did the Ute. We won't let them do to us what they did to our grandparents in the 2020s. Surely they won't tolerate the abuse for long and they will leave." He paused in his pacing and smiled for a moment before he frowned and started to pace again. "But they'll be back, no doubt. And in greater numbers, as well."

"I'm sorry," I murmured again. I'd never felt such shame in my entire life. The more I thought about it, the deeper I sank into guilt. It was all my fault and that thought repeated over and over in my head. If we were a normal tribe, we could seek help from outsiders like the people of Standing Rock had done so many times, and then the Ute a few years later. But we had our secrets to keep, so we were on our own, just like our grandparents had been during the last relocation when half of our tribe was murdered for standing up for themselves.

"It's okay, Mama," Sandra said as she crouched next to me. She laid her hand on my arm and rubbed it reassuringly. "We'll figure something out. And it's not all your fault. I, too, should not have left you in Washington. If we had been there," she said with a glance at her twin, "we would not have allowed you to kill him, either. I'm sorry we left you alone to hunt. Especially since you've never really been taught all the rules we hunt by. You've seen us hunt many, many times, but we've never really explained to you why we do what we do."

I raised my eyebrows in question and she continued to explain.

"We always hunt outside. We never enter the homes of our victims. We never leave witnesses behind, especially when they are certain of what they've seen. And then the others you do know. We only kill criminals, or evil people. We never hunt children. We don't orphan children. Stuff like that."

"I'm sorry," I repeated. "But he *had* to die."

"No, I'm sorry," she told me with sad eyes.

"So am I," Deema said, squeezing my hand again.

"I'm sorry, too, Mama," Aleks said as he hung his head.

"I guess I should not have left you, either," the male angel said from the corner.

Deema growled but stayed at my side. "What were you doing with my wife?"

"Trying to comfort her and win her back while you'd left her alone and vulnerable. At least I'm actually making an effort to teach her, rather than changing her and leaving her to wonder what she is supposed to do with herself," the angel replied coolly.

"Enough! It doesn't matter who is sorry. What's done is done," Brian grumbled. "And now we *all* have to deal with the consequences," he said as he cast an infuriated glare around the table. I could see his "angry vein" throbbing in his temple again.

White Buffalo glanced around the room. "How can we fix this?" she asked.

"Maybe we should sleep on it," Silverwolf suggested. "How about everyone comes back for lunch or dinner tomorrow, and we can figure this out then? Could the elders join us, too?" he asked my older brother.

"That's fine," Brian grunted. He pushed away from the table and stood up. "We'll come over for dinner at six o'clock." He walked out the door without another word.

"It'll be okay, sis. We'll figure something out," Will assured me. He squeezed my shoulder and kissed me on the forehead before he followed Brian out the door.

"Aren't you going with them?" Deema said, glancing at the angel.

"No, I believe I would rather stay here."

"I'd rather you didn't," Deema replied bitterly.

"And I could not care any less than I already do about what you want. Hope is my only concern."

"I'm going to bed," White Buffalo announced as she stood and walked up the stairs to her room. Silverwolf followed her silently and Deema gave a low growl in the back of his throat.

Fierce Lion gazed at Singing Sparrow and raised his eyebrows.

"I'll be up in a while," she said in a distracted tone. She seemed to be deep in thought.

He gave her a kiss on the cheek and walked up the

stairs. I heard the shower turn on after a minute.

After several quiet minutes, Taniya picked up her son and carried him up to their room. Then, one by one, my children all decided it was time to go to sleep, and they silently filed upstairs to their bedrooms.

"I don't have to leave you, do I, Mama?" Silver Panther asked me sadly.

"No, baby. Wherever I go, you go." I offered her a weak smile. "The whites would notice you growing so quickly, and I would never risk having any of my babies taken away from me."

She smiled at me and wrapped her arms around my neck to give me a hug. She ran upstairs and changed into larger clothes before she climbed into bed.

The twins stood up and announced that they were going to go outside and tend to the smokehouse, garden, and chickens. Once they were outside, Deema and I were alone with the other angel. Something inside of me wouldn't let me tell him he had to leave, so I just ignored him as much as I could.

I snuggled into my husband's stony chest. "I feel so stupid," I mumbled. "I can't believe I messed up so bad." My body started shaking with tearless sobs and he wrapped his arms tighter around me.

"It'll be okay, love. We'll think of something." He sighed forlornly. "If only there was someone out there who could vouch for your good intentions. Or, if only we could travel through time."

"Yeah, if only," I mumbled as my sobs slowed. Then an idea hit me like a lightning strike. I pulled away from Deema and gazed into his eyes, a smile spreading across my face.

"I left other witnesses behind that night, too."

He gawked at me in disbelief. "You *what?*" he demanded as his eyes turned to stone.

"We found a woman being raped and we killed all of her attackers. Long Falcon took her to the hospital. Then I saved another woman who was about to be kidnapped plus one more woman who was cornered and about to be raped. If all of those women came forward separately, and went to the authorities to report me and what they've seen, maybe that would get them to ease up and leave me alone," I explained hopefully.

His eyes softened while he gave it some thought.

"That might work, or at least help. Why don't you check the future and give it a try?" he suggested.

CHAPTER 22

I walked out to the back patio and sat down in the hammock. I hung my wings over the side of it and leaned my head back to rest on them. I thought about my decision and figured out the details of what I would tell the women before I checked on the future again.

I decided to visit all three women in their dreams and get them to report what they'd seen to the FBI. I would instruct them to tell no one else of what they'd seen, but they needed to tell the FBI everything so that they would not want to come after me anymore.

As I slowly rocked forward and back in the hammock, I heard the soft swish of the door opening and closing behind me. The footfalls of the male angel were nearly silent, but I could still discern them. When he walked past me, his wing brushed against mine for just a fraction of a second. I gasped so hard that I choked on the air and pitched myself forward to escape the startling sensation. It was far from painful, and actually might have been the most pleasurable split-second of my life.

"Dmitrius," I gasped as he came rushing around to stop me from smashing my face on the stone wall that encircled my patio.

'*Yes, my love,*' he said inside of my mind.

"You can't say that," I choked. "You can't do that."

"But it is how you must learn. You need to know," he insisted.

Deema bolted outside and tried to pull the angel away from me. "Get away from my wife," my husband snarled.

Dmitrius didn't budge. He slowly turned his head to peer over his shoulder at the vampire while he stood up straight and released me. Deema shrank from his glare and did his best not to cringe.

"She's still my wife," he said with a touch of defiance in reply to whatever Dmitrius had mentally said to him.

"So, now you know my name. I can teach you so much more if only you would allow me to do so." With that, the angel disappeared into thin air just as quickly as he'd arrived earlier.

I sighed and settled back into the hammock before I turned my mind to the future and waited for the haze to clear. I saw a room full of men, arguing quietly on the dark side of a one-way mirror. On the lit side of the glass was the first woman I'd saved that night. She was in tears while she described what had happened to her and how I'd come to her rescue. Per my instructions, she did not mention the other blood drinkers—just me and Long Falcon.

The vision twisted and cleared again to reveal the same men watching the second woman I'd saved that night. This time, in the middle of her story, Sarkovski burst into the darkened room to join the other men. He sat down and listened intently while he was caught up on what had been said so far. After Lucia was done with her story, they asked her a few questions she couldn't answer, followed by more questions that basically made her repeat her story over again.

"She's telling the truth," one of the men whispered. "She has not lied once," he assured the other men around him.

My vision grew hazy once more before it cleared and I saw the last woman I'd saved that night. She told her story while the men listened intently behind the glass, and then she also got a long line of questioning. Once she'd gone, the men left the tiny room behind the glass and sat down in a conference room.

"So, what do you all make of this?" one of them asked the rest.

"I believed every single one of them," the human lie detector asserted. "Each one of these women was saved by the same woman who killed the congressman."

"So if she saved these women, why would she kill one of our officials?" the first man asked him.

"She told each of the women that she only kills evil men and, according to the times given to us by the four women who have seen this supposed angel, she killed the congressman in between saving the first and second women. She must've known something about him that we do not," one of the men chimed in.

"She claimed to be a mind reader," Sarkovski commented.

"She proved herself to be a mind reader to all three women who came in today," the human lie detector reminded him.

"What do we do with all this information?" the first man asked the group. He was clearly the one in charge.

"I will still go investigate, but I will not take as many soldiers with me. If she is trying to clean up our crime, then perhaps we should not fear her. Maybe we should, instead, seek out her help," Sarkovski replied.

"What if she proves to be difficult?" the man in charge asked. "If anything, I think you should take more men with you to bring her in dead or alive. She killed over a dozen men in one night, and all by herself at that!"

"Well, if she's impervious to bullets, then it doesn't

really matter how many guns I bring, does it?" Sarkovski retorted. "I think we need to use logic and reason with her. She can read our minds, so we need to have good, pure thoughts when we approach her."

"When are you scheduled to leave?" one of the men asked him.

"I'm flying out to Denver day after tomorrow. I will go to the army base to pick up some soldiers and a vehicle. We plan on arriving at her home on June thirtieth."

"And if she's not there? What if she's still here in the city? Or in some other city?"

"Then I am prepared to wait for however long it takes," he said with confidence. A pair of men burst into the room. "Sir," one of them addressed the man in charge. "We've heard back from the teams sent to check out where the women were attacked, and there is evidence of a recent bloody struggle at each one of them. A body had been located and removed from one of them by the local police. They haven't figured out who he was yet. And we're still checking with trash companies to see where the trucks assigned to those areas are or where they dumped."

The boss scratched his chin. "What? No bodies in the dumpsters?"

"It's been picked up already. But we're working on it."

"Fucking trash day," the boss grumbled.

The pair who'd interrupted them left.

"I'd like to request that he comes with me," Sarkovski asked his superior, jabbing a thumb at the human lie detector.

"What do you say, Charleston?"

"I'll go," he conceded. The men all stood and dispersed from the room as my vision faded.

I turned my mind to the first woman that I'd saved in Washington DC. I found Lexanna sleeping in her bed, and I pushed my way into her mind. Her dream twisted, grew hazy, and then shifted into the scene I created for her. I faced her with my wings spread as we stood in a forest clearing. "Lexanna," I said gently, holding my arms out to her. She took a tentative step toward me and I took her hands in mine. "I know I instructed you before to never tell anyone of me, but plans have changed. I need you to go to the FBI and ask to speak to Walter Sarkovski. Tell them that you have some information concerning the murder of a congressman on the same night that you were assaulted."

She opened her mouth to speak, but I held up my hand to silence her.

"They will tell you that he is not available, but they will put you in a room to be interviewed by another agent. There will be a one-way mirror in the room through which Sarkovski will observe you. I need you to tell them of how I saved you."

She burst into tears.

"I know this will be very painful for you, but my life depends on you doing as I ask. Please, Lexanna, I need you to do this for me. In this life, I was born as a Hopi Indian and I have put my entire tribe at risk by coming to the capitol that night. Without your help, I, and many of my tribe members, will die. Tell them all that I have told you and all that you have seen. Except, you cannot tell them of the group I had with me. You will have to tell them of Long Falcon, because the hospital knows that she brought you there. But the less you tell them about my other children, the safer they will be. Do you understand?"

"Please don't make me do this," she sobbed.

"I'm sorry, sweetheart, but this must be done. Can I count on you?" I pleaded.

She stared into my eyes for a few moments and read the desperation in them. "Your people will really die if I don't?"

"They will," I said with a sad sigh.

She lifted her chin and squared her shoulders. "Then I will help you. It's disgusting how those in power have been treating Native Americans for the last sixty years. I want to help you."

I smiled down at her. "You sweet woman—it has been far longer than that that we've been abused. Be brave, Lexanna. And thank you so much. I'll never forget you."

"Will I ever see you again?" she asked hopefully.

"Perhaps." I smiled as I faded away and forced her to wake up. She sat up in her bed, tears still streaming down her face. '*Remember*,' I pushed into her waking mind. '*First thing in the morning. Walter Sarkovski at the FBI.*'

I cleared my mind once more and searched for Lucia. I also found her asleep in her bed. I pushed my way into her mind and produced the same scene that I had for Lexanna.

"Lucia." I gave her a big grin, opened my arms, and spread my wings. "How are you feeling?"

She allowed me to enfold her in a hug before she answered me. "I'm fine, I suppose. Why are you here? Where are we?"

"This is a dream I am creating for you. I could not risk coming to see you in person because I am too far away and I needed to speak to you immediately. Tomorrow morning, I need you to go to the FBI and ask for Walter Sarkovski. You must tell them that you have information for him about the woman who murdered a congressman on the same night you were assaulted. If you don't believe that I am really here, asking you to do this, then ask your roommate in the morning and she will tell you that I came to her as well."

"So it *was* you," she whispered.

"Yes, dear. I saved you both that night, and another woman as well. But I also killed a man who has ruined countless lives, and he was writing a bill that would steal the rights of millions more. The FBI is coming to my home in a few days to try and kill me. That is why I need you to help them understand that I am not an evil creature. Tell them all that occurred that night, including the exact location of where he tried to abduct you."

"I will," she said as she nodded fervently.

I huffed a big, relieved sigh. "Thank you." I smiled and hugged her before I faded away and left her with empty arms. I forced her to wake up and spoke to her again in her waking mind. *'Remember—Walter Sarkovski.'*

"I will," she murmured. She laid her head down and went back to sleep.

I drifted my spiritual presence into the next room and found her roommate fast asleep. I pushed my way into her slumbering mind and had almost the exact same conversation with her as I'd had with Lucia.

The only thing different was that I told her to be sure that she went separately from Lucia so that they didn't think that they'd made it all up. She agreed to do as I'd asked and I faded away.

She bolted upright in bed when the dream ended.

'Remember,' I said inside her head. *'Walter Sarkovski at the FBI.'*

"I'll remember," she whispered before she fell back asleep.

I pulled away from the apartment and returned to my body on the reservation. Before I opened my eyes, I decided to check on the future again to make sure it was still the same as I'd seen before my visits to the women. Once I was satisfied that it would all still happen the same, I slowly opened my eyes and realized that it was brighter than it should be. The sky was just starting to show signs of predawn. Deema stood a few feet away, watching me patiently. "How long was I gone?" I asked as I turned to the east.

"Several hours," he told me, kneeling beside my left

knee. He took my hand in his. "What did you learn?" he asked me anxiously.

"Before I tell you, I'd like to drink," I said as my right hand flew reflexively to my throat. "The burning is unbearable."

He disappeared up the stairs and was back in a flash with an armful of blood bags clutched to his chest. He dropped them in the hammock beside me before he sat down on my other side. He waited patiently while I drained all twelve pints and listened to the house start to wake. By the time I finished my blood, the twins had returned from a hunting trip. They each had two gutted deer which they dropped unceremoniously when they realized I was "awake" and had finished with my mental journey.

"I'd like to repeat this story as few times as possible, so let's wait until the others are all out here, too," I told them when they sat on the ground in front of me like little kids waiting for their teacher to read them a book.

One by one, my entire family came downstairs and joined us on the patio. Silver Panther was the last to come outside. She sprang over the heads of her siblings and landed squarely in my lap.

"Will you tell us now?" Deema asked anxiously.

I smiled and gave him a brief nod before I told them what I'd learned while they had all slept. When I finished my explanation, they all sat in silent thought for a few moments. I felt satisfaction rolling off of Silverwolf in waves.

"And just what are you so smug about?" I asked him teasingly after I caught the tiny smile that played on his lips.

"I knew it'd be a good idea to sleep on it," he said as his grin grew wider.

I laughed. "Yeah, except I don't sleep."

Everyone got a kick out of that and I started to feel relief rolling off of the entire group. Everything would be okay now and they all knew it. We could probably even bring our stuff back from Taniya's house.

"So, they will still come, but without the intention to harm us?" Taniya asked once the laughter subsided.

"Yes. But Sarkovski will have a human lie detector with him that he wasn't planning on having before. So, while you all eat breakfast, I'll have to look at the night of the meeting again and see how that changes things."

"Well, speaking of breakfast…who's hungry?" Taniya asked as she turned to go back into the house.

Everyone stood to follow her except for us vampires. The twins returned to the yard and strung up their kills on the side of the smokehouse to skin them and prepare them for processing. The bears they'd retrieved from our Rocky Mountain excursion had mostly been parsed out to others in the tribe who had their own smokehouses. They were helping us get as much dried meat stored up as possible. Deema stood and tossed the empty bags of blood into the compost bin while I leaned back and started to search the future again.

I turned my mind's eye to the night of their expected arrival, but I saw nothing new. It was all the same as before. I was severely confused. I tried to see it again, but still nothing had changed. Deema came back and sat down next to me.

"I don't understand," I confessed. "It's not working. That night is still the same. If he's bringing that Charleston man with him, why can't I see him?"

"Hmmm," Deema mumbled as he gave it some thought. "The women have not yet gone to the FBI, correct?"

I nodded.

"Then these men have not yet made the decision for him to come here. So, wouldn't you not see the future change until they make the decision to change it?" he postulated.

I thought about it for a few seconds before I realized he was right. "Yes," I said as I ducked my head. "I suppose it makes sense that the choices of the women would change the future, but since the men at the FBI haven't made their choices yet, I wouldn't be able to see the result of choices that they've not yet made. I'll search again after lunch and see if there's any change."

"Should you go tell the elders now? Or do you just want to wait until they come for dinner?"

"We can wait. The more we know, the better. And I think I'm going to be learning a lot today."

He stood and started toward the door. "Are you coming in for breakfast?"

"Not today." I leaned back against my wings. "I'm going to peek in on the women again so that I can make sure they are doing as I've asked. Will you stay with me? I don't like going into my trances without being watched over. It makes me nervous and I can't concentrate as easily."

"Of course." He sat down next to me again and took my hand.

CHAPTER 23

I searched the capitol for Lexanna and found her exactly where I wanted her. She stood at the front desk inside the FBI building, waiting for the receptionist to speak to her. I peeked into her thoughts because she seemed terrified. She'd forgotten the name of the man she was supposed to ask for. '*Walter Sarkovski*,' I pushed into her mind. Shock crossed her battered and swollen face for a brief second before comfort took its place. She wondered if I was still watching over her, and I assured her that I was. '*I'll be here for you throughout the entire interview if you'd like.*'

At that moment, the receptionist asked if she could help her, and Lexanna nodded for both of our benefits. "I need to speak to Walter Sarkovski in regards to the murder of the congressman several nights ago," she told her.

"Do you have an appointment Miss…" the receptionist asked politely.

"Sanatori. And no, I do not. But I have some information for him that is pertinent to his investigation," she replied.

The woman typed on her computer for a moment before she frowned. "Agent Sarkovski is not in right now, but you can speak to another agent who is also working on the case. Please go to the third floor and ask for Agent Ludwig. He can take your statement." She pointed to a bank of elevators and picked up the phone to inform the agent of the woman's arrival.

Lexanna was alone in the elevator for the short ride up to the third floor. "Can you hear me in my head? Or do I need to speak to you aloud?" she whispered while she covered her mouth, pretending to yawn.

'*I can hear you in your head*,' I replied.

'*Good*,' she thought with a sigh of relief as the doors slid open to reveal a man waiting for her.

"Miss Sanatori?" he asked in a gruff voice.

"Please, call me Lexanna. You must be Agent Ludwig." She offered him a weak, lopsided smile and extended her hand that wasn't in a sling.

He returned her dim smile and awkwardly shook her left hand before he led her down a hallway.

Once they'd sat down in the interrogation room from my visions, he cleared his throat. "I understand you have some information for us concerning the murder of a congressman in his home last week. Were you in the area at the time? Did you see the culprit flee? Or were you attacked by her, too?"

"Yes, sort of, and no. She saved me."

He watched her with thinly veiled shock.

"The, um, creature who took the life of that man saved my life that night. I was in the hospital at the time of his death. But I can give you an exact description of her. I can tell you her name to verify what you already know from your DNA testing. I can even tell you why she's done the things that she has."

She paused and wondered if she could tell him that I was there with her now.

I told her that I would allow it. This was not part of what I'd intended to do before, so I figured I was changing the future once again. I hoped that would be a good thing.

"In fact, she is with me right now in spirit," she told the man who was staring at her with great skepticism. "You may ask me questions that I do not know the answers to, and she can answer them through me."

"Who is this 'she' you are referring to?" Ludwig grumbled, glancing over at the mirror.

Lexanna paused for a moment while I fed her the answer. "The name on her birth certificate is Hope Dancing Bear—though her last name has changed since then—and she was born on the Hopi Indian Reservation about twenty years after they were all forcibly relocated to Colorado. She says that Walter Sarkovski was planning on visiting the home that he thinks is hers with six armed men. But she says she does not live there any longer, and it is the home of the tribal elders now. She says she is a nomad who flies around the world killing criminals."

"And how does she buy plane tickets if she has no income?" he asked with another glance toward the mirror.

She laughed. "Plane tickets? She doesn't need plane tickets. She has, like, a fifteen-foot wingspan. She is an angel incarnate. She can read minds even at great distances, and that's how she knows the evil in a man's soul."

"Can she read my mind right now?" he asked in a sarcastic, disbelieving tone.

She paused for a moment and listened to what I told her to say. "Yes. She says that you think that I'm lying, but there is a human lie detector behind that glass who knows I'm telling the truth. She says that your name is Albert and your wife's name is Carlinda. You have a dog named Cocoa, but it's a breed she's never seen before, so she doesn't know what it is." Surprise spread across his face before she continued. "A Chow-chow. God, Hope, you've never heard of a Chow-chow?" Lexanna giggled. I reminded her that we didn't get many fancy dogs on the rez and she straightened her face.

"How long has this supposed angel been among us?" he asked her with a twinge of interest.

"She says just a few years."

"And how did she save you?"

"I was being raped and beaten by a group of men in an alley off of Fourth and Jefferson." She gestured to her still battered face and the sling she wore on her right arm. "She landed behind them and started pulling them off of me. Once I was free of their grasps, she ripped out their throats and drank their blood," she said while she stared at the one-way mirror.

"You need to talk to me, not the mirror," Ludwig grumbled as he scratched down some notes.

"Why? Doesn't Charleston need to see my face to know I'm telling the truth?" she asked innocently.

"How do you know the names of these men? How do you know my name?" he demanded.

"I already told you. The angel is telling me. And now she says that there are two more women coming today whom I have never met, but she also saved them that same night. One of them is here, asking to speak with Sarkovski. But he will not arrive until the middle of the second interview. He's rushing to be here as we speak."

"I'll be back in a moment. You just sit tight," he told her as he turned around to leave the room.

"Could you bring me back a Coke, please?" she asked before he slammed the door.

A few minutes later, the door opened again and the human lie detector entered with a can of soda in his hand.

"So you're Agent Charleston?" she asked him once I'd fed her the knowledge.

"I am," he said. He took a seat across the table from her and slid her the can of Coke. "How do you know these things that you could not possibly know about us?"

"The angel is feeding me the answers. She says she does not want any harm to come to her tribe because of her actions so she is trying to change the future. She says that last night you got test results back from the DNA you ran on a feather that was left behind in the congressman's house and you confirmed her identity. She says that you have her DNA on file because she donated blood to the Red Cross about a decade ago."

"She can see the future?" he asked skeptically.

"Yes, she can," she replied simply.

"Can you give me a description of her?"

"She's about five feet, ten inches with long black hair that reaches just past her knees. That night she was wearing a long, white, flowing dress. Her wings are massive and covered in sparkling white feathers. She appeared to be in her mid-twenties and she had a woman with her who she claimed was her daughter, but she looked to be about the same age. It was the second woman, the one who could not fly, who took me to the hospital and then escorted me home. But one thing I don't understand is that they were both a very pale shade of white, yet she claims to be Hopi."

"She is indeed Hopi," he mumbled, more to himself than to her.

"Oh," she said after a moment. "She is a vampire," she gasped. She thought back to a few minutes ago when she'd told them that I drank blood. She hadn't seen me do it, so it hadn't really registered with her what I'd been having her repeat. "Of course," she muttered to herself.

He peered up at her and shock ran across his face. "There is no such thing," he insisted.

"Oh, but there is. You may not have come across any in your time here, but some of your colleagues know them to be real. She says that the FBI has recently gotten involved in a string of murders in Las Vegas. Countless criminals have been found dead and drained completely of their blood with bite marks on their necks. The Vegas police are baffled. I know I saw a lot of blood on the wall in the alley where I was assaulted and the other two women can tell you where they were attacked. But now she's also telling me that the bodies are already gone. The congressman had the same wounds and no blood left in his body," Lexanna informed him as I fed her more information.

He studied her face while she spoke and decided that she believed everything she was telling him. "Please wait here," he said once he stood. "One of us will come back in a little while." He left the room and I told her to be patient.

'*I can only be in one place at a time, so I need to check on the other women briefly. I'll be back soon, okay?*' I pushed into her head.

"Okay," she muttered weakly. I could see the strength and confidence running out of her when I floated my spirit from the room and back down to the reception desk. I entered the mind of the woman who sat there and saw that she'd just sent Lucia upstairs to meet with Agent Ludwig. I searched the area for Lucia's roommate, and found her across the street at a coffee shop. She'd decided to wait about an hour before she went in to ask for Agent Sarkovski.

CHAPTER 24

I found Lucia when she exited the elevator. Ludwig was waiting for her and he silently led her to the same room that where Lexanna was sitting.

"Do you know this woman?" he demanded.

"No," she said weakly.

"Tell me what you know of this supposed angel," he said, slamming the door.

She stared at him in shock. She had made no mention of an angel to anyone in the building so far. I spoke to her inside her head and told her that I was there in spirit to help her tell her tale. She relaxed a bit and sank into the chair next to Lexanna.

"A man pulled me into an alley and put his hand over my mouth when I started to scream. The woman landed in front of me, spread her wings, and told him to let me go. Once he did, she drank his blood and threw him into dumpster at the back of the alley," she told him matter-of-factly.

"Where did this occur?"

"You know where Providence Park is? It was half a block west of there on E Street. There's an alley between two buildings that goes back to split the block."

The large mirror vibrated a bit when the door in the observation room opened and closed.

"And what did she look like? What did she say to you? What time did this occur?" Ludwig asked her as he paced.

While she told him what he wanted to know, I slipped into the tiny room behind the glass and saw that Sarkovski had just arrived.

"She's telling me that Walter Sarkovski is here now. I would like to speak to him," Lexanna said once Lucia had finished speaking.

Ludwig turned toward the glass and stared at it as if he could see through it. After several seconds of silence, the mirror trembled again and Sarkovski entered the interrogation room.

He sat down across from the women. "You two seem to know much that you should not," he said in a casual tone.

They both gave him a curt nod.

"The other agents tell me that this supposed angel is here now, in spirit form, and that she is telling you what to say."

"Yes," they said together.

"May I ask her some questions?"

"She says she will answer your questions if you promise not to harm her people. She knows of your plans to go there with armed men. She knows that you will try to abduct her *if* you find her, and that when you *don't*, many of her people will die," Lucia informed him.

"All right then," he muttered. "I promise to not harm any of her people. Does her tribe know about her? Will she consent to meet me somewhere if I agree to come unarmed?"

"She says she is in Rio right now and she has no desire to meet with you," Lexanna told him quietly. "Even armed, there is nothing you could do to harm her. Bullets crumble against her skin. Needles cannot puncture her, so tranquilizers do not work on her. She is faster than your eyes can see, and she can fly at speeds faster than an airplane."

"Do her people know about her?" he repeated.

"Some do, but they will deny her existence to their graves. You have no place among them, she says. Whites are only welcome in their lands if they are pouring money into the casino that keeps the tribe alive in these capitalistic times," Lucia answered.

"Will she speak to me in *my* head?" he asked with great interest.

'*Yes, Wally, I will,*' I pushed into his mind.

His eyes widened in shock and fear as the two women stared at him, confused.

"She's not saying anything," Lucia whispered after a moment.

Sarkovski held up his hand and bid them to be silent while he listened intently for me to say something else.

'*Close your eyes, and I will show you myself,*' I commanded inside his head. He did what I asked and I showed him the same scene I'd shown the three women the night before. "You must not harm my people, Walter," I said as I took a step toward him. "They have done you no wrong, and neither have I."

His lips pressed together into a tight, angry line. "Why did you kill the congressman? *He* had done you no wrong."

I laughed bitterly. "Oh, really? That bastard Whip was writing a bill that he intended on passing through congress by any means necessary. The details of this bill would have taken away the sovereignty of every Native American reservation." I narrowed my eyes and began to walk toward him. "It would have required us to pay taxes to your government from our casinos that were more than double what non-natives pay for their casinos. It would have dissolved land treaties and taken away sovereignty. In one way or another, it would have destroyed my people, along with every single other tribe in this nation," I explained through gritted teeth. Rage was building inside of me and when I could no longer contain it, I screamed in his face, "This is *our* land! We were here first! You stole our homes and decimated countless tribes. Your government has stolen from my people too many times. My grandparents tried to be peaceful and move to yet another reservation when you forced everyone to leave Arizona fifty-some years ago. Your government slaughtered my people for attempting to defend our Treaty Land and cut our numbers in half. And now you have the gall to try and take our lands again! I will *not* allow it!"

He was shaking in his boots, terrified that I would somehow kill him in this vision I was forcing upon him. I took a few deep breaths to calm myself and I retreated several steps back.

"I mean you no harm, Walter. I just need you to see my point—where I'm coming from. Your dead congressman was on the committee that has been building secret concentration camps all across this country. He had every intention of stealing our lands and building camps there, too. And I can have none of that. I was born an angel incarnate to protect my tribe. I have ten thousand lives to keep safe and I love each and every one of them. Do you see my point, Walter? Do you see why I had to do what I did?"

His face was still filled with fear. His mind was spinning, trying to understand everything that I had told him.

"I will have to confirm that what you've told me is true, and if it is, then we will not come after you," he finally conceded.

"I will visit you again tonight in your dreams," I assured him before I disappeared.

His eyes popped open and he glanced around the room like he was expecting to see me standing there.

"This is all just too much," he muttered, shaking his head back and forth.

"What happened to you just now?" Charleston demanded as he burst into the room.

"She showed me a vision and explained to me why she killed the congressman. He was writing a bill to take away the sovereignty of all the Indian Nations. He would have taxed them all to death," he said sadly, still shaking his head. "I have to confirm that this is true." He jumped up from his chair and bolted from the room.

The two women stared at each other curiously before they shrugged and turned back to Ludwig. He seemed baffled.

"Do you need us anymore?" Lucia asked Ludwig as she glanced at her watch.

"Leave your information with Charleston and we will contact you again if we need to speak with either of you," Ludwig said dismissively. "And don't leave the city," he said as they exited the room behind Charleston. They both followed the human lie detector to his desk so he could write down their contact information.

The two women left the building together and crossed the street to the coffee shop. They sat down at a table, ordered some coffee, and, in hushed tones, exchanged stories of their encounters with me.

CHAPTER 25

Lucia's roommate was already across the street, going into the FBI building. I entered her mind and told her that I would be watching and listening in case she got nervous or stumped. She breathed a sigh of relief when she entered the elevator and pushed the button for the third floor. She had no one waiting to greet her at the elevators, so she followed my instructions and walked down the hall to the interrogation room.

"Who are you and what are you doing in here?" Ludwig demanded after she seated herself.

"I'm here to tell you about the angel who saved me," she said as if he were dim-witted for not realizing that. She glanced at the mirror. "I'm not late, am I?"

"Who told you to come here? How did you know to come to this room?" he asked her with a touch of irritation.

"The angel called Hope told me," she said with a smile.

"And I suppose that she's in your head right now, feeding you answers?" he asked mockingly.

"She is indeed, Albert," she said as her grin widened.

He threw his arms into the air. "I can't do this anymore. Someone else is going to have to interview this lunatic. I'm done!" he exclaimed before he turned to stomp out of the room.

'*Wait*,' I said inside of his head. '*Perhaps I can convince you that I am real.*' He stopped dead in his tracks. His hand that clasped the door knob started to shake. '*Sit down, Bertie,*' I instructed him.

"Only my mother called me that," he muttered in disbelief. He released the door knob and turned to sink into a chair.

'*Well, I'm not your mama, that's for damn sure. Now close your eyes,*' I instructed once he was seated.

He did as I commanded.

I created the forest clearing scene once more and stood before him with my wings spread wide. "If you do not believe your ears, then certainly you will believe your own eyes."

"But you're not really here," he said.

"Not physically, no. But that does not mean that I'm not actually here, because clearly I am. If you cannot bring yourself to believe what these women have told you, if you cannot believe that I am really here speaking to you, then you should remove yourself from this case."

"Tell me something that I don't know," he said after a quiet moment of contemplation. "Tell me something that I can find out later that I don't already know. Then I will believe that this is real," he challenged me.

"Well, let me think about that. I've given so much information today, I'm not sure what else there is to tell you. Oh! Okay. The woman sitting before you now…You've yet to ask her name. It is Loretta Marie Sanderson. She grew up in Wisconsin on a dairy farm. She moved to DC five years ago and found a roommate through the want ads. Lucia is that roommate. By some odd coincidence, I saved them both on the same night."

I extended my hand to him. "Go ahead. Open your eyes and ask her for yourself." I disappeared from the vision and he bolted out of his chair.

"Woman!" he shouted at Lucia's roommate. "What is your full name? Where were you born? How did you come to be in this city? Who do you live with?" he demanded in a single breath.

"I am Loretta Marie Sanderson, but everyone calls me Mary. I lived most of my life on a dairy farm in Wisconsin and I moved here to get into politics. You know, maybe working as a secretary or something. But that never panned out, so I'm a waitress at Hooligan's. I live with a woman named Lucia whom I met through the want ads. She needed a roommate, and I needed a place to live. We've lived together for about five years now. She was actually here earlier because on the night I was assaulted, so was she. The same angel saved us both. She also appeared to both of us in our dreams last night and told us that we had to come here and tell our stories."

He stared at her with a slack jaw for almost a full minute before he told her to leave the room. "Agent Charleston will take your information so we may contact you later if we need to. And don't leave the city," he told her on her way out the door.

Charleston was waiting for her in the hallway and escorted her to his desk. He pulled a form out of the drawer and filled it out with her name, address, etc. He thanked her for coming in and sharing what she knew before he bid her goodbye.

'*You did great, sweetheart*,' I said inside her head.

She got into the elevator. '*Will I ever see you again?*' she wondered hopefully.

'*Perhaps*,' I replied. I moved my focus back to the room where the men were discussing what to do next and I listened in on them.

"Sarkovski just called," the head suit informed the others. "He found a file on the computer confirming that the congressman was indeed writing a bill to take away the sovereignty of the Indian lands. Land treaties would have been canceled, taxes levied, and certain customs outlawed. It would have ruined them financially and culturally if the congressman had gotten it passed."

A phone rang behind him then and he picked up the receiver. "Yes?" He listened for a moment before he hung up without another word. "Some bodies have been found. Three at the dump and two others in trash trucks. There was also a body pulled from an alley the morning after these…attacks. They all appear to have bite marks on their necks and they seem to be drained of blood. They are comparing the bodies now to confirm that they were indeed killed like the congressman."

All of the men watched him in quiet contemplation.

"So where do we go from here?" Charleston asked the other gathered men.

"I'm not sure," the man in charge replied.

"Perhaps we should wait for Sarkovski to return before we decide," Ludwig suggested.

"That's fine. Let's all take a break for a late lunch and meet back here in an hour."

CHAPTER 26

W hat are you doing now?"
Brian's angry voice roused me from my vision
just as I was about to pull away. I grinned
mischievously. "I was changing the future."

His furious face softened once he realized the implications of my statement. "What did you do?" he asked suspiciously.

"I sent the three women I saved that same night to the FBI headquarters. They all told their stories to some agents who are working the case of the congressman I killed. One of the men was a human lie detector, and he believed them all. I also entered the minds of the agents and spoke to them. I convinced them that I'm not an evil creature and, in an hour, they will all gather again to decide what to do next. Sarkovski no longer has any intention to kill me or bring me back for testing. I may even convince them to not come here at all." My grin threatened to crack my face in half.

"And what if they do decide to come here? Even after all of this?" he asked, still unconvinced.

"Well, I had the women tell them that I'm in Rio de Janeiro and since they believed me, they did not appear to be lying. Thus, Charleston, the human lie detector, believed them. Sarkovski knows that it is useless to come here to search for me since I told him that I'm not here and that the elders now live on my land. He asked if my people knew of my existence, and I told him that only a few out of 10,000 do, and that they would deny it to their graves. He swore to me that he would not harm any of our tribe, and I believe his intentions are true."

"He seemed so hateful in your first vision."

"In that future that can now never come to pass, I believe they must have told him some pretty awful lies about me. I mean, he seemed pretty mad today about the congressman before I set him straight, but not *that* pissed, you know?"

"Yeah. So, what now?" Brian wondered.

"Now we wait an hour and look in on them again."

"And until then?" Deema asked me with raised eyebrows.

"Until then, I feed and spend time with my children," I told him as I playfully swatted his arm. I knew what that expression meant and I knew that our alone time would have to wait until our problems with the government were resolved.

I stood up and went upstairs to our dwindling supply of blood. I drained another dozen unpalatable bags before I went back to the living room and picked up my youngest daughter. "You wanna go play outside with me?" I asked her while I swung her up toward the ceiling.

She giggled and agreed as I pulled her close to me.

I was on my way outside when Long Falcon stopped me. "Mama," she said hesitantly. "I think my wings are growing." I rushed to her side and ran my hand over the back of her shirt.

"They should emerge in an hour or so," I told her.

"Will I be able to fly by the time we need to leave?" she asked hopefully.

"Maybe," I told her with a smile. "But then, we may not have to leave. All morning I've been working on changing the future to keep them from coming here. In a little while I'll check on the FBI agents again to find out what their decision is."

"Oh," she muttered. "So what do I do when they break through my skin?"

I laughed. "Take a shower to rinse off the blood."

Her face fell at my attitude.

"I'm sorry, honey," I said more gently. "I'm just so happy that I may have stopped them from coming here. It could've been very disastrous if I hadn't intervened."

"It's okay," she mumbled, staring at her feet.

"Why are you so sad, baby? I thought you'd be happy that you can fly by yourself," I asked her as my eyebrows scrunched together.

"I'm afraid," she confessed.

"Of what?"

"What if I'm not good at flying?"

"You'll be wonderful," I assured her. "It's in your blood." I gave her a wink. She attempted a smile, but it was weak. "Would a hunting trip later make you feel better? Just you and me? A little quality time with your mama?"

Her eyes brightened a touch at my suggestion. "Where can we go?"

"How about Denver? It's only an hour or so away," I suggested.

"Okay," she smiled.

I carried Silver Panther outside and tossed her high up into the air. She flew up over a hundred feet while she squealed and giggled with glee. I caught her gently and kissed her cheeks before I tossed her into the air again. By the tenth time or so that I threw her, she was begging me to stop.

"Why, baby? Aren't you having fun?"

"Yes," she laughed breathlessly. "But I can't breathe." It took her a few minutes to catch her breath, but once she did, she wanted me to start throwing her again. By the time she needed another break, Deema informed me that an hour had passed and it was time to watch the FBI agents again.

CHAPTER 27

I walked back to the patio and situated myself in the hammock before I surveilled Sarkovski again. I invited my brother to join me in my remote viewing so that he could know everything that transpired. He sat across from me and we both slipped into a trance.

I caught Sarkovski just in time as he stepped out of the elevator and walked down the hall to join the other agents.

"So what are your thoughts on all of this?" Ludwig asked his partner when he took a seat.

"I think we should let it go and forget about her," Sarkovski said bluntly.

His superior stared at him like he was crazy. "She killed a congressman, and now we have all but a confession tying her to about a dozen other murders in this city alone. Plus, there's the entire year's worth of unsolved murders in Vegas that those women claimed she was a part of. How can you possibly suggest that we just let this go?" He was obviously not willing to take his subordinate's suggestion.

"Well, first of all, she could kill all of us if she wanted to. Her skin is impenetrable, so bullets are useless. She can't be tranquilized for the same reason, and she can move faster than our eyes can even see. She wants peace, not war. And I feel that if we go to her lands with soldiers, war is what we're going to get. With the way the media works in this country now, all it would take is for her to 'out' herself to the public and the general population would take her side," he argued.

"Yes, but would she be willing to go that far? She won't let us see her in the flesh, so why would she appear at a television studio and show herself to the world? Secrecy is what she wants," Charleston chimed in.

"If you won't go to the reservation to collect her, then I will," the boss-man spat at Sarkovski.

I decided it was time to convince him that Walter was right in thinking that they should just drop the whole thing. I slipped inside his mind and dug around for a few seconds before I made my presence known to him.

'*George,*' I said firmly inside his mind. '*I would suggest that you follow Walter's suggestion and forget about this whole thing. I can make your life a living hell from half a world away,*' I assured him. The expression on his face was priceless when I spoke inside his head.

"What kind of witchery is this?" he whispered, sinking into the chair behind him.

"She's in your brain, isn't she?" Sarkovski asked smugly.

The man I now knew to be George Smith nodded dumbly in response.

"What will you do to me?" he asked out loud with a trembling voice.

'*If you come to my lands, then you are as good as dead. I'm watching you now, Georgie-boy, and I will return to my people if you go there. I will kill you on sight because it is men like you that I strive to rid the world of. None of the men in this room and none of the people in your daily life have the slightest idea of the skeletons buried in your closet. But I know all about how you kill homeless people to take out your anger and frustrations. I know about how you like to get drunk and beat on your wife. And I know about how you rape her when she is too weak to fight back. You're one sick, twisted, son of a bitch.'*

"Oh my God!" he murmured in disbelief. "This can't be real…can't be happening," he muttered as he put his head in his hands.

'Oh, but it is,' I assured him. *'I can also haunt your dreams every night so that you can't sleep well anymore. Or, I could just leave you alone if you agree to no longer pursue me and just let me do as I do. I only kill criminals, after all. It is just the scum of the earth that I feed from. If anything, you should be thanking me for taking so many criminals off your city streets,'* I said smugly.

"Vigilante justice is not justice," he disagreed.

'It is when you can read the minds of your criminals,' I said with a chuckle. *'I see things in the minds of men that no court could ever prove. And you cannot hide who you really are from someone who can hear your every thought.'*

"I can't," he said, shaking his head again. "I won't give up on this. You will pay for your crimes," he said more firmly.

'I have committed no crimes. But be aware that, if you continue to hunt me, you will be the one who pays for his crimes. I can kill you before you ever even lay eyes on me.'

"Give me your plane ticket, Sarkovski. I'm taking your place on this trip to Colorado," Smith said.

Sarkovski laid his briefcase on the table and opened it. "I really don't think that's wise, sir. I think we need to just let this go."

"Just give it to me!" Smith demanded.

Sarkovski reluctantly handed his boss the ticket and snapped the case shut before leaving the room without another word.

'You are committing suicide,' I assured Smith.

"Get out of my head!" he boomed as he stomped out of the room.

'*I can stay in here as long as I please,*' I said inside of his mind. '*Unlike you, I do not require sleep and I can torment you for days on end until you give up. Or, I can meet you on your drive down from Denver and stop you from ever reaching my reservation. Perhaps you'll have a little wreck and die on impact. Or maybe you'll just be found dead on the side of the road with your throat cut and your wallet gone. Maybe they'll find your car wiped of prints at the bottom of the Grand Canyon. There are all sorts of ways that a man can die an accidental death.*'

He climbed into his car. "Leave me alone," he muttered.

'*Tear up that plane ticket. Promise you'll never set foot on Native lands. Keep your promise, and then I will leave you alone.*'

"I'll kill you, bitch, if it's the last thing I do," he screamed when he pulled out into traffic.

'*You'll die first,*' I promised.

I pulled myself from my trace and shook my brother to rouse him as well. "We need to stop him," I said when his eyes opened. "When he blinks while he's driving, can you help me pull him into unconsciousness or something so that he doesn't open his eyes again? Can we cause him to get into an accident or something? This bastard is relentless."

He gave me a slow, reluctant nod. "Yes, you're right. I don't think he'll ever give up. It's not in his nature to. I've never done anything like that before, and I don't know if it's possible, but it's worth a shot."

We both sank back into our trances and waited for the perfect opportunity. George blinked when he was about to make a turn, and instead of pulling onto a side street, he plowed right into the side of an empty brick building. His airbags deployed and knocked him unconscious, but they did not deflate as they should have. Before rescue workers could make it to the scene to treat him, he suffocated from the airbags surrounding his face.

I pulled myself up from the hammock. "Well, I guess that's that."

Brian stood up and stretched. "We should check in on them again tomorrow to make sure that the others still agree to leave us alone."

I nodded in agreement and turned to walk into the house. A glance at the clock that hung on the wall told me that the other elders would be arriving for dinner in less than an hour.

CHAPTER 28

During dinner, my brother and I explained to the elders how I'd spent my entire night and most of the day changing the choices of the FBI. After dinner, we all sat around the backyard and smoked a pipe to ask our ancestors for assistance in making the agents want to leave us alone.

"I can't say that I approve of you two killing that man," the chief said while he wrapped the pipe in the leather in which he kept it stored.

Dmitrius appeared at the corner of the patio. "I cannot say that I approve, either."

I decided to ignore the angel and just focus on my tribe. After all, they were the ones I was tasked with protecting. "I think I skipped over much of the detail of my conversation with him." I leaned forward to meet the chief's eyes. "He was just as evil as the men I kill for blood. He murdered so many homeless people that he had lost count. He would relentlessly beat and rape his own wife. If I'd seen him on the streets, he would have certainly died by my hands."

"Well, then—I guess that makes it okay," the chief mused after a moment of thought.

"And, it was clearly an accident," Brian pointed out.

"There is no way that the other agents involved with hunting Hope could ever connect her to this. If anything, we could make them think that it was an act of God. They all seemed to be somewhat faithful men. At least, I never got the feeling that any of them were atheists while I scanned their minds."

"And what is the next contact you will have with these men?" my grandfather inquired.

"I will appear in Sarkovski's dreams tonight to make sure he will keep his promise to stay away. Then tomorrow when the men all meet again, I will watch to make sure their official decision is to let the matter drop and never come here," I replied.

"And if they don't? If they still insist on coming after you?" the chief asked me.

My jaw flexed and my eyes narrowed. "Then I will enter their minds again and convince them that it is in their best interest to stay away."

"I could try to enter some dreams tonight," Brian said pensively. "I've never tried it before, but it's worth a shot. They don't know me from Adam and maybe I could make them think I'm an angel, too. Like one that's not in a body, ya know?" He started speaking quicker as he got more excited at his idea. "I could tell them that God took the life of their superior because he was hell-bent on taking the life of this holy protector who was put here for a reason—for the very purpose that she is fulfilling. I could make them change their minds. I'm sure of it."

"Well, that sounds like a plan then," the chief grunted as he rose from his chair. "We'll check on you again tomorrow. And thank you for dinner. It was wonderful." He turned and shuffled away. The other men stood and followed him.

My vampires gathered the chairs and put them away in the shed while I went upstairs to change into my hunting

clothes. I jumped out the window and found that Long
Falcon was already waiting for me so that we could go to
Denver.

"We'll be back later, love," I told Deema before I kissed
him on the cheek. "And we'll be good," I promised with a
wink.

I pulled my daughter into my arms and pushed off into
the sky. We landed in Denver about an hour later and I
scanned the area for someone worthy of death. Much to
my surprise, I found no one. We switched locations twice
before I finally found an evil man.

He beat his wife savagely on a regular basis. He kept
her barefoot and pregnant most of the time, but never allowed her to go to the doctor. There was no phone in his
house, and he literally locked her in every day when he left
for work. Of all the times she had been pregnant, only two
children had lived because he'd beaten her into so many
miscarriages.

Every cell in my being wanted to hurt him worse than
he'd hurt his wife. I wanted to crush every bone in his
body. I needed to make him feel pain like he'd never
thought was possible. He had to suffer and understand
exactly why he was suffering.

"Ronny," I said in a steely voice when I landed behind
him.

He swung around, pulled out a Bowie knife, and tried to
stab me with it. I took a step back that was too fast for him
to see before I stepped forward and ripped the knife from
his grimy fingers.

"You have caused much suffering in your life, Ronny."
I spread my wings wide and tossed his knife to the ground
behind me. "And now I will cause *you* much suffering."

He stumbled backward, fear starting to take over the
anger that creased his features. "What the fuck?" he muttered.

I placed my hands on his shoulders and forced him to his knees by crushing his collarbone. He started to scream in pain, so I smashed his Adam's apple.

"You have beaten your wife and killed your own unborn children. She will never be the same, and now neither will you," I said while I snapped his arms like twigs. "You want to beat up women? Does that make you feel like a big, strong man? How does it feel now to be beaten and crushed by a woman?" I slapped him twice and demolished both of his cheekbones. I held a fistful of his hair in one hand and kicked him in the ribs to punctuate each word. "You—will never—hurt—a woman—again!"

I heard his heart start to stutter when a bone fragment punched through it, so I decided I needed to go ahead and finish him off. I roughly pulled him to his feet by his hair and sank my teeth into his neck. I drank most of his blood, but I did not kill him because I wanted to prolong his suffering. I took his wallet to check his address, but I left it laying on his chest when I flew out of the alley. I scooped my daughter off of the neighboring roof and flew away with her in my arms.

"I've never seen you so vicious," she whispered with a shaky voice.

"He's been beating his wife for years," I growled. "He never lets her out of the house. She hasn't been to a doctor since they got married. He's beaten her so much, that she has had many children die before they could be born. He was one of the top five most evil men I've ever fed from. I found it very hard to stop, but I wanted him to suffer as much as possible," I explained to her while I made the short flight to his home.

We landed in the backyard of Ronny's house. "Where are we?" she asked.

"This is where he lived. I have to free his wife," I whispered, mounting the back steps. I ripped the door off its hinges and saw her in my direct line of sight. She stared at me with a terrified look in her eyes and I quickly searched her mind for pertinent information.

"You are free now," I said to her gently. "He will hurt you no longer, I promise. Go to your sister and she will care for you."

She crumpled to the floor and burst into tears of relief. "Thank you," she blubbered.

"That's why I'm here, honey. And I suggest you get some therapy before you try to have another relationship so you don't end up with a similar man. The police should be contacting you in the morning and you can tell them your story. I only ask that you do not mention me. If you are asked about your door, tell them that Ronny did this," I said, gesturing to the back door that hung from a single hinge.

She nodded shakily and she thanked me again. I turned and walked away from the doorway before I picked up my daughter.

We flew away and I scanned the minds that roamed the streets below for someone else to feed from. We landed in an alley and I whispered to her that she could have this one. Long Falcon murmured, "Thank you," as I set her down.

CHAPTER 19

My daughter approached the pimp who was searching for his prostitutes. "Excuse me," she said.

He turned to face her, ogling her up and down like she was a piece of meat.

"How you doin' sweet thang?" he asked in a thick, slurred voice as he staggered toward her.

She laid her hands on his shoulders. "I'll be doing a lot better once I get to drink you up," she said sweetly.

He stumbled and bumped into her. "Oh yeah? How much you gonna pay me?" he slurred. He put his hands on her hips and started to grind himself against her.

"Oh, I'm not paying a thing," she cooed. "But you're going to pay with your life."

His eyes widened for a split second before she latched onto his neck and sank her teeth into his jugular. He tried uselessly to push her off, but he gave up when I stepped out of the shadows behind her and spread my wings. He gawked at me and his arms fell to his sides.

"You die here tonight at the hands of a woman for your crimes against women," I told him seconds before he lost consciousness.

She dropped his lifeless body to the ground, and we

quickly gathered the cash from his pockets. She flipped him over to remove his money belt. "Hurry, there are people coming," I urged.

"Can we eat them?" she asked hopefully.

"No. They are generally innocent." I scooped her up and pushed off into the sky.

We traveled a few blocks south before I heard another evil man's thoughts. He was crouching in the shadows, waiting to pounce on a small group of drunken women walking home from a bachelorette party. I could hear the ladies laughing and making crude honeymoon jokes while they stumbled down the street.

I landed silently behind him. I covered his mouth with one hand, and yanked his gun away with my other hand. Long Falcon grabbed his shoulders and we pulled him farther into the shadows just in time for his intended victims to walk by safely.

"You will never hurt another person again," I whispered into his ear before I sank my teeth into his neck. After I drained him, I tossed him into the closest dumpster.

"I still thirst," my daughter reminded me when we lifted into the air.

"So do I." I searched the surrounding streets for more killers and thieves.

I turned toward the negative thoughts that I'd finally found and we landed in an industrial area. I pointed toward an abandoned warehouse and we silently walked toward a rusted loading bay door. I saw her head cock to the side while we both listened intently to the robbery they were plotting. Once we were sure that they all deserved death, she gave me a small nod.

I grabbed the bottom corner of the door and peeled it back like a can of sardines. When the shrieking metal stopped moving and I stepped through the opening I'd created, a volley of gun fire struck me in the chest and face. I inspected my clothes and frowned at the charred holes the bullets made in my white dress before I turned my scowl on the armed men.

I stepped toward them and spread my wings wide. "That wasn't very nice," I said.

Gasps and murmurs of disbelief echoed through the empty warehouse when they realized what I was.

"This can't be real," one of the men shouted. He took a step forward and aimed his gun at me with a shaking hand.

I crouched and pushed off into the air, soaring around the confined space. I laughed while they all stared at me in shock. "Is this trickery as well?" Chuckling, I dipped low and snatched up the man who had spoken. I pulled him close to me and sank my teeth into his neck.

While their eyes were on me, my daughter slipped silently into the warehouse and started feeding from the man closest to the door. We dropped our kills at the same moment and that was when the others noticed Long Falcon's presence. The remaining four men turned their guns on her a split second before I landed in front of her. I stepped forward into a slight crouch, ready to spring on any of them who pulled the trigger.

"I wouldn't do that if I were you," I warned them through bared teeth.

"And what are you gonna do about it?" one of them scoffed. He shot at me again.

I scowled at him when the bullet crumbled against my impenetrable flesh. "I'll kill you," I grumbled through gritted teeth. I sprang at him and tackled him to the ground as my teeth found his throat.

I heard Long Falcon behind me, stalking closer to one of the men. I could hear their hearts beating quicker with every step she took while their thoughts screamed with terror.

Once we had each killed three of the six men, we

emptied their pockets, set the building on fire, and took to the sky.

"I feel sloshy," she mumbled through a yawn as I sped toward the reservation. She didn't look like she'd last until we were home before she fell asleep.

"Me, too," I agreed, pushing my wings to their limit. I sped through the air for only a few minutes before she drifted off to sleep.

CHAPTER 30

"Hope," Dmitrius whispered in my ear.

I glanced around and saw him flying about five yards to my left.

"What?" I sighed.

"Can you land so we can talk?"

"Why should I? And what about my daughter?"

"I can make sure she stays asleep. And you know that we need to talk."

"Fine," I grumbled. I watched for an open area in which we could land.

"Thank you," he said emphatically as he swooped down to follow me.

I gently laid my sleeping daughter on the ground and turned to face Dmitrius. "What?" I said in a flat tone.

"Where to begin?" He began to pace back and forth in front of me, clearly agitated. "Hope, you cannot keep killing people. This is not the real you. Please, come away with me for a few days so that I can reteach you who you are. You have to trust me, Hope. I only want to help you."

"But I don't even know you!" I exclaimed, throwing my hands in the air.

"Are you certain?" he asked, walking around me in a circle. He brushed the edge of his wing against mine for a split second and I nearly fell over from the shock of the sensation.

"And what of the memories?" he mused when he'd completed his circuit around me.

"I...I..." My brain was still reeling from the small puzzle piece that had been filled in my memories of my former selves.

"Chew on it for a while," he suggested.

"But you're—"

"Yes, my dear. I am your true soulmate. You and I are the reason that the term even exists. Now that you know that, will you agree to come with me for a while?"

I watched the wind blow eddies of dirt around my feet. "I can't," I whispered.

"But this is not you, Hope," he pleaded. "You are not a killer. You never before had a cruel bone in your body. I do not eat, but what you did to that man tonight nearly made me sick. Do you know how hard that is to do?"

"No. But let me guess—I should?" I retorted in a sharp tone.

He gazed at me with the saddest eyes I'd ever seen. "Hope," he implored.

I narrowed my eyes. "I'm not just a killer," I snapped. "I am a killer *of* killers. Doesn't that distinction make a difference?"

"Two wrongs do not make a right, Hope."

"Is it wrong to prevent a wretched creature from killing over and over again? Is it wrong to save the lives of innocent people? Huh? Is it?" I demanded as I shoved him.

He didn't budge an inch.

"Damn. You're strong."

"Stronger than you are. Stronger than your so-called husband, too. I have to be stronger than all mortal creatures."

"We're not mortal."

"Trust me, you are. I could still decapitate him and kill him. He may be too stupid to realize the distinction, but surely you are not."

"Immortal means impossible to kill and not just one who doesn't age," I guessed.

"Yes, my dear. You, your vampires, even your children—all of you have reached a point of being ageless. That does not mean that you cannot die."

"Jesus tits," I muttered.

"No, no, he was quite fit and trim. Being a carpenter back then did that, you know."

I cast him a disparaging look.

"What can I say or do that will convince you? I would really rather not have to kidnap you."

"If you take me against my will, then I can only believe that you are my enemy."

He gazed at me with sorrowful eyes. "God help me," he muttered.

"You wouldn't really kill him, would you?"

"Only because you asked me once to spare him. That promise still stands until you rescind your request."

"I never would," I swore.

"Never say never. Once, you said you would never choose another one but me. Then Russia happened." His wing began to extend and inch closer to mine.

I pulled my wing away from his. "Stop that."

"I cannot stop gravity, Hope."

I scowled at him.

"Please, my love, will you not reconsider? This is not the real you."

I turned my back on him. "I just can't believe you."

"I know you do not fully have faith in those words," he replied as he stepped closer to me. "At least listen to my words, even if you refuse to feel what I wish to share through our connection."

I shuddered.

"Oh, I know." He used his abilities to whisper in my ear from several feet away while he also caressed my face and shoulders.

"Stop it," I said, trying to step away from his invisible touch.

"You used to love it when I did that." Dmitrius sighed. "Listen, Hope—you cannot save this tribe if you lack full command of yourself and your own abilities. I will pretend to have patience and wait for you to ask me, but I can force it if I have to. So until you let me really share," he said, gently running his hand down the edge of my wing, "I will just have to give you some things to think about."

"Whatever," I grumbled and stepped away from his touch again. It bothered me that I was beginning to want his touch, but I still felt like I had to resist.

"You are not an angel. You, vampire, are far from holy. You need to stop this business of claiming to be so. Vampires are a mere necessity for crime control—like police and judges. Believe me when I say we *have* had to step in before and cull some numbers. Especially when some develop a taste for innocent blood. But you are no more doing God's work by killing thieves and murderers than a shark pup is doing God's work when it eats its sibling while still in the womb."

"Wait—really? That happens?"

"Yes, actually, it does."

"All of them?"

"No, just certain species. Now, come on, Hope. Focus." I rolled my eyes at him.

"You are not an angel. You are a vampire who just so happens to have functional wings. It is a genetic mutation in your tribe of shapeshifters that gives the women wings."

"You're lying to me," I observed.

"Very good, Hope. I was just barely lying. You see, the

mutation that allows women to grow wings does originate with you. Or rather, your soul. But since you lack your memories, this is not really you. Right now, you are merely a product of your own environment—here in this life."

"How did—"

"Questions! Good. That means you are listening and processing. You see, we lived here a very long time ago. We had a single daughter. Circumstances arose that caused the need for us to transform into our immortal forms. She was still inside of you when you changed. The transformation also caused the need for her to be born a month early. And something happened to her DNA that allowed her to grow wings once she reached maturity. All of her daughters grew wings, but none of her granddaughters ever did. That is, until you."

"Okay." I was fairly stupefied.

"The elders call you a winged woman, which is the correct description. You are the one who began to call yourself an angel. You are the one who called yourself holy." He scoffed. "Child, you are nowhere close. So, the next time you present yourself as such, and you are not, I will turn your victim's blood to acid. It will not kill you, but it should hurt enough to deter you from doing so again."

"That's fucked up, Dmitrius."

"Filth and pleasure in the same breath," he said with a sigh. "Will you say my name again? It has been decades since I have heard it with real ears."

"Dmitrius," I growled.

"So angry. That is not the Hope I know."

"Well, I'll be this Hope for a long time, so get used to it. This time, my kids won't die. I won't die. My husband won't die. We'll be a big, happy family forever."

The angel broke his eye contact. "Ageless is not immortal," he said sadly.

"Is there something else you'd like to share?" I asked suspiciously.

"I know a war is coming. I know you and your family plan on fighting on the front lines. I know that front lines take high casualties. It is merely extrapolation that leads me to the conclusion that you all will not be together for even decades or centuries, let alone forever."

I began to walk away from him, but he appeared right in front of me. "How do you do that?" I demanded.

He shrugged one shoulder. "It is one of the gifts we have from God."

"And what of my gifts now?" I wondered.

He snorted a laugh. "Again, that is all from your tribe's magic, not anything God did to make you special. You are not an angel."

"Stop saying that," I snapped.

"Then take your true form so that I can no longer say it," he retorted.

My eyes narrowed. "And just what does that entail?"

"Shedding that body and taking on your immortal form," he said in a tone that suggested I was slow on the uptake. He swept his hands down his body to gesture to his own chiseled perfection.

I sneered at him. "So, by dying."

"That is one way to do it," he said with a shrug.

"There's another way?"

"Maybe," he said, staring into my eyes as if he was searching for something. "It would be up to you. Though, I could help if you asked me to."

"How?"

He chuckled, reached up, and grasped my chin to make me look at him. "I told you that you are an original. We are still trying to figure that out. Of course, if you knew your own memories and had control of some of the powers that lay dormant in your soul instead of just the ones in your DNA, then maybe you could help us figure out how to change you without killing you first."

I tried to jerk my head away, but the angel was too strong. He kissed me over my third eye and quickly beat his wings forward to touch mine again. I crumpled in pain when his sorrow over losing me rushed through my body. My breathing grew rapid and shallow, and my hands covered my face. A sob broke in my chest and Dmitrius's invisible hand caressed my cheek. For once, I couldn't pull away because his sorrow mirrored mine.

The angel snorted a laugh. "Surely you must mean some kind of funhouse mirror," he said, releasing me from his unseen grasp and turning his back on me. He strode a few paces away before he turned around to watch me. I was still crouched down on the ground, recovering from the shock of his last infusion of information.

"Will it always be like that?" I gasped once I was able to speak again.

"No, my love. Sometimes it will be much, much worse. Sometimes it will be much, much better."

I put my hands flat on the ground and peered up at him. His face was a mask of sorrow.

"Hope," he whispered. "Please, come with me. I know that part of you already wants to. You are far too curious to continue with all of these refusals. I know that even though you cannot remember who you are, your inner nature will still shine through at times. It is why you want so much to be an angel—because you really are one underneath it all. Please, Hope," he begged.

I slowly stood and turned to watch my daughter where she slept. "I can't leave her. I can't leave any of them. Not for a few days, anyway." I spun around to face him again.

He glanced away to avoid my gaze. "I am not sure how

to make it any shorter than that. How am I to fit thousands of lifetimes into a few hours? How am I to fit millions and millions of years of existence into a single afternoon?"

"How about you just keep it to the key points?"

Dmitrius cast me a dispassionate look. "You already have an idea of how this works. It is not a matter of words, it's a matter of—"

"Of memories? Of thoughts and time?"

"Yes." He sighed and met my eyes again. "Hope?"

"Yes?"

"You have to see how bad he is for you! Please, do not turn away. Do not stop listening now. I need you to remember. We all need you to remember. If you continue to refuse, then this whole tribe—this whole region—"

"Is toast?" I interrupted him.

He gave me the sweetest smile I could recall ever seeing. "Yes, I believe that is an appropriate colloquialism. How interesting English is as a language. For some ideas and concepts, there are no words. And yet for others, there are endless ways to express virtually the same idea."

"I'm not going with you tonight," I told him when his wing began to stretch toward mine again. I turned back to my daughter and he followed as closely as he dared.

"I will be back every day until you agree to come with me," he promised.

"You'll only piss off my husband," I said under my breath. I carefully lifted my sleeping daughter.

"I do not care about him. I care about you. And believe it or not, I care about this tribe. They were my people once, too, you know." With that last sentiment, he disappeared into thin air.

I pushed off into the sky and followed my internal compass to find my way home.

CHAPTER 31

I landed in the back yard and gently set my daughter on her feet. She swayed for a second before she regained her bearings and stumbled into the house. I heard her fall into bed and then she was fast asleep.

Deema crept up behind me and wrapped his steel arms around my waist while he kissed me on my neck. "So what do you say?" he whispered between kisses.

I turned around to face him. "Say to what?"

He grinned at me impishly and I instantly understood.

"Maybe later, lover," I said as I lowered my head in chagrin. "I still have to infect some dreams tonight."

He ducked his head to catch my eyes with his. I peered up and met his gaze, expecting some disappointment. He offered me a weak smile and released me after another brief kiss.

"I guess we'll have plenty of time when all this is taken care of, huh?" he asked.

I turned to walk to the patio and my waiting hammock, settling into my seat and closing my eyes. "All the time in the world."

"Don't worry. I'll watch over you."

"I know," I whispered with a smile and faded away.

I searched for Sarkovski and found him in no time,

slumbering in a small, fairly plain room. I made my way into his mind and pushed aside the dream he was having about his childhood dog.

The forest clearing materialized around us and I grinned at him. "Greetings, Walter."

"Hello again, angel," he replied with a nod. "I suppose you are aware that my boss died in a car accident today," he said timidly, shuffling his feet.

"My name is Hope. Please address me as such. And yes, I heard that he had passed into the afterlife. I'm sure his wife is relieved to be free from his abuse," I replied offhandedly.

My words, or perhaps the casual way in which I said them, caused him to start. He stared at me in shock for a few silent moments before he murmured, "His wife? He beat his wife?"

"Yes. He'd also killed countless homeless people. He would tape their mouths shut while they slept and then he would gut them. Sometimes he just shot them, and sometimes he simply beat them to death. He would kill them to release his anger and frustrations," I told him dismissively.

"A—are you serious?" he stammered.

"Absolutely," I said with unwavering sincerity while I met his gaze. I sighed wistfully. "If he had crossed my path in the streets, I would have killed him myself. How I wish I could have tasted his blood."

"So, you didn't kill him?" he asked cautiously.

"How could I have?" I asked him, feigning confusion. "I am so far away, and I cannot control people's actions. I can only enter their thoughts so that they hear me."

"Oh, good," he sighed, obviously relieved.

"So, you know why I'm here," I said, getting down to business.

"Yes," he said with a frown. "I found the files on the congressman's computer and you were right. When I go into work tomorrow, I will destroy your feather. I will delete and shred the files with your information. It will be as if we never knew about you."

"Except for all of the agents who already know about me," I reminded him.

"You won't kill them, will you?" he asked, suddenly startled by the thought.

"No," I said pensively. "I will not. But I will be keeping an eye on you all to make sure you will not be harming my people. If anyone shows up on my reservation, I can be there in just a few hours."

"And then you will kill them," he breathed.

"Perhaps. That depends on their intentions."

"What if *I* show up on your reservation? Will you meet with me? Please?" he begged.

"I will not," I replied coldly.

"Please?" he repeated desperately.

"I am not to interact with anyone but my people," I said in a voice that sounded like stone—cold, hard, and unmoving.

"But I feel so drawn to you," he continued to beg. "What if this was fate? What if I was meant to meet you? What if I was assigned to this case because God wants me to be a part of this? Be a part of your protection?"

"I will not meet with you. You only feel drawn to my mystery and vampire charm."

"I still have my plane ticket. The hospital gave it back to me since it had my name printed on it. I could still be there in less than two days," he said, grasping at threads of hope.

"No," I said in the same stony voice. "My people will not accept you. And neither will I. Now promise me that you will destroy that plane ticket and that you will not come to my lands."

He watched me contemplatively for an entire minute

before he finally gave me a sad nod. "I promise," he said in a glum tone.

"Fine. I will be keeping an eye on you and your coworkers over the next few days or weeks to make sure that you keep to your promise. Sleep well, Sarkovski."

I pulled myself from my trance and met Deema's eyes. They were still burning with his desire for me.

"Can we go now?" he asked hopefully, caressing my face.

I leaned into his hand. "Yes, love," I said. "We've still got a few hours before the sun rises."

He scooped me up and took off into the sky. In a matter of seconds, we landed in the valley and he ripped my tattered dress from my body. "I'll get you a new one before you hunt next," he promised as his kisses left a trail down my side.

I couldn't help but think about Dmitrius. Not once that I saw had his eyes roved down to leer at my body where my dress had been torn and burned by the bullets in Denver. I was almost certain that the angel didn't covet my body, but my mind. It wasn't pleasures of the flesh he was after, but more in the vein of intellectual intercourse. That appeared to be the polar opposite of my husband, who only seemed to want to be inside of my vagina and not my brain. That had always been fine before, I supposed, but now I was starting to feel just a little less okay with it.

We made love for hours until the sun broke over the horizon. I reminded him that the children would be waking up soon, and I needed some clothes before I could return home. He reluctantly released me and took off into the sky. He returned about a minute later with a clean pair of shorts and a corset which I put on in a rush.

"Is anyone awake yet?" I asked while I dressed.

"They will be waking any minute now," he replied, watching me with hungry eyes.

"Good. I'm anxious to see how the girls' wings are progressing."

We pushed off into the sky and hurried home.

CHAPTER 32

"G"ood morning, Mama," Sandra said in greeting when I landed in the back yard.

I smiled at her before I hurried into the house. I could hear footsteps on the stairs and knew the children were awake. My mind was filled with my desire to see my girls and perhaps give some flying lessons after breakfast.

"Mama!" Long Falcon cried when she saw me. Tears were streaming down her face and I rushed to her side.

"What's wrong?" I demanded as I placed my hands on her shoulders.

"My back," she blubbered.

I spun her around so quickly that she lost her balance and I had to keep her from falling into the wall. Her wings were much larger than the night before and the feathers were breaking through the surface.

"It hurts so bad. Can you make the pain go away?" she begged.

"Oh, baby." I sighed, my worry dissipating. "Did you sleep flat on your back while they grew through the night?"

She bobbed her head and the tears splattered off of her face and chin.

"You'll be fine, honey," I said after I was sure her wings were still growing properly. They looked just like mine, Taniya's, and her older sisters' wings had when they were that size, so I was confident that they were not going to be deformed. "Just give it a few hours and, from now on, I would suggest sleeping on your stomach or your side. My wings always hurt when I slept on them. Well, when I still slept," I added with a grin.

She peered at me like she was still unsure.

"Maybe you should try flexing them to work out the kinks in your muscles," I suggested.

"Okay," she agreed in a skeptical voice. She moved her wings slowly, as if she wasn't sure how to control them, while we walked into the dining room.

Aleks was cooking in the kitchen. Sandra was carrying large plates of food into the dining room while everyone else settled into their seats.

"What's on the agenda today?" Taniya asked as everyone dished out their food.

"I thought we could have some flying lessons and practice," I replied with a smile.

My two oldest daughters grinned back at me. "Cool," one of them said.

They all scarfed down their breakfast while our daughters' boyfriends debated on whether they should join us or not.

"Are you all ready to leave?" I asked once everyone was done eating.

"Yes, Mama," White Buffalo chirped as she pulled Silverwolf to her side.

"Long Falcon, do you want to come and watch?" I asked while my eldest two daughters towed their boyfriends through the back door.

"I don't know." She hesitated, staring at her youngest two sisters, and seemed slightly wistful. "Maybe next time. I'll hang out here today with the girls," she said after a moment.

"Okay, baby. We'll see you for lunch."

Taniya was still having trouble taking off from the ground, so she climbed the stairs to the top floor while I waited in the backyard. When she threw herself out the window, she was a little slow to open her wings. She fell toward the ground, and I darted underneath her to be ready to catch her. But she caught the wind just right and glided over my head before she turned west toward the valley.

I promptly pushed off and followed her. When I landed in the five-mile long valley, Taniya remained airborne and made wide lazy circles to avoid landing. I found my daughters standing about fifty yards apart. Both were wrapped in the arms of their mates and latched onto their lips. Deema landed behind me and cleared his throat.

Singing Sparrow blushed and she stepped away from Fierce Lion. "Sorry, Papa."

The Navajo grinned impishly as he continued to stare at my daughter longingly. I frowned when I realized that they would become intimate soon, and they would risk pregnancy if they weren't smart about it.

"All right. That's enough. Girls, fly," I ordered. "Deema, try to shoot your daughters."

Taniya giggled as she circled overhead. "That just sounds wrong," she said when I regarded her questioningly.

The girls pushed off into the sky, and my husband proceeded to fire at the three of them with the paintball gun. I called out tips to them while they flew back and forth through the length of the valley and we chased them.

"Tuck your wing to make a sharp turn," I yelled.

White Buffalo pulled her right wing close to her body and made a hard turn to the right. She kept it tucked until she'd pivoted a full 180-degrees. Then Deema shot at her again. He hit her right underneath the top joint in her left wing. She screamed out in pain, her wing fell to her side, and she spiraled toward the ground. I raced to my daughter and caught her just before she crashed.

"Are you okay?" The orange paint showed me exactly where she'd been struck and I carefully ran my fingers over her injury.

Deema also rushed to her side, all the while sputtering apologies.

"It's okay," she moaned. "I'll be fine. I think it's just bruised."

When I felt her wing, I was sure she was right. No bones felt like they were broken and I breathed a sigh of relief.

"Okay, that's enough for today," Deema mumbled with sorrow and regret still filling his voice. "I'll fly you home." Before she could object, he scooped her up and flew her back to our house.

"What's going on? Where's White Buffalo?" Silverwolf demanded as he ran around the corner with Fierce Lion right on his tail. "I heard her scream. Where is she?"

"She made a bad turn and the paintball hit her right here," I said and extended my wing, pointing to the spot where she'd been hit. "It's a very tender and vulnerable spot." I frowned. "Probably just about the worst spot to be hit. She's bruised and can't fly anymore today, so her father flew her home. But don't worry. She'll be just fine. She may be able to fly again by dark."

"Okay," he said hesitantly. He still wasn't entirely comfortable around or trusting of the vampires with whom he now lived.

I scowled at him and he wilted slightly. "Neither of us would ever intentionally hurt our children," I nearly snarled. "I understand that you care for her and you want to protect her, but *I* gave birth to her. She is *my* blood. She is *Deema's* blood. *We* are her protectors, too."

"I'm sorry," he mumbled.

"I'll take you home," Singing Sparrow said as she approached him.

"Thanks," he said with a sigh of relief.

After they took to the sky, I turned back to Taniya and Fierce Lion. "We should probably call it a day," I conceded.

"Okay," she quickly agreed. "I'm getting a little worn out already."

"Do you want some help for a takeoff?" I asked her, pushing my idea into her mind.

"That'd be great," she agreed and approached me.

I clasped my fingers together and held out my hands for her to step into them. While she pumped her wings, I boosted her into the air and she took to the sky.

CHAPTER 33

Once Taniya was out of sight, I turned to the Navajo. "Lion," I said with a sigh. "You know I can read minds and so can your father-in-law-to-be. But I can also see the future. When we get home, I will give you some cash and my car. You will go to the grocery store to buy food for yourself and the others. You will also buy some condoms."

His lovely tan skin turned a deep shade of red.

"I cannot permit you to impregnate my daughter just yet. And if you are not careful, you will."

"I'm sorry, Hope," he muttered, shuffling his feet nervously.

"And I would suggest that you wait until my husband is out of the house. You weren't here for when he flipped out over Silverwolf and White Buffalo simply for finding each other attractive."

"What happened?" he wondered.

"Later," I said with a frown and swiftly picked him up. "They're calling us home," I muttered, hearing Sandra's voice in my head.

I flew back to the house and gingerly set him down in the backyard. He followed me inside and waited in the living room while I retrieved my car keys and a fistful of cash.

"Someone should write up a grocery list," I announced, descending the stairs.

"Why?" Singing Sparrow asked suspiciously. She stepped to Fierce Lion's side and grasped his hand.

I smirked when I handed him the money and the keys. "I'm sending him to the store since he appears to be a normal human."

Taniya and my daughters threw together a grocery list and gave it to the Navajo. He cast a glance back at me before he walked out the door, and I gave him a significant look. He blushed when he turned away, and I heard Deema's teeth snap together. I put my hand on his arm and pushed the thought into his mind that he should calm himself.

"It's the only way," I murmured after the door clicked closed.

A hiss slid between his clenched teeth and his glare turned toward our grown daughters.

I pulled him back to my side. "Enough," I roared.

"Not in my home," he growled as he continued to glare at our winged children.

The girls gawped at each other, confused, before they turned their baffled faces in my direction.

I sighed, long and loud, before I stepped in front of my husband and began to speak. "I did not send him to the store just to buy groceries. I told him to buy condoms as well. I cannot allow you girls to get pregnant before the tribe is safe."

The girls gasped then blushed.

"I also told him that sex while your father was in the vicinity is forbidden," I continued. "That goes for you as well, Silverwolf." I gave him a hard glare and he withered.

Deema stepped around me. "I forbid this. I want these men out of my house and I want them to stay away from my daughters," he growled.

Silverwolf sucked in a quick gasp and my husband viciously snarled at him.

"Enough," I roared again. "They are allowed to stay and you will shut the fuck up!" I screamed in Deema's face. "Need I remind you of how you would feel if this were your son and a woman rather than your daughter and a man?"

He took a deep breath, but he continued to shake with anger and hostility.

I positioned myself between him and the kids. "What if my father had forbidden you to be with me? Or my sister? What if my elders had banned you from our lands? I suggest that you would take a lesson from those who surround us and learn some acceptance."

"Fine," he grunted before he stormed out the back door.

Aleks moved to go after him, but I laid my hand on his shoulder. "No," I told him. "Give him some time alone."

"But—"

"But nothing," I interrupted. "Leave him be. He'll come back when he's calmed down and had some time to think about all of this."

"Where does this leave us?" the wolf asked me cautiously.

"Nothing changes. You will continue to stay with us, as will the lion. If any of my other daughters fall in love, then they will also move in with us as well. I will not discourage my children from having relationships. I will, however, council all of them to be smart in their choices. Hence, I'm having Fierce Lion buy condoms."

"Lunch is ready," Sandra said quietly when she set the last dish on the table.

Everyone silently and uneasily sat down at the table and began to dish out their food.

I closed my eyes and slipped into a trance while I checked in on Deema. He was sitting on a ledge overlooking my practice valley. He seemed very conflicted, but also like he was deep in thought. I quickly searched the future to see when he would return. I frowned when I realized that since he didn't know yet, I could not see.

I opened my eyes and glanced around the quiet table. Everyone was eating silently and they all avoided my gaze.

"You all should relax. Everything will be fine," I assured them.

Suddenly, I was gripped by an unsolicited vision. I saw Sarkovski speaking to a little old man while they stood beside a small red airplane.

"How long do you think it will take me to get my pilot's license?" Walter asked the elderly man.

"Oh, not too long. A few months, maybe less. All depends on how quick you learn," he replied in a creaky voice.

The vision shifted to the agent flying in a different plane. He was alone and he was directly over my reservation. He anxiously stared through the window. I assumed he was hoping to get a glimpse of me.

The vision faded and I thrust myself into the mind of Walter Sarkovski. I saw through his eyes and determined that he was on a commercial flight—headed west.

CHAPTER 34

*W*hat the hell do you think you're doing?' I demanded with a booming voice inside his head.

He was so startled that he nearly jumped out of his seat.

"I'm—" he mumbled, trying to figure out how to speak to me without appearing to be a lunatic.

'*I can hear your thoughts, you idiot. Why are you flying toward my people? And why did I have a vision of you learning how to fly small planes? I have forbidden you from going to my reservation. I have forbidden you from trying to find me. And yet still I see you in a small plane, flying over the lands of my people. If I choose to return to them, I could crush your little plane like a soda can. Or I can peel it open like a tin of tuna and toss you to your death. So do you have a death wish? Is that why you have disobeyed me?*' I screamed in his mind.

He glanced around anxiously, worried that others may have heard me. My voice was so loud it was as if it hurt his ears, though he knew that wasn't possible.

'*Answer me!*'

'*I had considered it, but I had not decided,*' he finally replied in a clear, direct thought.

'*It will not come to be,*' I growled.

"Mama," Sandra said as she shook me. "Calm down."

"Not now," I snarled, shaking her off.

"You're yelling really loud. I bet they can hear you a mile away."

"Let me deal with this," I replied before I turned my mind back to the idiot agent.

'*So you really are a mother,*' he mused. '*I don't believe I was meant to see that or hear that, but I did. Just how many children do you have? I believe that you really are on the reservation.*'

I snorted. '*Then you are sadly mistaken. You must be pretty dumb if you don't realize that most people in South America look more like Native Americans than families of European blood. Of course those around me look like Natives. Idiot.*'

'*You're good at dodging questions,*' he smirked. '*She wasn't Native, and she called you Mama. So how many children do you have?*'

'*None of your business. Will you fly back to DC when you land?*'

'*I have put in a request to transfer to the Denver office. They have no reason not to give it to me.*'

'*Stay away,*' I growled before I lost the connection. As usual, a loud noise jarred me from my vision and I automatically went on defense mode.

"It's just us," Brian said after he closed the door. Deema was also with him. I gleaned from Sandra's mind that she'd called him to come home.

I hissed as I re-sheathed my sword and started pacing the length of the dining room. That son of a bitch, that asshole FBI agent was never going to give up. He was determined to see me in the flesh. I noticed out of the corner of my eye that Brian was confused for a moment before he started listening to my mind. He silently sat at the table and waited patiently for my mental tirade to end.

After several minutes, I took a calming breath and explained to everyone what was going on.

"What do we do?" Long Falcon whimpered.

"We wait," Brian said simply.

I stared at him in shock. "We should kill him," I snarled.

"How is that preserving life?" he asked calmly.

"It's not," Deema said as he laid his hand on my shoulder.

I glared at both of them.

"We will wait and we will see what he does next. Perhaps you can scare him into staying away by threatening his life in his dreams," Deema told me while he led me to the couch. He pulled me down to sit beside him, and I stiffly took my seat. "If you can scare him enough, then he might change his mind and actually stay away."

"And if he tells others?" I growled as I tried to bolt off of the couch.

He pulled me back and held me down beside him. "We will ensure that he does not."

I let out a deafening roar of anger and everyone pressed their hands to their ears. I struggled to free myself from Deema's grasp. "Release me," I snapped. He shook his head and held me down even tighter.

"She wants to fly to the forest to tear up trees like you do whenever the girls piss you off," Sandra said quietly.

He let me go and I bolted out the back door. Ever since I'd become a vampire, flying was absolutely effortless—everything physical was. Without even thinking about it, I took to the air and reached my top speed in a matter of seconds. My internal compass let me know which way I needed to turn for the Grand Canyon and I unerringly went straight toward it.

'*Not too long,*' Brian said inside my mind.

I simply snarled in response.

CHAPTER 35

When I got home the next day, I was greeted by an empty house. No notes, no hybrids, no humans, no vampires. Anger coursed through me. I trudged up the stairs to where we kept blood in the attic. After I drained over a dozen pints, I felt much calmer and searched the area for the minds of my family.

I wasn't surprised to find them all crammed into the meeting room at the Hall. My ire started to flare again when I realized that the whole purpose of the meeting was to discuss my mental stability.

Deema sighed and shook his head. "She won't hurt anyone."

"It's not in her heart to hurt those who don't deserve it," Sandra agreed. "Sarkovski has no evil in his heart. No matter how angry she was or is, she could never actually harm him."

"How can you be certain?" the chief asked cautiously.

Aleks scoffed. "We wouldn't allow her to, for one."

"Then where is she now?" Great Falcon asked.

'*I'm in my house, left behind by my entire family while you all discuss me behind my back,*' I pushed into every mind in the room while I dove out the top floor window.

"She's on her way," Brian told them after he latched onto my mind.

I was pissed. Furious. Enraged. And yet I was perfectly calm. One piece of my mind was the calm little center of the storm raging within. And that calm little center was explaining to the rest of my mind why this was all necessary. Something else was nagging me, trying to remember flashes of a vision I'd had while destroying trees that I'd not yet examined or forced into clarity. Something about my past, before this life, but I was too angry to really look into it.

I took a few calming breaths before I was sure that I could enter the building without tearing off any doors. Once I made it to the meeting room, the calm center of my brain had grown by a large amount. My rage was entirely under control. I appeared composed when I sat on my stool and waited for everyone to stop talking over each other.

"That's it!" my big brother finally bellowed over everyone. "Shut up and let her speak for herself now that she's here."

Everyone did shut up and they all turned to stare at me with a wide variety of expressions, ranging from hostility to sympathy to worry and everything in between. But I wasn't quite ready to talk yet. I was still trying to organize my thoughts so that I could speak. I took a few more calming breaths to allow my calm center to finish spreading and my racing thoughts to find the words I needed.

"Thanks for waiting for me," Dmitrius said after he appeared out of nowhere. He gave a small chuckle and winked at me. "You have no idea yet just how true that is," he said to me in a quick aside.

"Welcome, Dmitrius," the chief said as gave the angel a small bow of his head. "You are always welcome here, of course."

Deema growled, but stayed where he was standing. The chief glared at him, but Deema ignored the old man. All of the vampire's focus was on his assumed rival.

"Stay out of this, blood drinker," Dmitrius said with a small sneer twisting his lips. "No one wants or needs you here. This is not, and never has been, *your* family."

"I want him here and I need him here," I interjected in the calmest tone I could muster.

Dmitrius raised an eyebrow at me. "I am sorry, Hope, but that still remains to be seen."

"All right, let's just keep this to the business at hand, okay?" Brian said, glancing back and forth between my two apparent suitors.

CHAPTER 36

Okay. Um…Well, first of all—what the fuck, you guys? I have a temper tantrum and you start saying I'm unstable? Deema freaks out all the time. The twins have had a flip-out or two. It's a vampire thing. Do I not always calm myself? Even if it takes tearing up some trees—"

"Which I've done *far* more often than she has," Deema interrupted.

"—or having a couple of meals, I always calm down and see reason," I continued.

"So you don't intend to kill him?" Nallia asked quietly from the back of the room. There were three women I didn't recognize with her, but I could see small wings peeking over their shoulders. I knew they had to be Austyn, Chelsea, and Cassandra.

"Only if he lays eyes on any of us with wings," I replied with ice dripping from my words.

Dmitrius appeared right in front of me again and seized one of my wings. His grip was not hard or painful, but the look in his eyes was both. "I will not allow you to harm innocent people. If it is the presence of wings that is the problem, then should I do all of you pretenders the courtesy of removing your wings?" His harsh words and tone were such a shock, that he might as well have slapped me. I wrenched my wing away from him hard enough that I lost my balance, tumbled backward, and landed on my rear. He let go easily, though I knew he was strong enough to follow through with his threat. Something in his eyes told me it was an empty threat anyway. The corners of his lips turned up in agreement when I considered that all he'd wanted was my attention.

Deema flew toward him as a growl started in his throat, but he stopped short, frozen in place. I studied the angel and saw that he now held the hand with which he'd gripped me behind himself, like he was signaling Deema to stop. I immediately realized it was more like a signal for the use of the angel's telekinetic power.

Whoa.

"Do not act so surprised," he murmured as he stared down at me. "You could do it, too, if only you would listened to the whispers." He moved his other hand and I was lifted to my feet. Once I was stable, I felt as if hands were smoothing my hair and wings and gently caressing my face.

"What do you mean? Whispers?" I could not stop my voice from shaking. I'd been extra careful to never mention or even think about the whispers around others. The whispers almost always only ever came when I was alone. They were so quiet, so sudden, and they could not be controlled, so I couldn't even listen to them over again. They were in a language I didn't understand, and they'd frightened me ever since I'd started hearing them. I'd soon realized that I could not hear the voices if I had music playing and, from then on, I took to either keeping the stereo on, or humming to myself. Once I'd become a vampire, I stopped listening to music in the house and instead listened to music from other houses around mine or even from passing cars. And really, with my perfect memory, I could constantly listen to anything I wanted to inside of my own head.

He sighed heavily. "If you had listened to the whispers rather than fearing them…if you had realized that the whispers were also a part of your wing growth, you would have soon begun to understand them. It is a language that you know, if only you could allow yourself to remember it. It is the language of our kind." His expression fell and he closed his eyes for a moment.

"Focus," my brother whispered from beside our grandfather.

Dmitrius shook his head as if to clear it. "You cannot kill the agent. He means you no harm. He is even willing to leave his job, if that is what it takes to gain the trust of the tribe and be accepted here," the angel told me in a way that was so odd.

Oh, how this man confused me! He was stern, but casual in how he spoke. And yet, he was also neither. But even more importantly, I *felt* his words. I knew that he spoke the truth, and I'd do exactly as he said.

"Okey dokey," I murmured in a daze.

Deema was suddenly unfrozen and seemed uncertain for a moment before he hesitantly walked to my side. "I will not let you be alone with my wife," he calmly stated, lightly putting his arm around my shoulders. But calm tone and actions or not, I could see the rage brewing behind his obsidian eyes. Deema was ready for a fight if this angel mouthed off to him again.

"Yes, you will," I answered for Dmitrius as he opened his mouth. I'd decided that I couldn't put this off any more. I was far too curious about my past and my secret powers to keep denying his offers of help. I knew I still didn't want to change what I was, but what could it hurt to gain some extra powers?

Deema turned to gape at me. "What?" His tone was

flat—stunned. His rage was deflated and an empty shock took its place.

"I may have been your wife 500 years ago, but I've known him since—"

"Since before the beginning of time," Dmitrius finished for me.

"No," Deema nearly growled.

Still, I could sense the pain behind his jealousy. "Don't fight me on this," I said softly. "We're running out of time. I will not argue with you. We will not fight over it. You will trust me. Are we clear?" I met his eyes and saw an unsureness growing there that I hadn't seen in a long time.

"Okay, Hope," he said. He broke my gaze and turned for the door. I wanted to tell him I loved him, but I hesitated and then he was gone. I figured he knew, but still...

I closed my eyes and hung my head for a second before I remembered the room full of elders, hybrids, and vampires.

"Grandfather?" I asked, turning back to the elders.

"You will not harm the agent?" he asked me.

"No, Grandfather."

"Then we are done here." His eyes moved to the angel, who gave him a tiny nod. It irked me a bit to not be able to penetrate the exchange.

Dmitrius stepped to me and gripped my left shoulder in his hand while he caressed the side of my face adoringly with his other hand. "Thank you," he whispered fervently before he kissed my forehead.

I blinked and we were suddenly nowhere. I peered all around at nothing and no one. I was nothing—I glanced down and there was no substance to me. I could sense the presence of the other, but I could not see him either. I felt like I blinked again, though I was certain I had no eyes. Then again, if I had no eyes, how was I seeing?

Before I could figure that out, I saw that I was standing

near the top of a mountain, holding hands with the angel. Far below us, I could see a small village of goat herders. I was incredibly thirsty for the blood that ran through their veins. I felt him squeeze my hand and I knew that he was definitely stronger than me. I also realized that the whispers were back.

CHAPTER 37

"W here are we?" I asked. It seemed that the wind
swept my words away. But when I saw him
smile, I knew that he'd heard me.

"We are somewhere they will never search for us, so
they cannot spy on our talks. Please, have a seat if you
would like." He gestured to what appeared to be a natural
rock formation, but it was molded perfectly so that I could
sit down and be comfortable with my wings. Across from
it, there was another formation just like it. I immediately
realized how close it would cause us to be if we both sat.
Close enough to lean forward and feed from him.

I avoided meeting his eyes. "No, thank you. I never tire
now," I said. "Wait—talks? As in plural? I thought you
said you could make this quick."

He chuckled lightly and leaned toward me. "Many, I
pray," he whispered in my ear. "And a few days *is* quick.
To do this right, we really need much longer."

"I've so many questions," I blurted out.

He released my hand and walked around behind me. "I
know you do, my dear," he said.

I tried to track him with my mind, but I couldn't.

"I have us blocked from their sights," he said while he
continued his circuit.

I couldn't tell, but I thought maybe he was caressing me again. Though, I hoped it was just the wind. "They cannot find you if they search for you. You were lost to them from the moment we disappeared. Do not try to look in on them," he warned the instant I considered it. "Then they could find you. We do not want that, now. We will be needing our privacy," he whispered and swept my hair back over my shoulder to expose my neck.

"Please don't do that, Dmitrius. You know that I'm married." I sidestepped away from him and the warm, suddenly very aromatic blood that was pumping through his veins. But he stayed right there beside me, as if we were attached.

"Oh, but we are attached. We are of the same ilk, cut from the same cloth. Whatever bindings you have given yourself while in this body do not matter. You will remember that soon enough." He took me in his arms, beat his wings just once against mine, and held me tightly for a few seconds before he released me.

I stumbled backward and plopped down into the stone seat. He sat down in front of me and turned me by pushing on my knees so that we were not only facing each other, but our knees were interlocked. I didn't know what to say or think. I did actually feel very drawn to him. Even my wings seemed to want to stretch out and touch his wings more than I'd ever noticed before. I felt like I'd been holding them away from him for so long.

"Do not fight it," he whispered, leaning forward and stretching his wings toward me. "It is exactly what you need to remember yourself again, but you must choose to accept it."

"Yes," I whispered. I gave in and allowed my wings to be drawn to his.

When our wings touched, it was glorious. We were suddenly one, his voice speaking in my mind in the language he'd called ours. And all of a sudden I understood it perfectly. I also knew everything I'd ever known before I'd been born into this body. I could remember every previous life, every stretch of time between lives—I could even remember the Fall. I could remember him standing beside me while we watched friends of ours fall from Heaven.

"Dmitrius," I whispered against his mouth when it covered mine. It took me a few moments to remember the other Dmitri in my life—my husband. "No, please," I mildly protested as we both held each other more tightly and his lips trailed along my jaw. The edges of our wings were still lining up perfectly and pressing together in a soothing yet sensual way.

"Drink," he murmured against my jaw, guiding my lips to his neck.

I was so thirsty that I didn't even give it a second thought. My teeth pierced his tender flesh. His Light exploded in my mouth, poured down my throat, and spread through my whole body.

Time ceased to exist or even matter. It was like I was back in the Void, only I knew I wasn't because it was different. It was more like I was everywhere instead of nowhere. But I was still grounded in our embrace and in the joining of our wings. Then his voice brought me back from the Everywhere and Everything that I couldn't help but feel and know and revel in once again.

"See, my love? You shall forget about him soon enough," he whispered into my ear.

"But things are different now," I nearly sobbed. I finally found the strength to push at him rather than pull at him. "I had children with him. They are ageless and so am I. You said it yourself—I'm different from the rest of our kind now."

"We can change you back," he said tenderly. He traced

the edge of my face lightly with his fingertips and his wings pressed more firmly against mine. "And you will forget about them someday, too."

"No, I won't." The hardness in my voice stopped him short. "They are my children. I carried them, birthed them, and raised them. They are part of me and now I am part of them. It's one thing to have mortal children who die. I can move on and forget the pain of their losses. But these will not die, and they will always be part of me."

"You are mostly right. They are part of you right now. But when we change you back, they will no longer be a part of you."

"That doesn't make sense. If you change me to what I was before I was a vampire, then I'd be the same as I was when I gave birth to them. Their wings and shapeshifting are a part of them because I was a mortal angel. That was the DNA I gave them. Deema gave them the vampire genes."

"No, my dear. You must not have understood when we talked about this before. You would be changed into what I am, which is far from what you were before. You have not taken this physical form in a very long time. Your children would no longer be important to you, I promise."

We were still joined and I knew he meant what he said. The thought of not caring about my children—or my brothers or my tribe—was so jarring that I was able to separate my wings from his and move away a bit.

"That," I gasped, "I am not ready for." I stared at him in shock for a few moments while my racing mind continued to process what I'd learned and remembered through our joining.

I had no more questions for him. I understood everything I needed to know about the Void through which we'd passed to arrive at where we were. I knew how to return to my tribe, or to go wherever I wanted to now. I could feel various powers coursing through me that I'd never known I'd had before in this body and I knew how to control them all.

He smiled sadly. "We have time."

"I don't know how to choose," I blurted out without meaning to.

He lost the smile and the sadness in his eyes grew. "We have time."

"You kept things from me," I realized.

"Some things I kept from you to spare you the pain of prior knowledge."

"I need to return." I turned away from him and almost jumped off the mountain, but then I remembered that I could travel much more easily now.

"I can follow you anywhere, you know?" he called after me, almost desperately. "You cannot stop me. You know that I have been following you for weeks before I took you away."

"But do you really want to alienate me any further?" I asked him over my shoulder.

"*I want you to remember*," he said in our language.

"I do," I replied. "I remember…" I trailed off.

He knew. He had full access to my mind, even though he'd managed to keep parts of his mind secret from me.

"Please." The word did not just sound in my ears, it spoke inside of my very soul. I felt all of his pain, his anguish, his desperation, and his desire to be my partner once again. I'd missed him immensely, without even knowing he was gone. It seemed so clear to me now why he'd been so hostile, indignant, and aggressive. But promises to him were not the only ones I'd ever made. I had my own pride, too. I knew my life had just gotten even more complicated with this new knowledge and fount of emotions.

I sighed and stared down at the village to avoid his mournful gaze. "You know that I chose this life."

"Not *this* life!" He was radiating misery when he landed in front of me and gripped my arms, lifting me from my feet so that we were eye-to-eye. He trembled while tears streamed down his cheeks and he roared in my face. "You chose that tribe, not that blood drinker! This is not what you chose when you agreed to be born there! To be born to them without me!"

He set me on my feet, but I collapsed to my knees, feeling his frustration and sorrow over my current path continue to wash through me. Suddenly he had an Immutable Blade in his hand. His face became a mask of calm when he lifted the Blade and took his aim.

Of course, I knew how to send it into the Void so it could not touch me, but I was so stunned that he held that particular knife that I hesitated. Then both of my cheeks were sliced through so that my jaw flopped open and unhinged. I felt no pain, which surprised me for only a second. Of course the Blade was sharper than vampire teeth, so why would it sting when nothing else did?

Without touching me, he pushed my jaw back into place and my flesh began to knit together. Despite my painless and damn-near instant healing, I was angry he'd cut me. I used my newly remembered telekinetic powers to take the Blade from him. He did not fight me for it.

"You know what it will do to me," he said in a steady voice while he watched me with sorrowful eyes. His cheeks were still wet with his tears. "But if you can wait for a minute or two, you will see that it is not the same with you now."

I could already tell that he was right—the Blade would not leave a scar on my flesh. But how could that be? Then again, I already knew that answer. This body wasn't what my soul was meant to wear. It might stand up to the abuses of traveling through the Void, but it was far from ideal for such travel. His current form, on the other hand, would forever be scarred if I cut him. His soul would be scarred. Every human form he ever took in the future would be marked in some way, early in his life, so that his mortal form would match his immortal soul.

"I can't think this through while I'm here with you. I'm sorry, my love." I slapped my hand over my mouth.

"Old habits die hard," he whispered into my soul like he had before.

I pushed off into the sky. "Please, don't follow me," I sobbed.

He knew my heart, so he knew how much I meant it. He stood there on the mountain and watched me fly away while his sorrow over my choices poured into my soul, devastating me all the more, since it was now a mirror of my own.

CHAPTER 38

I flew northeast, though it really didn't matter which way I flew. We were on the complete opposite side of the world—in Tibet. But it seemed just as well. I needed the time to think. It was startlingly disorienting to have so many tens of thousands of years of memory surging through my brain. So much knowledge was right there at my beck and call, just as if I'd never forgotten it. Some was so violent it even made me shudder. Other memories were so beautiful or passionate that they made me shudder, too.

I could remember thousands of lifetimes with my soulmate, my partner, my equal—my Dmitrius. Each one had been filled with both good times and bad, and we'd endured it all side-by-side. He'd fathered myriad children that I'd borne across the millennia. Had I the time, I could have listed each and every one of their names. Each one, he'd treated with the loving kindness that was the core of his nature. Had he ever been angry? Most definitely. But that was part of the human condition. Just like the love we'd shared—the love I was denying us both by staying with my family. The desire to be with the other angel tore at my heart, warring with my undeniable need to remain with my children and beloved husband. I couldn't recall a single time in all of my existence when I'd ever felt so irresolute or anguished.

Now that we were connected—or rather, now that I had my powers back and could find our connection—I knew he wasn't following me, but he was still watching me.

"Damn it all, Dmitrius," I muttered. "If you're going to watch me, you might as well follow me physically, too."

'*How can I not watch you? You know how much I have missed you,*' his voice sounded inside my head.

And I did. That was the thing with our kind—we were of one mind, even though we were all still individuals. That could actually get pretty complicated since there are hundreds of millions of us, but emotions keep it in check. While I *could* know anything that any other angel knew, I only *did* know the hearts and minds of those I was closest to—so I did know exactly how much he missed me, how much it hurt him that I might choose blood drinkers over him, and how much it scared him to think that I could choose another partner over him. Yes, I knew. It wracked my soul as it wracked his.

I could not deny that I ached for him. I knew that he knew that it took all of my restraint to not turn around and go back to him. But I had to return to my children. I'd missed most of Silver Panther's childhood since I'd been gone for so long. Traveling through the Void almost always took a long time unless one was very skilled at skimming it to travel a short distance, but it was never really consistent since time didn't actually exist in the Void. Joining like we did by lining up our wings also took weeks. Similarly to when we were between lives or deep in the Void, time seemed to pass at a faster pace when we were joined together in that manner. If our time spent in angelic form passed as slowly as it did for humans, it would seem interminable.

It was only out of my respect and—let's face

it—affection for Dmitrius that I waited until I was well beyond Japan and far out over the ocean before I tried to look in on my family. I knew they had to be worried sick about me. Sure enough, immediately upon my connection with Brian, his head popped up. "I found her!"

I couldn't believe what I saw. My brother had a strap of leather tied over his eyes, but he was turning his head as if he actually saw my family crowding around him, all talking over each other to ask things about me.

"Shut up!" he finally shouted while I continued to dig through his mind. I quickly discovered that Dmitrius had told my brother telepathically to wear the leather in order to increase his powers. I went over their conversation in less than a second while other thoughts and memories percolated into my mind. Sarkovski had arrived. The elders had accepted him without question, based on the word of Dmitrius. He was in the next room, listening, but staying out of sight so as to not anger me should I remote view them. I almost laughed.

I couldn't get over how easy it was. I knew everything I could ever want to know about my brother. Ugh. And many things I didn't want to know. I also knew he had no access to my mind except for what I purposely sent to him.

"Hope?" he said aloud. His quavering tone startled everyone in the room with him to stillness.

"Hello, brother," I replied aloud. I figured I'd let the other remote-viewers have the chance to watch our talk while also illustrating my new abilities.

"You're alive and you appear to be whole, but why can't I access your mind? Why do you feel...different?"

"I am different," I said flatly. "Not as different as he would've had me be, but different nonetheless. My mind is permanently closed now to all but those of my kind."

"Taniya?"

"She is not of my kind." It took an enormous amount of

self-control to keep my tone even and my face blank.

"Yes, he said that before. But why? I mean, if the other women aren't like you, then why do they have wings?"

"That doesn't matter right now," Deema grumbled. "Where *is* she? Where has she *been*? Is she coming home—" He choked himself off with a sob that he tried to hide.

"Why can't I find you?" my brother asked.

"Because you've no access to my mind. You'll never be able to remote view me again unless I seek you out first…"

"And?" Brian prompted me.

I sighed. "I am over the Pacific. Yes, I'm coming home." I hesitated while I dithered. "I—I cannot tell you where I've been. It is a secret place."

I watched Deema's face fall and he turned away from my brother. "Secret," he whispered forlornly. "So she *will* leave us when she returns."

"Don't put words in my mouth, Dmitri," I growled. I pumped my wings harder, anxious to return and look into his eyes, to hold him in my arms again.

"It's only a matter of time," my husband whispered. It was an eerie, twisted echo of my angelic partner's words, '*We have time.*'

"I'm coming home," I repeated in a hard tone. "Would you prefer that I not? Is your insistence that I'll be leaving merely your desire to me rid of me?"

"Of course not. Please, come home," he sobbed as he fell to his knees.

"I am. Further conversations can wait until I get there. I have all the answers we need now. I'll probably need at least a week alone with the elders to tell them all we need to know."

"We all love you, sis," Brian reminded me. "We'll see you when you get home."

"Yes," I replied before I cut off his end of our connection. I couldn't help myself—I just had to see them for a while longer. Tall Filly was almost completely grown. Silver Panther was the size Filly had been when I'd left. They all seemed so sad that I wanted to cry.

I carefully slid back into Brian's mind to search for more pertinent information about me. I was not happy with what I found. Dmitrius had been talking to several of the elders inside of their minds the whole time he'd been at the Hall with us. He told my elders that I would only be with them just long enough to keep them safe. My fellow angel had told them that I'd choose to leave them once they were safe, otherwise I'd be trapped with the tribe for centuries until I felt like I was little more than a slave to them.

I wanted to punch him. I wanted to pummel him into the dirt for sticking his nose where it didn't belong. My hand flexed around the Immutable Blade that I'd taken from him. Part of me wished to scar him with it, but the rest of me cringed away from the idea of marring his immaculate flesh.

Thinking of his flesh caused shivers to run down my spine. I couldn't help but recall the last time we'd been together when we were both in our physical angelic bodies. Words could not even begin to describe the ecstasy. It had been sublime to hold him earlier, but this body was not what my soul needed to truly be the same as him again. Without my immortal form, the bliss I felt with him when we joined our wings was only a shadow of what it could be. This knowledge was tempting, but I remained resolute to hold him at a distance.

But the Immutable Blade—it had been eons since I'd held one. The rarest of rare blades, their creation only began after the Fall and ceased a mere 10,000 years later. Of course, it took a full year to forge each blade, so there was less than one knife per 150,000 devoted angels. Oh, yes. A very rare blade indeed…

And I desperately needed a sheath for it. Damn. Without the proper sheath for an Immutable Blade, it would cut through everything it touched, even if very little force was applied.

CHAPTER 39

I was nearing the California coast when I felt him exit the Void fairly close to me. It was like an explosion of sensation coursing through my body. *Lover is near, lover is near, lover is near...*

"A sheath, my dear?" He held it out to me, knowing very well that I could not reach out to take it from him without our wings touching. I shuddered against my will when I remembered a flight we'd taken many millennia before. Unable to resist himself, Dmitrius had embraced me mid-flight. Our wings had touched and the sensual rapture was so great that we could not pull away. We'd crashed into the ground so hard and from such a height that it had left a crater.

"Snatch," I gasped once I was able to pull myself from the memory.

He gave me a perplexed expression before he realized that his hand was empty and both of mine were now full. "You are getting good at that," he mused.

I slid the rare Immutable Blade into its home. "It is what it is," I mumbled, securing the sheath to my belt right next to my katana.

He gave me a tender smile. "You always were so good at anything you put your mind to."

"So, am I actually an angel now that I have my memories back?"

"You are closer than you were before, but honestly? No, Hope. You are still not a real angel. Not until you have your immortal form. Every time you travel into the Void, you will be taking a hit to this body. I do not know for sure, since your case is unique, but I think that every time you go into the Void, it forces you to be a little bit more of an angel."

"Are you returning with me?" I asked flatly, trying to ignore his proclamation.

"Do you want me to?"

Anger and desire both swirled through me. I didn't have to answer him, just as he hadn't needed to ask me. He knew how torn I was. I'd missed him so much. It was disorienting to feel so strongly for someone that I'd not even been able to recall six weeks ago. But the pain that his presence and existence caused my husband cut through me like a knife. As incredibly selfish as it was, I wanted them both, even though I knew that was insane.

When we flew over LA, I heard a woman singing on stage in a club. "These days of rage have left their stain on me," she began, immediately capturing my attention. Her voice was a raspy growl, singing words that I would have recognized anywhere.

"Shh!" I snapped when he almost began talking again.

I was entranced by her voice and the words. I'd known them by heart since I was a teenager and had happened across a music video from the early 2000s. I'd soon become obsessed with the music of Otep and had memorized all two hundred and thirty-two of her songs, as well as all seventy-three of her spoken poems that I could find. Then there were the books upon books of poetry, artwork, short stories, and more. I'd obsessed over them, memorizing much of her work and finding solace in her assurances that

I was not alone, no matter how different I felt. I'd tried to find her once, but was crushed when I found out she'd been dead for nearly a decade.

"I've broken these men of blood. Now I wake, naked in the debris. But I'm sick of fighting, sick of crying. Everything mounting up sky high and I must thus trust no one. Stay frozen. My moment is here. The enemy's drawing near." The singer's voice was ragged and raw. At times, she sounded like she was on the verge of tears. Others, I thought she might be about to pummel someone to death in her rage. Oh, and that roar! No one could ever say that she wasn't skilled at her craft. It gave me chills how this impersonator could match the original so well.

I sighed as I felt each word for my own reasons and she continued chanting, "Stay away. Stay away. Stay."

"Come away, Hope," he murmured. He left the wide arch I was making and turned back toward my reservation.

I began to follow him, but then I caught a few more lines that really stuck with me and I hesitated. "All I'll ever do is hurt you. Stay. No, go away. Stay. No, go away. Stay. No, go away. Don't go. Trust no one. These days of rage have left their stain on me."

I could hear her pain in her wail. It was like she was saying that it hurt to be together, but it also hurt to be apart. How could she ever choose? How could she make her choice of whether to stay or to go? She was so scarred, tainted, and stained from her rage, how could she ever know that she was making the right choice?

I wondered if I was reading into her song excessively. Was I placing too much of my own slant on her words? If only I could ask the original artist, but she was long gone. Or perhaps she had intentionally left it ambiguous, to be interpreted freely by fans in all sorts of different situations. Like—*Hey, I'm damaged and I don't think you can handle all this baggage that comes with me.*

That really would apply to a lot of people.

I needed to know if this woman truly felt the pain she sang, but hadn't written, or if she was just acting. She murmured, "Hope hurts," right before I delved into her mind and found the most tortured soul I'd ever encountered. She was right. Hope hurt. It hurt to hope for something that could never happen, like happiness with all of those whom I loved. It hurt to hope that they'd love me back, despite things from my past that couldn't ever be undone. And *this* Hope hurt. I hurt. Her pain actually caused me to curl in on myself in a sob of desperation. And yet at the same time, I could feel the immense strength that her pain had given her. Part of me wished, for a moment, that I had her resolve and her passion.

'*Leave her be*,' he whispered into my mind while he fed me the emotional strength I needed to uncurl myself and resume flying. "She accepted the challenge of this lifetime and body because her soul is strong enough to use that pain to help others. Come away, Hope, and leave her be. It is not the first time she has been herself, and it won't be the last. Her duty is to help people, though in a different way than your duty."

But I couldn't help it—I turned around and flew back toward the club. I wanted to hear her music with my own ears. "Who says she cannot help me?" I murmured when he chased me. If she was another angel, and she had the strength she did, maybe she could teach me to be brave, strong, and confident like she was.

She was chanting again, still irresolute as to whether she wanted this hated loved one near. I felt it. I didn't want Dmitrius around. He only brought my family pain, and by extension me. The singer was begging the other to stay. I sighed, feeling that, too. I didn't ever want him away from my side. I wished to never be apart from him ever again.

But she was also angry. Her fists wanted to fly. So did

mine. I wanted to pummel his face for abandoning me, for stranding me, for erasing me and my tribe from his life until it was convenient for him to return. But he'd neglected me. Now, he wanted to dissect me, to emotionally purge me of my family.

Otep gave me the words, but I knew then that I infused my own meaning into them. That was how it was meant to be. She showed her rage, and I felt mine mirror hers, though for very different reasons, I was sure. Maybe that was how the impersonator could mimic the original Otep so well. She'd found her own way to interpret the words, to feel them herself, just like I did while I flew over the club to listen to the music.

"Abandoned, stranded, betrayed. With friends like these, I need my enemies. Dissected, neglected, erased. With friends like these, I need my enemies," she roared.

"How fitting," I mused, circling the club, high overhead. I wanted to throttle the angel beside me for not joining me in this lifetime of incarnation. If he hadn't abandoned me, none of this would've happened. It would've stayed easy. I wouldn't have married a vampire and produced such unnatural hybrids as my children. I could've saved my tribe and moved on to the next life. But now? Now I was something that never had been—never should have been—and yet I didn't want to change at all. I wanted to remain exactly the same. I feared the transformation that he wanted—the change that would remove my love for my children.

"Hope," he murmured, trying to fly closer to me. "You know it is not like that. Come on. Can we please land?"

I knew what he wanted—to touch his wings to mine again.

"No," I managed to whisper as I tried, unsuccessfully, not to shudder with desire.

He sighed, but continued to follow me. "I miss you so much."

I turned away from the club when she went into a piece of poetry spoken over background music. It was an original, but still in the style of the previous incarnation of Otep. As much as I hated to admit he was right, Dmitrius did have a point about me not intruding on her. She probably wouldn't know who she really was when she was between bodies. It would taint her purpose to know that she was truly an angel on a mission to help victims of abuse, bullying, and rape. "I'm going home. They're expecting me."

"I will not be a distraction," he offered hopefully.

I scoffed. "You'd be nothing but."

"Can you at least tell me…" He trailed off and turned away.

"What?" I didn't really feel like delving into his mind, lest I lose all of my self-control and turn away from my family and my tribe for him.

"But that's not what I want. Not really," he said, contradicting my thoughts. "What I want now is the assurance that someday we *will* be together again. I do not want to lose you forever to this ossified body and that cold blood drinker."

"He is my family, too, now. As are our children. Dmitrius, you know my heart. How can you ask such things of me? How can you cause me such pain?"

"I do not mean to or want to. Hope, I only want to bring you joy and satisfaction. I love you. We are where the term soulmates came from. How can I not beg you to return to me?"

I sighed again. Yes, we were the first pair of immortal souls who'd kept returning to Earth to be born of mortals, to have the challenge of finding each other without our knowledge of ourselves or our angelic natures. Time and time again, we'd found each other as humans and fallen in love all over again, never to know until we'd died what we really were.

We'd also spent eons unincarnated, roaming all over God's Creation. I could recall with perfect clarity the first time he'd expressed his preference for me over all of the other angels in existence. It had been rapture to know that I was his, and he was mine. We had been Watchers back then, which was how we fell in love with being human to begin with. Observing those mortal bodies with their mortal souls had made us curious. Curiosity had led to embodiment, which led to enjoyment, and then the inevitable tens of thousands of years of reincarnation that had followed.

"My love," he whispered into my soul.

All I had to do was say the words, and he'd leave me. All I had to do was speak them in our language, and he'd be banished from my sight for however long I said. But how could I? I wanted him, needed him, and craved him. I knew he could and would help me. He'd do anything I asked him to do if I really meant it. Yet I could not mean this. Yes, I wanted my husband desperately, but I also wanted my angel. This whole conundrum had me internally wallowing in misery. I wanted to be angry with him, but I could not find the strength or true logic for it because I knew his heart just as he knew mine. We were both tormented by the pain this triangle was causing everyone.

"What if…" He trailed off again and looked away from me. "What if he were to die?"

Without even thinking, I turned to attack him, but he was ready for that. He threw his weight back so that he reared up and I missed him by inches.

"Hey! I did not mean I was going to kill him!"

"I would not forgive you if you did," I snarled. I drew my sword and turned to chase him. But he went into the

Void, knowing I wouldn't follow him and risk losing more time. I forcefully re-sheathed my sword and pumped my wings even harder. I was getting close to home, and I was so anxious to hold my children again.

CHAPTER 40

"Mama!"

I barely heard the shout over the distance, but I could see Sandra far off in the night sky, racing toward me. In just a matter of moments, we were crashing together in an embrace. The thunderous boom of our hard bodies colliding echoed off of the surrounding mountains.

"Aleksandra," I whispered into her hair while we squeezed each other tight.

"Mama, I've missed you so much!" She wept without tears as she supported our weight and turned to fly us back home.

"I've missed you, too, baby," I managed to blubber between my own tearless sobs.

"Why can't we hear your mind or feel where you are anymore? We've been so worried about you. Everyone freaked out when you disappeared and we couldn't find you anywhere. Dad is so distraught. I've never seen him like this before, even when he used to search the woods for us in the beginning after we were changed. Your brother just sits on the floor all day with that leather over his eyes, constantly searching for you. When you disappeared, everyone else's wings started to grow as fast as White Buffalo's did. Everyone with a bird's name can fly now.

The elders have made every woman who can fly practice all day long and every man who can shift is made to practice shifting and practice fighting in all of their spare time, too. Everyone's been so worried that you'd never come back. We thought he'd taken you out of this world entirely," she rambled.

"He did," I said before she could start a new sentence or question. "But I've returned. He does want to take me away, but I told him no. He wants to change me so that I'm not a vampire anymore."

"He can do that?" She squeezed me even tighter. "Will he do that? Give you a mortal body so that we'll lose you to death someday?" Sobs shook her body again and she used all her strength to hold me to her.

"I would not be mortal," I assured her. "I'd be a different type of immortal." I ran my hand through her hair to try to soothe her. "I'd still be strong and fast and have all of the powers I have now. But my skin would change and I wouldn't need to drink blood anymore."

"But you would not be human?"

"No, baby," I soothed. "I would be a true immortal. Only by my own choice would I ever leave this world. No one would ever be able to kill me in that body, should I choose to be changed."

"Then do it!" she exclaimed as the reservation came into view on the horizon. "We are not true immortals in this form. If someone decapitates you—if, when, they come to destroy us—we can't lose you."

"It's more complicated than that," I hesitantly replied. "He claims that if I change my physical form…" I trailed off, searching her eyes and her mind while I also tried to find the right words. "He believes that I won't love you anymore. He thinks that my tribe won't matter to me. So I told him no."

We landed in my backyard. "But you could still die," she said through her sobs.

"But I won't," I assured her while a flood of people rushed out of my house toward us.

For a moment, I was petrified. I had no idea who to hug first without offending anyone else. I wanted my children, but I wanted Deema, too. Luckily, I didn't really have to choose since almost everyone crushed in around me in a huge group hug. They all talked over each other, expressing their love and concern for me along with their relief that I'd returned.

"Mama, I shifted," Tall Filly informed me.

"You did? When?"

"Just a couple of days ago. Uncle Brian helped me by being inside of my head."

"Well, that was awful nice of him. Did you thank him?"

"Yes, Mama. And my wings grew and then White Buffalo shifted."

"I see that." I watched her with curiosity when Silver Panther pushed her way through the crush and climbed up me. I peered down at her in amusement. "You're getting too big to ride my hip like a little one. You're mostly grown now."

She put her arms around my neck and laid her head on my shoulder like she'd done when she was small. "I know." She sighed and squeezed me with her arms and her legs. "But you missed the rest of it." *'Your last child, and you missed the last of her childhood. I'll grow wings, too. Very soon, you know. But I'll never be a little one again. I'll never be your baby again,'* she thought toward me while she softly cried into my hair.

"Oh, honey," I murmured. I hugged her in return and stroked her hair. "You'll always be *my* baby, even if you aren't still a baby. I'll always love you, even if I have to go away sometimes."

"So you will be leaving us again," Deema whispered from where he leaned against the back of the house, watching us all.

"Sometimes, I may have to. But that doesn't mean, in any way, that I ever will or did intend on leaving for good. I'm already getting really sick of your sullen attitude. If you want to push me away, keep it up. But right now, as far as you're concerned, I'm not leaving you in a marital way so drop the fucking attitude."

"Ignoring a problem won't make it go away," he snapped back.

"And handling it like this—arguing in front of every-one—isn't going to fix it either. But have you even given me a chance to discuss this with you? Have we sat down and talked about it? No. You have no idea yet what has really happened to cause me to have been gone for so long. You take the word of someone who is a total stranger to you and just assume I will leave you, and so you treat me like a dick for it. Fuck you, man. The only problem we have right now is this—you and your assumptions. When there is time, you and I will go away to have a long talk alone. But here? Now? This is not the time or place for this. So either act like everything is normal until we can really talk, or go the fuck away."

Without another word, he flew away into the dark night. Whatever. I almost didn't even care. It was just one less thing that had to be dealt with *immediately*.

I turned to Silent Wolf, who still wore the leather across his eyes. My brother seemed even bigger than I remem-bered him. I wondered what he'd been doing to add even more bulk to his already muscular form. "I assume I am to meet with the elders first thing in the morning?"

"We will be waiting for you by eight."

"Good," I muttered. "That gives me almost nine hours to start to set things straight around here."

"Do you need to hunt, Mama?" Aleks asked me hopefully.

"No, baby, I'm good for now. I'm going to try to hold off for another day."

"Another day?" White Buffalo wondered. "How long has it been since you've hunted?"

I pondered that for almost a whole second before I realized just how long it had really been. "When Long Falcon and I went to Denver," I announced to the shock of all.

"That cannot be," Aleks said with certainty as he shook his head. "That was almost two months ago. You must have had blood since then. You'd be insane with bloodlust by now." He stopped and observed me more closely. He took a few steps toward me and ran his finger down my temple and across my jaw to the tip of my chin. "You are different, and yet still the same. You *are* still vampire, but...What is it about you now, Mama?"

"I have had blood, I just have not hunted for it. I'm guessing that the immortal blood I drank has been sustaining me for much longer than normal human blood does." I shrugged and tried to avoid eye contact with any of the blood drinkers. They all knew what an intimate experience it is to drink blood from another. That I'd done that with the angel? Well, that was almost tantamount to cheating on my husband. It was a good thing they didn't know just how intimate it really was to join our wings as we had.

"You fed from him?" Jumping Wolf asked in a flat tone. His lips were pressed into a tight line and his eyes were narrowed. I watched his nostrils flare a few times before he unclenched his jaw just enough to speak. "You held another man in your arms and fed from him? Did you not think that that would hurt our father?"

"Child, do I not feed from mortal men? Is that any less intimate?"

"Considerably less," Black Horse cut in. He was fuming with just as much anger as his brother. "Those are evil strangers. This is a man who is trying to take you away from us. Not someone you're trying to or going to kill, but someone even more immortal than we are who wants you for himself. How could you do that?" By the end of his little rant, I could see the pain showing through the cracks of his indignation. I saw in my son that he felt that I had betrayed not only his father, but him and his siblings, too.

"I had no choice. You hybrids are so lucky that your need for blood is not as great as ours is," I said while I gestured to the two remaining vampires. "But I spent a whole week in the Void just to travel to our secret place—" I wanted to curse myself for saying *our*, but tried to just brush past it rather than cringe once I'd said it. "—and I was in desperate need by the time we arrived. I had no other choice. There was no other blood around and I could not wait any longer."

"The Void?" several of them asked at once while my boys grinned at each other.

"I'll explain in a bit," I told them with a quick glance.

"So you attacked him?" Jumping Wolf asked hopefully.

"No, he offered. He knew how badly I needed it."

They didn't like that version, but at least they weren't as mad at me as they had been. Of course, I was also suspicious that their father was getting them riled up over it from wherever he was.

"Anything else you all want to yell at me about that just can't wait? Anything imminently important that must be addressed tonight?" I scanned everyone's faces while I waited for an answer. They appeared everything from sullen to guilty to suspicious to madly curious, but they all shook their heads. "Good."

CHAPTER 41

I clasped my hands before me and turned to face the back of my house. '*Walter,*' I pushed into his mind. '*Why haven't you come outside to meet me yet? You might as well since you've already invaded my home.*'

I could feel his fear swirling with his resolve, each one weakening the other.

"Should I—d—d—do you want me t—to come outside? Or—or to leave?" he stammered from where he stood on the second floor, watching us from a window.

I sighed. "Outside, Walter," I nearly growled, beckoning him with my fingertips. I watched him swallow hard before he turned away from the window. I could hear his shuffling steps progressing unsteadily across the floor and down the stairs.

"Be nice," Brian warned as he stared hard and waggled his finger near my direction, but he was off by a bit.

I almost laughed out loud when I realized that even this close he was unable to sense where I was standing. The leather seemed to be great for everything else—his third eye was perfectly functional in allowing him to see even inanimate objects. But he still could not see me. I did at least crack a smile. I just couldn't help it.

Walter Sarkovski walked hesitantly through the open

sliding glass door and peered over at me beseechingly. I'd considered meeting him halfway and walking across the yard as well, but I quickly decided against it. After all, we were not equals in any way, so why should I make a gesture of equality? Better to let him come to me.

While he took tentative steps across the yard, I dug through his mind for all of the answers I wanted. When he stopped a dozen feet away from me, I stared directly into his eyes for the first time.

"Whether you are close or far, I can get you before you'd even have time to realize it," I told him casually. I sighed after his heart began to race and my brother glared toward me again. "Not that I plan to. I'm just saying—you don't have to stay so far away from me. You wanted a good look at me? Now is your chance. Don't let your fear stop you."

He gave me a weak, forced smile before he took some halting steps toward me. "Your wings are different from the other women," he observed. "When I first saw the others, I'd assumed that you had made your wings seem so sparkling and luminescent just for appearances in the dreams. But, you are exactly like you were before. Actually, I guess if anything, you are even more beautiful in real life. Why *are* your wings different?" he asked with burning curiosity.

I took a deep breath before I stared into his eyes and told everyone the truth. "Many centuries ago, when our prophesies were written, my soul had been born into this tribe. At that time, the souls of our elders were also incarnated here. We had all agreed to return to this place and assist our descendants so that our tribe would survive.

"In that time, when I was here before, I discovered my true nature after I'd conceived a daughter. It was the latent genes in her that have been passed down through the years to other women in the tribe. Everyone who has grown wings is my great-granddaughter, to some degree. Including myself, actually. I am my own granddaughter." I laughed out loud when I realized how preposterous that sounded. "So, all of our angels, except for me, have wings only because of the magic our tribe contains. I am the only true angel among us. Only I have a soul which has and will always exist. Because my soul is that of a true and genuine angel, I can now remember everything I've ever known in all of the billions of years that my soul has existed."

He gasped. "So you know the answers of Heaven?"

"I do. But that does not mean I have any intention of telling anyone things that they ought not to know."

"Can I ask questions anyway?"

I snorted a laugh. "You can ask, but that doesn't mean I'll answer."

"How many angels are in Heaven?"

"That I can sort of tell you. It says in the Bible that there are myriads of myriads of angels. A myriad is ten thousand. Just doing the math yourself, that works out to be over four hundred million if you count the plurals as only two myriads multiplied by two myriads."

"There are four hundred million angels in Heaven?" he whispered, staring at me with wide eyes.

"No, there are more. But I will not give an exact number because no one else ever has. Our exact numbers are a secret."

"So you cannot tell me how many fell?"

"A third, and that's all I'll say. Most of us chose to stay with The Creator."

"But if you've not fallen, then how can you be here?"

"Fallen doesn't quite mean what you think it does," I said with a touch of frustration. "Those of us who refused to join with The Opposer are not bound to the spirit state. There always have been and always will be angels incarnated on Earth at any given time. But we who have sided

with The Light are not here to do bad things. We are usually born so that we may help others. But sometimes we do
choose to be born merely for the enjoyment of being incarnated. I have actually lived thousands of lives."

I scowled as I stared off into the sky for a moment.
"Those who chose darkness, defiance, and evil were cast
out. They also can and do reincarnate whenever they want
to. They come into human form so that they can wreak
havoc on the world. One benefit those like me have over
those who were cast out is that they cannot take a physical
immortal form. If they are on Earth, they are in human
bodies with human limitations. For them to use their angelic powers, they must be in spirit form. But in that form,
they have limited influence. They cannot control mortals,
but they can whisper and guide them. Those like me,
however, can choose to take a physical immortal form. In
that form, or in the form I'm in now, which is different
from all the rest, we can use our angelic, God-given
powers."

"So," Walter drawled, then hesitated.

I knew what he wanted to ask me, but I wanted him to
say the words himself so that the others wouldn't feel as
left out of the conversation. I raised my eyebrows in
question and gestured for him to continue.

"So, you know God?"

I allowed myself to laugh. "Yes, but, really, that is a
terrible word. It is a misnomer because it denotes gender.
The Creator is not man or woman, nor plant or animal, nor
water or stone. The Creator is The All. I may use the word
God sometimes because that is the common word in this
language, but that is the only reason. Calling it The Creator, or Deity, The All, The Everything, The Infi-
nite…Those are all better choices, but still do not even
begin to give an accurate title to The One responsible for
every single thing in existence."

My children were fascinated and my brother was staring up at the sky, absentmindedly scratching the knot of the leather on the back of his head. Walter seemed like he might faint.

"I feel like I've always been a faithful man," he began after a moment of thought. "But am I offending God by using that term? Am I going to Hell for my own limitations?" He lost the remaining color in his face while he further considered the implications of his questions.

"No," I said gently. "You are not an evil man and The Creator doesn't punish mortals simply because they are ignorant."

"Thank God," he breathed before he flinched. "I mean, thank The Creator," he quickly corrected himself.

I couldn't help but laugh at him again. "Old habits are hard to break. But don't worry. It really isn't a big deal—it's more of a personal preference for me."

"You know others of your kind?"

"I know all of my kind."

"Are they coming to help you? There is so much I've found out." He stared off into the distance for a moment before he took a few quick steps toward me and fell to his knees. "Oh, Hope," he sobbed. "There is so much I need to tell you of what is being proposed against your people. I have to help you. I must stop the destruction that is being planned."

"I know all about it, child," I soothed, laying my hand on top of his bowed head while he sobbed. "There is another who would return to help me, but I doubt that I'll need it or accept it."

He gazed up at me quizzically. "Why would you not accept help?"

I looked away from everyone's curious eyes. "It's complicated," I muttered. "Besides, we don't need his help," I said with a touch of attitude that was entirely for

Dmitrius's benefit since I knew he was still watching me. "We have plenty of warriors right here in the tribe and, now that I have access to all of my powers again, we'll be fine."

"You don't know what they have. Or what they have planned," he pleaded as he looked up at me in supplication.

"Yes, I do. I know everything."

He shook his head and wore a vehement expression. "You can't," he said with certainty.

I turned west toward my valley. "You know I've access to your mind," I reminded him. "I also have access to…well, pretty much everything that any other angel has ever known. It's complicated and hard to explain, but it is what it is. It will be very difficult to leave me stumped ever again now that I have my abilities back."

"You keep saying that. Didn't you have all these powers before?"

"Only some. That's why I had to go away for a while—so that I could relearn to use all of my latent skills. Now, I am the most powerful creature you've ever met."

"I—I—I—" he stammered before he sat back on his heels and wiped his face with both hands. "I think I need to go lie down."

I turned away from him. "You do that," I muttered.

I waited for him to close the door behind himself before I began to speak again. "Don't think I've forgotten," I murmured in answer to the thoughts of my curious family. "The Void is a place of nothing. It is the nowhere that is layered over everywhere. Modern science calls it the fifth dimension. My kind, as well as those purely in spirit form, can enter and exit the Void as a means of travel or escape. It is not easy to traverse and since time does not exist there, it is very easy to lose large amounts of time while passing through it. We lost a whole week there simply because I glanced around for what seemed like just the blink of an eye. But for one who is skilled at it…well, he passed in and out of the Void without me several times over the course of less than a day."

"You wear a new knife," Will observed from where he stood behind Brian.

I gingerly fingered the handle. "Yes," I mused. "It is called an Immutable Blade. It is *only* for use by angels. No others may touch it unless it also touches me. Meaning, if I hug you and it is sheathed but presses against you, all will be well. But if it is taken from me, or someone else picks it up while I'm not wearing it…" I trailed off with a shudder.

"Bad things happen?" Will guessed.

"Very bad things," I agreed with a solemn nod. I dithered for a brief moment before I unsheathed my newest weapon. I crouched down and lightly ran the blade through a stray patch of grass. The knife cut through the bright green blades of grass with immense ease, yet the blades seemed to almost explode apart. Starting at the cuts and spreading in both directions, the lively green turned a sickly brown as the grass dried up and died. Everyone gasped and most took a step back out of fear of my demonstration.

"It is a blade forged by…I suppose the common nomenclature would be demon, but just as God is not what you think of 'Him' as being, and angels are not quite what you've always thought they are…Fuck it. It's just the limitations of this language. Demons forged these blades after their Fall from Heaven. The Creator had made the first Immutable Blade, which was used by Michael during the Battle. Afterward, the Opposer took advantage of the Void, since no one had really known how to make use of it before, and stole the Immutable Blade. His cohorts were able to reproduce the work, but each Blade took a full year to forge, even with tens of thousands of demons working on each one. They actually made 10,000 Blades before anyone in Heaven realized what they were doing. We've since managed to reclaim the vast majority of them. Only a handful are still unaccounted for—several hundred, maybe. Though, in order for a demon to use one on an angel, the angel would have to make the trip into Hell where they are still hidden."

"So there is no worry of a demon exiting the Void and cutting you up with an indestructible blade?" Brian asked.

"Immutable. And no, there is no worry of that. It cannot happen."

CHAPTER 42

It was only a few hours until sunrise by the time everyone had reluctantly gone to bed, and I was alone with my vampire children.

"Mama?" Aleks asked uncertainly.

"Yes, baby?" Again, I knew what he wanted to ask me, but I needed those few seconds it would take him to ask me in order to formulate my answer.

"Can you still see the future?"

I stared into his eyes while I waited to see if he'd ask what he really wanted to. When I was sure he wasn't going to ask yet, I allowed myself to answer him. "I can only see what will happen while on this path. If anyone involved changes their mind about something, then that changes the future. And if someone whose decision will affect an outcome cannot make up their mind, then I cannot see a clear end to that situation."

His eyebrows furrowed in thought while he processed that for a moment.

"So, you don't know yet if you will leave us?" Sandra asked for him.

"I only know my own heart. I cannot speak for your father nor can I speak for my—for the other one." I silently cursed myself for almost calling Dmitrius my soulmate in front of my children. The horrible thought of leaving them after they'd missed me so terribly for five hundred years and only had me back for one year was enough to make me want to curl into a ball and sob in misery.

"I remember when you were born," I blurted out before they could question me again. "It was the early morning, just before sunrise. I'd thought I was going to die. Aleksandra, you came out first, though you were backward. I bled so much, the midwife told Deema over my screams and tears that she was sure I wouldn't live. But I did." I smiled at them tenderly before I glanced to the west again.

"It took weeks longer than normal for me to heal, but I eventually did. After your first few hours of life, he told me that he wanted to find a nurse for you so that I wouldn't lose any more strength by feeding you both, but I refused. I told him I'd kill any other woman who tried to feed my children. I was so weak and pale from losing so much blood, but the vehemence with which I'd said that to him was enough to make him believe me."

Without another word, I turned from them and began to walk away. Out of habit, I glanced through my garden at all of the unappetizing food that grew there. I was just beginning to feel the hints of the thirst, but I knew I could easily last at least another day before I fed.

"I'll be back after the meeting with the elders later," I told them before I took off into the sky. I'd hoped that my tone and sudden departure would be enough to stop them from following me without my having to say it directly and hurt their feelings.

It was. I made it all the way to the valley by the time they went inside the house to find something to occupy their time.

I found Deema exactly where I knew he'd be—standing on an outcropping of rocks halfway up the mountain that marked the northern end of the valley.

Without saying a word to him, I tackled him and wrapped my arms and legs around him while we tumbled down the mountainside. My face crushed to his and I kissed him for all I was worth, desperately clinging to him. I was drowning and he was a life raft.

He used his ability to fly to stop our violent descent while he tried to pull his face from mine. My lips moved down his jaw and then to his neck when he pulled away even farther. His scent filled my nostrils and I shuddered with desire and desperation.

"Stop," he whispered while we hovered beside the mountain. "We need to talk first."

"No," I nearly sobbed. "Please," I begged as he continued to pull away from me. "I've missed you so much. I need you. I love you." He was still trying to pry my fingers from his clothes when I looked him straight in the eyes and choked out, "Don't you still want me? Don't you still love me?"

His eyes filled with pain and desire. He instantly gave up on trying to get me off of him and gave in to his mutual desire. We were a tangle of lips, teeth, flesh, and limbs during the flight down to the valley floor. We made a rough landing.

"My wife," he murmured against my mouth. He gripped my hair at the back of my head with one hand and held me tightly around my waist with the other arm.

"Dmitri," I whispered back, my voice throaty with desire.

"Please," he nearly sobbed, holding me even tighter.

"Hush now, my love, my husband, my vampire," I soothed, kissing his face. "Make love to me, please," I practically begged before I ripped his shirt off.

"We need to talk," he said while he held me so close that I could not remove his pants or mine.

I reached behind myself to unhook my corset. "No.

Later," I muttered. I threw my shirt out of reach. "Please, I need you, Deema. I need to know you still love me. I need you to show me." I pressed my bare flesh against his and clutched at his back.

"And the other one?" He bit his lip and averted his gaze, bracing himself for my response.

"There is no other here. Right now, it is only you and me. Please don't ruin this with talk of—Please!" Sobs wracked my body and I clung to him for dear life. "Don't you love me?" I asked him again. "Don't you want me anymore?"

Violent sobs shook his body. "You still smell of him. You still taste of him. How can you deny there is another?"

"Please," I begged him, but he tried to push me away. "I love you."

"Then say the magic words. Say that you choose me in your little secret language."

I hadn't expected that. I hadn't considered that he would know that I had to say the words. Damn. Dmitrius must have told him by being in his mind back at the Hall. I stared at him in open shock, watching the sadness grow in his eyes. He'd hoped that I would just blurt it out, but I didn't.

"What?" I managed to whisper.

"Didn't think I'd know? Yeah. He told me when he had me frozen. He told me a lot of things that day. It's why I didn't want you to go with him. I knew you were lost to me the moment you said you were leaving." He pulled away from me suddenly and flew to the other side of the valley, leaving fifty yards between us.

I stared down at my numb, empty arms before I peered up and met his gaze. "Deema," I whispered as I reached toward him. "I love you. Don't you love me?" I began to shuffle toward him.

"Does it matter? You won't choose me," he said in a sullen tone.

Anger suddenly coursed through me and I stopped in my tracks. "Would you?" I asked him, genuinely curious. "If it were you who had to choose, Deema, my love, if I were the one being the way you are, and if you were the one begging me—"

He turned his back on me and hung his head. "You can't ask me that."

"It is the same as before," I murmured. I began to walk toward him again. I sent him mental flashes of our daughters' faces and the faces of their mates. "Turn the tables and see if you feel the same. I am here begging you, and you are being so cold to me. He sees me as his equal, but how do you see me? Can't you see how your behavior would hurt me? How can you ask me to say the words that make the choice if you're not even willing to show me that you love me?" I choked on the last two words when I could no longer hold back my sobs. "Do you?" I whispered as I finished closing the distance between us and laid my right hand on his shoulder.

He was still and silent. He just kept staring at the ground.

I stepped closer and ran my hand down his arm. "Deema," I whispered. I held his hand in mine, and I pressed myself against his back. I felt him shudder slightly when he exhaled. "My husband," I murmured, running my left hand down his left arm.

He snatched up my hand and held it tightly in his as he pulled my arms around him.

"My lover," I whispered. I stood on my toes and pressed more firmly against him. "Father to my children," I said between the kisses I peppered onto his neck.

That was it—the breaking point for him. Finally! He turned on me suddenly and attacked me with a ferocity of passion that rivaled my own. "My wife, my lover, my angel," he said against my skin, crushing my body against his own. "Mine," he whispered with such intensity and possessiveness that I thought he might never let go of me again. And right at the moment, I wouldn't have had it any other way.

My lips found his and I was in a whole new kind of heaven. I ran my tongue along his sharp teeth and drew a drop of blood. When our tongues met, he moaned, gripping me tighter and kissing me deeper.

When I jumped up to wrap my legs around his waist, it broke our kiss. But that was fine. He was suddenly more interested in re-exploring me. His hands roved over my body while his kisses trailed down my neck.

Much to my surprise, Deema latched onto my throat and began to take deep draws of my blood. I moaned in ecstasy when he guided my mouth to his neck and my teeth pierced his flesh. I greedily drank his blood. I couldn't believe I'd forgotten how amazing it tasted to drink the living vampire blood. So delicious, so intense, so effervescent.

I moaned in ecstasy and misery when his emotions poured into me through our blood connection. Actually, we were both moaning like we were already making love, even though we still wore our pants.

With bloody lips, he let out a deafening roar when he ripped off my shorts and threw me to the ground. He dove between my legs and began to feed from my femoral artery. He reached up to my face with one hand so that I could still feed from his wrist and he wouldn't weaken me by taking too much without giving it back.

I gazed down to meet my husband's eyes in our moment of passion, but saw other eyes, too. Dmitrius stood beneath the tree from which I'd cut my first bokken. He watched us with the most miserable expression I'd ever seen him wear. '*How could you? How can you share my blood with that monster? That was my gift to you,*' he wept inside of my mind while silent tears poured down his face.

Deema saw, too. He saw the shock in my eyes and felt my whole body stiffen just before I met his gaze. Then he saw Dmitrius's reflection in my eyes. My husband tore his wrist from my mouth as he spun away from me and turned on the angel.

I curled into a ball and wrapped my wings around myself, sobbing in my tearless vampire way. "Please," I begged, not knowing how else to articulate all I wanted to say in that instant. I didn't want them to fight—I knew who'd win. But I didn't want either of them to win. I didn't want either of them to be hurt. I wanted Dmitrius to leave me to have alone time with my husband, but I didn't want him to be angry with me for it. I wanted Deema to return to me, not to stalk toward my soulmate as a predator does its prey. "Please," I begged again, peeking out from behind my wings to see if either was paying any attention to me.

Then I saw Deema stoop down next to the remnants of my shorts. When he began to reach for them, I realized that my sword and the Immutable Blade were right there, too. "No!" I screamed as I bolted toward him. "No!" I touched him just in time—only a fraction of a second later, he touched the handle of the Blade. He gripped it firmly, tugged it from the sheath, and began to stand up again. I'd tried to tackle him, but his rage seemed to be making him stronger. I wound up on his back and he continued to go for Dmitrius.

"You have to let it go!" I screeched while I struggled to reach for the handle of the Blade. "You don't know what it can do! You have to let it go!"

"I know enough," he growled, trying to throw me off.

"But it can kill you, you fucking moron! Dammit, listen to me! You cannot use that knife!" I was beating on his head and shoulders, but he held the Blade out in front of him.

"I don't believe you. You just don't want me to kill him."

"You cannot kill him. The Blade will only scar him. But it will kill you if you use it! Let it go!"

Deema turned his head to glare at me over his shoulder before he growled, "Liar. You never would have chosen me. See how you defend him?"

"I'm defending you! If I wanted you gone, if I wanted you dead, don't you think I'd let you fight him? He is truly immortal. You are not. Your body simply doesn't age and is difficult—*not impossible*—to injure. That doesn't mean you can't ever die. Will you fucking listen to me? Deema, drop the damned knife!"

We were still outside of striking distance of Dmitrius, who'd stood stock-still the whole time, just watching us while he continued to cry silently. '*I see how it is,*' he thought toward me. He held his arms wide in an open invitation to be stabbed.

"No!" I screamed again as Deema finally shook me off when he whipped the Blade back to throw it. The instant he was no longer touching it, I skimmed the Void just enough to beat the Blade to Dmitrius. I stood between them both and much to their mutual shock, the Blade struck me instead. I looked up and had to cross my eyes in order to see the Immutable Blade jutting from my forehead. It was buried up to the hilt. I could feel the curved tip of the Blade scraping against the inside of the back of my skull. I fell backward and Dmitrius caught me a split second before he took us into the Void.

CHAPTER 43

We instantly appeared in my bedroom, where he frantically dressed me and called for my vampire children. "Sashas! Help! Sashas!" he shouted hysterically.

Everyone in the house began running upstairs, but the vampires made it first. "No!" he bellowed when everyone tried to pour into the room. "Only the twins! Only they can help her right now! The rest of you—get out!" He was clearly enraged and no one was brave enough to demand otherwise.

"Please, what happened?" came the calls of several of my children from the hallway once he'd closed the door in their faces.

"Your *father*," he sneered, "threw the Immutable Blade that is now lodged in her forehead! Now shut up!" His roar shook the house and they all fell silent.

I was lying on the floor, staring at the ceiling. I could not close my eyes, nor could I take a breath. I could feel my wings sprawled out beneath me at awkward angles, but I could not get them to move. I wasn't sure if I was actually paralyzed or just in some kind of severe shock. I could almost feel my body, but it was all sort of numb. I soon realized that I couldn't even move my eyes.

"You'll be okay, I promise," Dmitrius soothed, brushing my hair away from the wound.

I could feel the blood pouring down my face, soaking my hair and the carpet beneath me. My precious, life-giving blood, just draining away like it didn't want to be inside of me anymore. Fitting, I supposed. Even my own husband didn't want to be inside of me anymore. Why should his blood want to be inside of me?

"Don't think like that," my angel said quickly while a bit more panic entered his eyes. He was worried that I would give up, that I would allow myself to die before I'd even saved my tribe.

"I have to remove the Blade. I need you to hold her down. It will not be easy," he told them while he crouched at the top of my head. He put his knees on my shoulders and held my skull tightly between his thighs while the twins rushed to secure my torso and legs.

When he began to pull the Blade from my brain, I started to feel everything again. Searing, burning pain ripped through me. I couldn't help but scream and thrash. It only took him a second, but that second might as well have been an eternity. When the Blade was free from my skull, he released me. The twins could no longer hold me on their own and I leapt to my feet, roaring in pain and savage need.

I turned on Dmitrius and sprang at him. He did nothing to try to stop me. He actually even turned his head a bit to give me better access to his neck. I ripped open his flesh and a hot jet of his blood shot into my mouth. I snarled like a feral beast and gnawed unnecessarily on his shredded, ragged throat, taking deep, hard draws of his blood. He fell to his knees after a moment and I went with him, unable to make myself stop drinking his blood while I crushed and broke his body.

'*But you must stop,*' he whispered into my mind. '*You*

*must feed from your children if you truly wish to remain a
vampire.'*

Of course. That's why I was a little different after
feeding from him before. I could drain him, take all of him
into me, and then I could shed this body. Or I could leave
him be for now and keep being a vampire and loving my
children. The thought of losing my love for them decided
it for me. I dropped Dmitrius to the floor before I stood and
faced my vampire children.

"I can finish him off and be reborn as what he is, or I
can feed from you both and remain a vampire. If I become
like him…" I trailed off, knowing they'd understand the
implications. They nodded and stepped toward me.

"We remember," Sandra said.

Aleks stood in front of me with open arms. "Please,
drink if you want to," he offered.

"My sweet boy," I whispered before I embraced him
and pierced his flesh. I only took a few draws before I let
him go and turned to his sister. She also allowed me to
drink from her and I knew I'd still get to love them. At
least, for a while longer.

"The others, too," Dmitrius panted from where he lay
crumpled on the floor.

Deema suddenly burst through the window, scattering
broken glass all over the room.

"*Get out!*" I screamed at him in Russian.

He glanced around and saw Dmitrius lying on the
ground, broken and bleeding. For a brief flash, he seemed
satisfied. Then he was terrified when he realized that I'd
done that to the one who'd saved me. What would I do to
the one who'd harmed me? He was back out the window
and flying away before I finished my lunge toward him.

The sparkling shards were still falling to the carpet
when I leaned out the window to go after him. I was
stopped short by the sunrise. I'd sat and watched many

dawns since I'd become a vampire, but this one was like no other before it. An artist would've wept to see something so beautiful, so perfect. I nearly wept myself. I lost any interest in chasing him—my rage had all drained out of me. I turned away from the rising sun, but something felt off so I turned back. When I studied my hands, I realized that my skin was not changing in the light like it always had.

"The others," Dmitrius whispered again. "You must feed from them all—hurry!"

I panicked, bolted for the door, and yanked it inward. "Come in, now, all of you," I insisted as I stepped back. "I drank too much of his blood," I said in a trembling voice, pointing at Dmitrius's prone and bloody form. "I'm changing and I can't change. I want to stay as I am until I can truly make a choice. Please, my children. Please!" I sobbed. I fell to my knees and covered my face with my hands. In shock, I pulled my hands away immediately and stared at them for half a second. "Tears!" I gasped. "I'm crying tears! Please help me!" I begged when they crowded around me in confusion. Yes, there were tears on my hands, but they were tinged with blood, just like they'd been the only time I'd ever before cried as a vampire.

"She needs to drink a few swallows of blood from each of her children in order to stay emotionally connected to them," Dmitrius informed them from where he still lay on the floor. His voice seemed stronger and it sounded like he was starting to sit up.

"You will drink my blood," White Buffalo commanded. She stepped forward and kneeled before me. She brushed back her hair, baring her throat to me. "I will not lose you," she said with fierce emotion as she gripped my shoulders and pulled me closer to her.

As gently as I could, I bit her neck and allowed her bitter, innocent blood to flow into my mouth. She made a small noise of pain and I let her know I was sorry by smoothing her hair.

"It's okay, Mama," she murmured. I swallowed another mouthful.

When I released her, I licked her neck a few times, willing the wound to heal and no longer bleed. It wasn't anything I'd ever had to do before, but regaining my knowledge had clued me in to the fact that I could do it.

One by one, my children allowed me to feed from them. The outsiders—the men my daughters had chosen—bristled with hostility, but one glance at Dmitrius—who had risen to his feet—caused them to be still and silent.

"How do you feel, my love?" he asked me tenderly after I'd finished drinking from Silver Panther.

I shot him a dirty look. '*Must you antagonize my children so soon after you've allowed me to stay with them?*' I thought toward him in our language.

He hung his head in shame. "I—I am—" He sighed heavily and his posture slumped in defeat. "Goodbye," he choked out before he slipped into the Void.

I collapsed to the floor in misery. I silently thanked my children, but bid them to leave as I wrapped my wings around myself so that I could hide inside of them while I wept.

My poor kids. They still had no idea what was happening. They couldn't even begin to understand why this was so hard for me. To them, it was a simple notion—I must stay with them and their father so that we could protect the tribe. And I intended to do so.

But what of after? And what of until then? I was miserable, no matter which one I was with at any given moment, because I was constantly hurting them both. I sobbed all the harder. Because I loved them both, I hurt them both.

Tears still fell from my eyes and, while it felt right to finally be able to cry real tears again, I knew it should not be happening. I pulled out a downy, fluffy under-feather and used it to wipe my eyes. But it did not grow back in a matter of seconds as it always had before—it was quite suddenly there. I blinked and my feather was just…there.

As the liquid tears continued to fall, I tried to analyze the changes that had and were occurring in my body. I still felt a desire for blood. Just thinking about feeding from some evil mortal set my throat to flames. Yes, I wanted blood, but I could feel that I did not need it as desperately as I had before I'd ever consumed Dmitrius' blood.

But the sun—I threw open my wings and made my way to the shattered window. The sun was almost completely over the horizon. I examined my flesh in the pure, clean light as it flowed through the broken window. I was still extremely pale—the mark of a vampire—but my skin still wasn't becoming translucent. I watched my skin for a solid fifteen minutes for any sign of change, but there was none. It was not growing darker to indicate my transformation into an immortal angel. But it also did not become clear like it always had before.

I examined my emotions, my attachments—they all felt the same. I loved my children and would do anything for them. I bit my lip in regret when I realized that wasn't entirely true. Because they would want me to always stay with them and their father, but I no longer knew if that would be the case.

Deema had hurt me. Not just with the Immutable Blade, but with his words, his actions, and his thoughts. He'd already given up on me, and he'd never even really fought for me.

I leaned against the window frame and began to pick out shards of the remaining glass. I supposed I almost couldn't blame him for giving up so easily. Dmitrius had told him so much to cause him to lose hope. And not just within the last month, but many years before, as well…

CHAPTER 44

It was 1550 when I'd first laid eyes on my husband. I was sixteen and my father had taken me to a market in a big city for the first time. I'd had no interest in any of the boys from our village who'd courted me relentlessly, and my parents were starting to worry that I'd never marry. Other girls were already teasing me for being the old maid among us.

But in my mind, I'd always heard a name that called to me, a name that sang to my soul. My parents had been confused about how I could have known the name since there were no men or boys in our village named Dmitrius. But even when I was very young, I'd tell my mother that someday, I'd marry Dmitrius.

Then when I heard another person shout "Dmitri!" aloud for the first time, I turned around and saw who I thought must be my Dmitrius right there in the market. I immediately tugged on my father's sleeve. He was in the midst of negotiating a trade, and I knew better than to interrupt, but I could not stop myself.

"Papa," I'd whispered. "That man—that man with the obsidian eyes. Th—That man," I stammered, my eyes following his every step.

"This will have to wait," my father said in a rush to the

tradesman before he pulled me away. "You there," he called out as we made our way toward him. "What is your name, son?"

"I am Dmitri Ivanov," he replied cordially, though obviously surprised. When his eyes fell on me, I knew he saw my beauty even though I mostly hid my face with my scarf. I'd known I was likely beet-red in embarrassment. It wasn't proper for a lady to point out the man she wanted. That was what men got to do in those days.

"This is my daughter, Anastasia Marie. I wish to strike a deal with you," my father had said casually.

"I would give you anything you want for her," he muttered as he stared deep into my eyes. "I can and will give your daughter a fine life. I promise," he said a bit more steadily. "If she is agreeable, that is," he quickly amended.

My father snorted a laugh. "Agreeable, she is not always. But she has a good heart underneath."

They worked out a deal for my bride price and a date was set for mid-spring, just one month away. After my father had agreed to everything, he told me to remove my scarf. I did and then I shyly exchanged pleasantries with Dmitri. His name ran shivers down my spine, so did his eyes and his smile. When he kissed my hand, it felt like he'd shocked me.

The next month was a blur to me. My sisters came home with their husbands and children to help prepare for my wedding a few days after my parents had sent out announcements.

Our wedding came and it was joyful, though I spent much of it embarrassed by the thought that everyone knew I'd lose my virginity that night. Our wedding night was not as exciting as my sisters had made it out to be. Mostly, it hurt. I was scared, but he was gentle and eventually he just left me alone when I asked him to.

Before the end of our first month, I'd turned a complete one-eighty and had developed quite a passion for him. I'd gotten over my shyness and my fear. I'd realized that this man would be with me until we were old and gray, so I might as well enjoy myself.

I remember the first kind thing I ever said to him. I woke up beside him on our third day of marriage and I saw the way the sunlight played on his dark hair. "Your hair is wonderful," I told him softly after he woke and met my eyes. "I hope you let it grow long like mine," I whispered as I ran my fingertips through his shaggy mane. He actually never cut it again until after the twins were born. That was when he'd begun to sit on it and he kept it trimmed to his waist thereafter.

I wrote many letters with my sisters in the first few years and I was very surprised by what kind of tips they had for me concerning my marriage and my wifely duties. Per the advice of my oldest sister, Dmitri and I tried many different things with our mouths that never would have occurred to us to try and we spent many nights enjoying those explorations of lips and tongues. My other older sister gave me mostly cooking advice—that was very good—but only a few good sex tips.

I learned in those nights that Dmitri would do anything to please me or bring me joy. Even in the days, he showed me in other ways that he'd do anything to make me happy. He taught me to hunt with him so that I would not have to spend long days away from his presence. He let me teach him how to make bread so that we could be together while I was in the kitchen.

The first four years of our marriage, I'd only been able to get pregnant five times. Twice, I had miscarriages less than four months along. Once, I gave birth at about seven months along, but she did not live. The second to last time, I gave birth to a son and we named him Dmitri. But he died of pneumonia when he was five months old. The last time I got pregnant was with the twins at the end of our fourth year. I was twenty and I knew I had to be strong for them so that they could be strong. The fact that they lived—that they continue to live—thrilled me more than I could ever convey.

I could still remember the exact feeling when I told him no other woman would ever nurse my children. I'd never been so furious in that life before as I was to think that another woman would try to give her strength to my babies. Outrageous! Only *my* strength was good enough for my children. Only I deserved to make that bond with them and impart my essence into them.

And I was strong. I pulled through like no other woman of my time ought to have. But I knew I had to be strong for them. Just something inside of me had always whispered that to me, like I already knew on some level that I wouldn't be around them for long enough.

The night Dmitri didn't come home, I was outwardly calm for the sake of my children. But inside, I was writhing in misery. Once I'd finally sung them to sleep, I paced the floor for the rest of the night while silent tears ran down my face.

Three nights passed and no word came of him. I wasn't eating or sleeping. I could barely make myself drink water. So when I saw him standing on a tree branch outside of my window, pale like a bone, his skin almost shimmering in the moonlight, I knew he had to be an apparition.

I threw myself onto our bed, a wail of misery that formed his name escaping my lips as my tears began anew. "Dead, dead," I sobbed. "And his spirit has come to say goodbye. No!" I wailed when I felt a touch on my shoulder from which I pulled away.

I peered up to see his misery painted on that pale white face as he stood over me. "Ana," he whispered, lightly

stroking my cheek with his icy fingers. "I cannot bear to be
without you. I must take you with me." He leaned over me.
He took a deep breath through his nose, smelling my flesh,
my hair, my sweat and my tears. With a shuddering sigh,
he exhaled through his mouth and drew me closer to him.

"Deema, you are a statue," I said when I felt how solid
he was. Not only was this not an apparition, but he was as
hard as granite. His flesh was chilled like a stone, and so
was his breath. No spirit could possibly feel so solid. I
touched his cheek as he'd done to me. His skin was like a
living rock—it would yield to my touch and to his
movements, but it felt so *solid*. I knew that no mere knife
could ever pierce his flesh again.

"Oh, my love," he whispered. "I am no spirit, and I am
no statue. I am your husband and I love you. I need you to
know that and remember that while I do this. Please, forgive me, my wife," he said while he nuzzled into my neck,
burying himself in my hair as he spoke. "We will return for
them someday." That promise was the last thing he ever
said to me in that body.

When his teeth broke through my flesh, it was like hot
knives had been jammed through my throat. I tried to
scream and to struggle, but it was useless. His grip was too
tight and his thirst was too great. I could feel my veins and
arteries pinching, collapsing, as he took a few hard draws
of my blood, and I knew I was going to die. I knew I'd
never again get to hold my Sashas or sing them to sleep.
My life was over and I easily accepted that. I detached
myself from the pain, even though Dmitri was no longer
taking deep draughts of my blood.

"No," he whispered, shaking me by my shoulders. But
my spirit had already left my body. Yes, my heart still
stuttered out a hap-hazard beat, but my awareness no
longer cared about the sufferings of that physical shell. I
was in spirit now and I knew *everything*.

"Come back," he begged between licking my still-bleeding neck.

I knew he had no idea what he was doing. He'd failed to ask his creator how he'd been made and now he'd botched my attempted transformation. That was very much in character for him—to assume that he understood how something was to work after only seeing it and never having had the unseen processes explained to him. Yes, we'd lost many new crops we'd tried due to his bull-headedness.

"No," he sobbed when my heartbeat faltered and then stopped. "Come back," he begged, staring into my lifeless eyes. He went back to licking my neck, like that would somehow return my soul to my body, or restore my heartbeat.

But there was no going back. What was done was done. My body was out of blood and my heart would never beat again. My spirit was slowly losing its connection with my brain. Though it took the actual death of my brain before my spirit was completely severed and that took a few minutes. I knew Dmitri could hear some of my spirit's thoughts through the blood connection. He frantically scanned the room, trying to see my soul as it floated away.

"Please," he begged. He tightened his hold and crushed my lifeless body against himself, all the while continuing to lick my bloody neck. I heard bones snap and watched with a sort of detached fascination when some poked out through the skin. Skin that only moments before had been mine.

Oh, but I had to go. My soulmate would be very upset with me that I hadn't found him in this life. I saw the desolation spread in my husband when he heard and felt the implications of that parting notion—Dmitri wasn't my true love, and he knew that I'd given up on my true love, or perhaps just deluded myself into thinking that he'd been the one. But he wasn't. And now I'd be off to try and be with my true soulmate again as soon as I possibly could.

Yes. My Dmitrius had been in the village to the east of mine. I could see that now that I was part of the Everything again. But my father had taken me west and that was when I'd met my husband.

I'd halfheartedly cursed myself for settling for the name, for not finding the right soul. Dmitrius was always upset with me for centuries after I made such mistakes and wound up with another in lives where we'd chosen to find each other.

He'd only made such a "mistake" once. But since I wasn't mad at him at all and found a happy life of my own in that body, he was all the more angry with me. I hadn't understood, but then again I had. He'd thought I should be just as hurt by his being with another as he was by mine. But why should I be? It was only flesh—bodies that decayed and rotted. It was not a true betrayal of our souls.

"It's not as if we are sleeping with demons," I'd scoffed at him before. "What does it matter if that flesh touches the flesh of another? It is not truly *your* flesh, is it?"

"It is while I'm in it. It is while you're in it," he'd replied in a miserable, sullen way. I could still remember the way he'd looked at me, the misery etched into his perfect face.

'*East*,' my Deema thought as my brain finally died and my spirit finished separating from the physical body.

Oh, no. Examining it all again, I understood.

He'd begun to go by Deema immediately following my death simply because that had been my name for him in private and my last thought of him.

East. Yes, he'd gone to find my true love and to confront him. I'd seen that at the time, though only because I'd been there and watching my Dmitrius when Deema had arrived.

My spirit soared at seeing my soulmate, even if he was in the flesh and I wasn't. I knew I could not be with him in this life. He'd have to die before we'd be born again to the challenge of finding each other.

Deema appeared in a rage by tearing the door from the house and throwing it into the woods behind him. "You," he snarled, glaring at the terrified mortal form of my true love. "You think you can take her from me?" he bellowed while he raged through the house, breaking clay pots and jars that lined shelves around the room. Mixed paint along with dry pigments splashed and blew around in the wind made by the vampire.

"Her who?" Dmitrius whimpered. "I have no woman. I never found the one I wanted."

"Because I found her first!" Deema bellowed in his face. "But now she is dead and her soul doesn't want me! Her soul wants *you!*" In one fluid movement, Dmitri ripped out half of an outer wall and threw it into the forest as well.

Dmitrius cowered on the floor, clueless about what was happening to him or why. My husband just glared at him and roared again. "I will find her again someday," Deema snarled, snatching up the other up by his collar. "She will be mine again," he said with glazed eyes.

"Who?" Dmitrius whispered while he continued to panic.

Deema did not respond. He tore into the man's neck without any attempt at being gentle. Dmitrius went rigid with shock and pain for a few seconds before he remembered to forget. When he released the pain, as I had done, he was able to leave his body and join me in spirit form.

"My love," his soul whispered to mine once he was outside of his body. "My only Hope," he continued as we came together.

"No!" Deema bellowed. He crushed the body he held.

He realized he'd made a strategic mistake again. By killing my soulmate, he'd given us the freedom to be reborn as soon as possible.

'*Oh, yes,*' my Dmitrius thought with a viscous edge. '*She will be my wife again as she has been thousands of times before. Too bad for you that you will never get another chance.*'

"Bastard," Deema growled before he crushed the brain, and thus severed the connection between spirit and body.

My soulmate gathered his strength and—more quickly than I'd ever seen him do it—he manifested his immortal body. His wings unfurled and filled the cluttered room while he glared down at my husband.

"She," he rumbled, pointing to where my spirit still floated. "She is mine. You will never have her again and if you try, you had better watch for my wings. I will destroy you. Even if I must do it slowly," he'd promised.

At the time, I hadn't really cared. Still, though, I just couldn't commit to it even when I really felt nothing for him anymore. "Leave him be," I'd commanded. "Let us leave this place so we can pick a new home in which to live and to love."

We'd entered the Void, where he shed his physical form, and then we'd traveled to India to be reborn.

CHAPTER 45

I checked the clock and saw that I was late to my meeting with the elders. I threw myself out the window and took flight toward the Hall.

"Sorry," I said when I entered and took my seat. "There was some family drama I had to deal with."

"Fighting with your husband?" Brian guessed.

I snorted. "Pretty much. I'm sure it'll come up again later. Or soon." I sighed. "But it's not relevant to our discussion today, so I'd rather not talk about it."

"Why would a marital spat matter to us?" one of the younger elders-in-training muttered.

"Because he tried to kill the other real angel, who wants to help us, but instead he almost killed me. Also, I drank so much angel blood, that I'm starting to transform and my skin doesn't change in the sunlight anymore. But none of that matters today. We are here because now I have all of my powers back. Aside from seeing the future, remote viewing, and reading minds, I can do all sorts of other stuff, too. Like, I can know everything. Yes," I said, meeting the suddenly doubtful eyes of several of the elders. "I can find out anything I want to by checking my connections to every single other angel in existence. We can at any time know anything that any other angel knows—or really, anything the Creator knows, since we are all of and by the Creator. So, we will not be surprised. I will always be forewarned.

"I have recently decided, however, that I will not be disclosing everything I know. There will be times that I must act independently, and I will not have the time, or perhaps even the inclination, to come running to you to inform you of my plan of action. Sometimes, I'll just have to do it. But, I am your protector so you must trust me. For almost three thousand years I've loved this tribe and I do not plan on letting you all be exterminated."

"But how long have you existed? Three thousand years must be a very short time to a timeless creature." The chief seemed torn between being disturbed and relieved.

"I've always existed, since there was anything *to* exist. Perhaps we came to be billions of years before there was physical matter, before the Big Bang, or perhaps it was only seconds. I do not know because time is immeasurable when there is nothing against which you can judge it."

"Are there other worlds? Other places where you go to incarnate and live lives?" Tall Grass asked me with a captivated expression.

I sighed. "We are getting off topic and frankly, guys, I've got other shit I need to be doing, too. Like mending my fucking family. Can we get on with it?"

"Touchy, touchy," the sixteen-year-old smirked. "Sounds to me like there are other planets."

"So what if there are? Did you ever think that maybe they don't have souls? Or maybe it isn't as nice there? Or maybe it's just the most fun to be a human? What the fuck does it matter? Really, in the scheme of all that's happening right now, does it really fucking matter? The father of my children buried an Immutable Blade in my forehead up to the hilt less than two hours ago. But I left dealing with that to come to this damned meeting. So if this is all merely for your curiosity? Fuck it. It can wait and I'm leaving." I put my hands on the table and started to stand up.

They glanced around at each other. "Immutable?" several of them muttered.

I groaned and fell back into my chair. "It is a very rare knife that can cut through anything and anyone. It is the only weapon that can harm or scar an angel. If it is used by anyone other than an angel, it kills them. Deema got around that because I was touching him while he held it, trying to get it away from him. Then he threw it, so he was not touching it when it hit someone. But I skimmed the Void, a place of nothingness that is layered over every-thing, and I beat the Blade to Dmitrius. But I was not fast enough to catch it with my hands and did not think to catch it with my mind. Instead, I caught it with my skull and my brain." When no one laughed at my joke, I picked up a piece of paper from across the table to display my teleki-nesis and began to fold and crease it as it was suspended in the air. Within a few seconds, I'd made an origami swan, which I then made fly around the room. After a moment of that, I was bored with it and burned it up in a flash, so that even the ashes of the paper became nothing but a small puff of smoke.

"It is not only small things that I can move," I said casually when the table smoothly began to rise off the floor. But it took the elders a moment to notice it since they, too, were lifted at the same smooth rate of the table and chairs. When they gasped and murmured, I slowly set them all back on the floor. "I could no doubt move a tank with ease. So, like I've said, the invasion will be no wor-ry."

"You could still be decapitated and die," Silent Wolf said. "You need to let the angel change you to an immortal form."

"No, I don't. You see, even if this body is killed—which it won't be—" I added viciously. "—I know how to materialize my immortal physical form myself. I've seen Dmitrius do it instantaneously. I can do it, too."

"Are you certain?" Grandfather asked me.

"Yes," I said with a serious nod.

"That's all I need, then," the chief said, sitting back in his chair. "I mean, God knows I'm curious about so much, but I won't waste any more of your time today. Anyone else have anything?"

He was only answered by many reluctantly shaking heads. They also burned with curiosity and questions for me, but they understood my desire to try to fix my familial problems.

"Okay, then," the chief said as he shooed me away. "Go back to fighting with your husband."

"Gee, thanks," I muttered. I stood up and turned to leave.

"Oh, Hope?" Brian said. I turned back to him. "One more thing. We want you to accept the help of Dmitrius. We fear to take any chances or lose any more lives than we have to."

"Yes, I know," I said in a defeated tone.

"I realize this causes you problems at home, and I am sorry for that."

"No," I choked out. "It's okay. I understand." I turned for the door again and took my leave. I didn't really know where I was going, but I knew I couldn't be within those walls anymore.

CHAPTER 46

I ambled outside and stared up at the pale morning sky. With lethargic motions I launched myself into the air and languidly made my way to my valley. I didn't particularly want to go there, but I definitely didn't want to go home.

Of course, I found Deema there, sitting inside of my dust-covered tent, crying tearlessly while he smelled my old scent on my blankets. But he heard my wings and came out in a rage, thinking that it was his rival who was landing near him.

"I'll never smell like that again, you know," I said as he stopped abruptly and stared at me in open shock.

"It is both of your old scents. But now you'll forever smell of him. You'll always taste like him. You'll never be only my Hope," he whispered helplessly.

His words sounded in my head, all twisted up together. The first time we'd met in this life, he'd said something about my only Hope, just as Dmitrius had said to me when he'd died five hundred years before. Now it seemed a cruel distortion.

"I guess I never was," I heard myself saying. I didn't know why I said it. I certainly didn't want to hurt him. But I had. I saw him crumble and it was as if I could almost see his heart breaking just a little bit more. "You've carried this around for five hundred years," I whispered to him before I took a few steps closer. "I remember it all now, you know. I remember the night you killed me." I hadn't meant for it to sound harsh, but I suppose the wording did, even if my tone didn't. "I remember you showing up at his house and killing him. I remember you reading his dying mind. I remember his threats to you and your defiance of him.

"And because I remember, now I also understand. I know now why you behaved the way you did in Taniya's apartment. I understand the looks, the comments, the uncertainty. I get it all now. The victory in making me your wife, in retrieving your children, and helping them to love you again. Am I just a prize to you? A useful tool in getting the vengeance you've been after all these centuries? You must realize that I'm the only reason you still live, right? You remember he said he'd kill you? He only didn't because he knew it'd take me centuries to forgive him, and he hates being away from me even for just a few decades."

His posture fell when I accused him of thinking me to be a prize and he sobbed silently while I'd finished my little rant.

"I don't think you're a prize. Not in the sense you mean, anyway."

"Then why give up on me so easily? Why can't you even fight for me? You've been searching for me for half a millennium and now you won't even fight for me?"

"How?" he begged hopelessly. "How am I to fight for you? You won't let me fight him."

"Ahh!" I shouted in frustration and threw my hands up in the air. "He'd kill you with ease. There is no hope for you in fighting him as mortal men fight." I peered over to the tent and shredded it into a pile of tiny scraps of cloth in a matter of seconds using my telekinesis. "How would you

fight a man who can kill you with a glance? You live because I say you do." I couldn't bear it any longer and I
threw my arms around his neck. "And I'll always tell him
to leave you alone, even if you turn away from me. Even if
you give up on me. God help me, Deema, I love you," I
whispered in his ear.

I felt his iron embrace slide around my waist and a
single sob broke in his chest. He buried his face in my hair.
"But you love him, too," he whispered back.

"Yes, and I always will. I'll not lie to you—he *is* my
soulmate. But that doesn't mean I can just give you up."

He pulled back and watched my expression. "So, you
want us to share you. Oh, how sick," he groaned when he
saw my cheeks color for a second.

"No, I *do* want to choose," I objected. "I *will* choose.
But I want to make sure I'm making the right choice. It
would not be the first time that one's soulmate had
changed. It'd just be the first time for me."

He gasped. "It can change?" He pulled me back to him
and held me even tighter. "You could really choose me?"

"Could," I stressed as I tried to catch his gaze. But
when I did, he came in for a kiss that melted my insides.

"I will fight," he muttered against my mouth. "You are
mine," he panted, pulling my legs around him. "My love,
my wife, my only Hope."

I pulled away from his kiss. "You still hurt me," I reminded him. "You still lied to me, even in this lifetime."

"I will atone for it all, my sweet angel," he said against
my skin.

His lips traveled down to my breasts. I melted into his
touch and was lost to intelligible words for many hours.
He was suddenly my Deema again, doing anything he
could to please me, to bring me joy.

"*Moi Deema,*" I moaned countless times that day.

When it seemed he was finally done with his mission

for the moment, we both lay there, panting. I turned to tell him that I loved him, but my words dried up in my throat.

All I could see was his jugular vein pulsing in my face, calling my name. I was overwhelmed with my need to consume his blood again and, without warning, I mounted him and bit into his neck.

He did not resist, nor did he try to drink my blood in return. He just lay back and moaned softly while he caressed the small of my back. I was shocked at how much like Dmitrius's blood Deema's now tasted. Finally, I decided that it must have just been the recent exchange we'd had. When I'd had my fill, I sat back, but stayed on top of him. I expected him to appear paler than he usually did, but he seemed to have an almost rosy glow. Again, I made an excuse and told myself it was just the tinted sky of the setting sun reflecting off of his shiny white skin.

"Do you want to hunt with me?" he asked softly. He gazed into my eyes and slowly rubbed his hands up and down my thighs.

"I suppose you need to now," I mused, tracing the planes of his solid chest. I gave his offer a brief consideration before I replied, "I don't feel like I need to. Honestly, I kinda just want your blood. And…" I trailed off, winced, and averted my gaze.

He tensed all over. "And the other one?" he guessed. His hands became fists against my legs.

"I will not lie to you," I whispered while I continued to look away from him. "Yes, I want blood from both of you. Funny thing, that…" I trailed off for a moment as he picked me up and set me back on the ground. "I was analyzing how I felt about blood earlier, and before we made up, I still wanted human blood. But now I don't. I wonder why that is," I mused. He put his clothes back on and threw mine at me.

"Who cares?" he grumbled. "I'm going hunting. I don't

care what you do." He took off without even a glance toward me.

I sighed when I realized that I'd probably just messed up our progress. "I'm going home," I called after him while he headed south. Probably to Phoenix, I figured. I quickly put my clothes back on and flew east to my house.

CHAPTER 47

When I landed in my yard, I heard Deema and Brian inside, arguing about me and the tribe. I walked inside and immediately told them to shut up.

"First of all, you have no say in this tribe, Deema. The elders let you stay, but they can also tell you to leave. I don't even need to know what you're arguing about to know the truth in that. And keep in mind that you are arguing with an elder," I said as I gestured to my brother, who was bristling with anger. "Second of all, I thought you said you were going hunting?" I put my hands on my hips and waited for his reply.

He looked toward me, but not at me. "I don't know what you're talking about," he said in a flat tone.

As I continued to watch his eyes, I realized he was staring past me so that he wouldn't have to meet my gaze. "You told me five minutes ago that you were going hunting," I said in a huff. "So why did you beat me back here just to start arguing with him?"

My brother turned to me and took the leather off of his eyes so he could see me. He blinked at the light before he could focus, but by then I'd already read his thoughts. He'd been arguing with Deema for over an hour.

My hand flew to my heart and I stumbled backward. "What?" I gasped. I turned to Deema and he finally focused on me. His eyes shifted to my pounding heart before he met my eyes.

"I haven't seen you since you screamed at me at sunrise. I went and hunted then. When I came back, no one had seen you since you left the meeting with the elders. You went missing again." He sighed. "At least it was just for one day this time." His eyes were as red as someone who'd been crying all day, even though he could shed no tears.

I began to hesitantly walk across the room to him. "No. No, I must have been dreaming," I decided. "I dreamed of you all day—that we had made up, and..." I reached him and ran my fingers under his collar. "Perhaps now I do sleep again," I mused when I stepped closer to him. "My skin is not changing in the sunlight, but I still want blood. Maybe I'm something else—something *other*..." I peered up into his eyes and I reached around to clasp my fingers behind his neck.

His face was filled with pain and he turned his nose away from me.

"Deema?" I said in a shaky voice. "Do you not want to make up? Do you not want to fight for me? The other may have always been my soulmate, but there have been other souls who were paired but then chose another. Do you understand?"

He tensed, put his hands on my hips, and gently pushed at me. "You reek of him," he muttered. "Don't touch me right now. I'm leaving for the night."

When I did not step away from him, he simply ducked under my arms and walked away.

I turned to face my massive older brother and he gaped at me. "You are not the same," he finally managed to whisper. "I never really scrutinized you—I never really saw you since you got back. I haven't taken this leather off for weeks except to wash my face. When I'm wearing it, I can't see you at all. Well, I could when you let me while you remote viewed us. But—holy shit. You are so different," he babbled uncharacteristically. He loomed over me, his head even taller than the top joint of my wings.

"What do you mean?"

"When I see you with my real eyes, I can now sort of see you with my other sense. I mean, not as much as I should, but still… Hope, you are so different," he proclaimed.

I searched for Dmitrius in my mind and found that he was watching me from just a few blocks away. I checked on Deema and he was soaring through the air, obviously filled with anguish. I called to my angel and he appeared in the room with us.

"How dare you trick me like that?" I growled as I rushed toward him and shoved him into a wall. Luckily, he stopped himself before I sent him through it.

He seemed stunned and abashed. "I thought that I could give you what you wanted. I thought that if I could be him for you, it would be like you got to have it both ways."

"Except that I'd still be hurting him!" I bellowed in his face.

"I thought—"

"Fuck what you thought! What about what I thought? You tricked me. You made me think that things were on the mend with him. He is my husband and I have loved him in two bodies now. Sophia only needed two lives to love another—to choose another soulmate."

"But Victor needed five before he switched and then he went back to Marcello a mere thousand years later," he shot back. "And besides—they were all of our kind. He is not. You cannot choose a mortal soul as a perpetual soulmate."

He seemed almost smug when he pointed that out to me.

"And when did the rules start covering vampires?" I mused in a casual tone while I continued to glare at him.

"They do not, because you ought not to mix with them. Just look at what you've created," he hissed at me.

"Hope," my brother whispered. I could see in him that he was afraid I'd anger Dmitrius to the point of him not helping us like I'd been instructed to allow.

I glanced over my shoulder at him. "Oh, he knows," I grumbled. "And no matter what I say or do, he'll always come back for me. Won't you?" I barked, turning back to him.

He reached out to touch the side of my face. "Always, my love," he replied tenderly.

"Oh, fuck off," I snarled, swatting his hand away.

I turned and ran up the stairs to the bathroom. I quickly removed my clothes and jumped into the cold shower. By the time the water had heated up, I was mostly done bathing. I quickly rinsed off and did my best to shake the water from my wings.

When I made it back to the living room, I found Dmitrius and Brian in deep discussion. I ignored them and left through the backdoor. I focused on my husband and found him almost halfway to Phoenix.

I took to the sky and beat my wings with all the strength and speed that I could in my effort to catch up to him. I hoped and prayed the whole way that he'd talk to me—really talk to me. I was so heartbroken over it all. Even more so now that I knew our reconciliation had been false.

I caught up to him just past Winslow, right before we passed over some national forests. "Deema," I called out when I saw him, my voice filled with my love and my sorrow. "Please," I begged when I'd closed some more of the distance between us. "Please, can we land in the forest and talk? I love you," I pleaded while I flew beside him and he turned away from me. "Deema," I sobbed. "Deema, please," I begged again, throwing myself at him.

He dodged me and turned to fly away from me, but really we just started flying in giant circles since I kept following him.

"Did he tell you?" he finally asked me in a flat, emotionless voice. Without waiting for me to answer, he continued in the same breath, "I'm taking the kids and we're leaving. You can have your fucking angel. You're not worth fighting for." His voice was cold, and so were his eyes. But I knew it was a front—it had to be. He'd been so hurt by me less than an hour ago.

"They won't leave me to go with you," was all I could think to say. I was just too stunned to ask him why he wouldn't fight for my love when he already had it.

He scoffed. "They'll see reason soon enough."

Still, I could see the lie in his confidence and I could hear his racing, nervous heart that usually beat so languidly.

"Don't think it makes you 'win' to be the one to leave me. It makes you lose because you gave up."

"It makes me lose because I don't have you anymore," he whispered so softly that I almost didn't hear him over the wind.

I threw myself at him again. "Oh, Deema," I sobbed. This time, he caught me and supported my weight while we flew. "Please, please," I kept sobbing as I gripped his shirt, tearing through it in places where I wasn't careful enough. I crushed him to me, relishing the feel of his granite body against mine. I sucked in his scent and shuddered out another string of sobs. "I love you so much," I bawled into his collarbone while he squeezed me back. "Please," I begged again.

He sighed, long and heavy before he sucked in a shuddering breath of his own. "I will fight for you for however long I'm able to," he whispered into my ear. He took us down to land in the forest. I let out a sob of relief and I finished shredding his shirt to remove it.

CHAPTER 48

I t was almost two whole days before we made it back to our house. I knew whenever Dmitrius had peeked in on us and he knew I wasn't happy with him. Oh, but God help me, I did still love him. I needed him like a fish needed water. Or like a vampire needed blood.

I also wanted to pummel Dmitrius for tricking me into drinking his blood again. I truly had no desire for human blood anymore. Even though I'd gone hunting with Deema twice while we were gone, mortal blood now held the same appeal to me as did the blood of animals.

What I really wanted was Deema's blood and I feared that he knew it. Twice he'd caught me listening to his heartbeat in the same way we listened to a victim's. Finally, when we were heading home, he asked me about it.

"You did not seem to enjoy your blood tonight," he hedged. "Is it because of your…changes?"

"I think so," I said bluntly. "I'm still a vampire, but really, I only *want* immortal blood. Be it vampire or angel."

"Demon," he muttered, shaking his head. "I'm no vampire. I'm a demon. A monster," he grumbled dejectedly.

"What?" I asked as I felt my white skin pale even further. "Are you really a demon? Are you really one of the Fallen?" I felt like my chest was constricting and put a few more feet between us while we flew.

"What? No! No. I just meant that as a metaphor. No, Hope, I promise," he said quickly. He tried to get closer to me.

"But really, how do I know? Demons don't always know what they are until they die. You've not died," I pointed out.

"No," he insisted, emphatically shaking his head. "You'd know, though, wouldn't you? Don't you have access or whatever?"

"Maybe I wouldn't know."

"Would that be the key?" he wondered aloud. "Is that what would break you free of me? That I were a demon—one of the Fallen?"

"No," I realized. "There are others who would not part when one chose to Fall and one chose to stay. It is harder for them, of course, but it does happen. What's not supposed to…" I trailed off and turned away, tears welling up in my eyes.

"What?" He moved to fly beneath me like he always used to.

"I don't want to keep hurting you," I blurted out when the tears spilled over. "But everything I say or do or discover about myself seems to do so." I let out a long, shuddering sigh before I finally spit it out. "I'm not supposed to fall in love with a mortal soul."

"Oh," was all he could say.

I tried to soothe him and caressed his face. "But I did."

"How can we know that, though? How can we know that I'm not really a demon?" His heartbeat started racing again.

I thought about that for a minute, waiting to see if the answer would just come to me like so many others did now that I had back my connections to the other immortal souls. No answer came. Well, no usable answer. All we needed to do to know what kind of soul he had was wait for him to die. Damn it all.

"There is no way to know while you still live," I whispered after a moment.

Deema said nothing—he just continued to watch me. After a while, I asked him why he stared at me so intently.

"I'm trying to memorize your face. I don't ever want to not see your face again. I want to always be able to recall with perfect detail every curve, every pore, every single thing about your face and all of your expressions."

"You act like I'll die," I said before I bit my lip and looked away.

"No, I act like you may still leave me. You *are* changing, Hope. Every day, you are a little different. And now you don't want human blood? Yeah, I don't think you'll be a vampire for much longer. Especially if you drink any more of *his* blood." Deema sneered when he thought about me drinking the angel's blood.

"The last time he tricked me," I protested. "He told me how to stay a vampire by feeding from the twins, but then he tricked me into drinking his by making me think he was you," I growled as my hands became fists at my sides. "I am so furious with him right now," I fumed.

My husband began to smile. "Furious enough to…" His hand moved to my belt and brushed the handle of the Immutable Blade.

"Don't you ever touch that again!" I roared, smacking his hand away. "Don't think I'm joking or only saying that because I'm mad at you for hurting me. Don't. Ever. Touch. My. Blade. It can fucking kill you. Are we clear?"

His eyes were as round as saucers and he withdrew from my fury. "I'm sorry," he whispered. I saw in his mind that he genuinely feared me in that moment.

"Are we clear?" I screamed at him again.

"Yes, baby. We're clear. I'll never again intentionally touch your Blade. I'm sorry." His voice oozed sincerity and I saw in him the unending regret he'd always have for hurting me instead of Dmitrius.

I held my arms open. "Come here," I whispered. He flew closer to me and we embraced while we soared over the desert. "I love you," I said in his ear and he squeezed me tighter.

"When will you choose?" he wondered aloud.

"Deema," I groaned.

"Do you know? Is there a time limit or anything? I'm not asking to be cruel," he said sincerely. "But the waiting, the not knowing—it's so hard. Even if you left me, at least it'd be a final decision. At least I could learn to live with your choice." He pressed his lips together in a tight line when he realized he'd lied to me.

I delved into his mind and saw the truth. If I left him and our children chose to stay with me and/or our tribe, he was going to try to find a way to die. I simultaneously wanted to clutch him to me in fearfulness of losing my love and kick his ass for considering suicide. He saw the change in my expression and felt the tensing of my body. His face pinched with chagrin.

"Baby, please," he gasped when my grip on him tightened in anger.

"You will not," I seethed. "How dare you even consider that?" I pounded a fist against his stony chest. "You will not!" I roared in his face.

"Hope, please," he implored, holding me to him even tighter.

His thoughts took on an almost reproachful tenor. He didn't want to out-and-out blame me for his desire to die. It was merely a side effect. But how could he not feel like I was culpable? It would be the result of my choice and actions that would make him want to die in order to escape the pain.

"You will not," I said again, my pain taking over my tone. I clutched him to me with more force than was necessary and he held me just as tight. The tears began to well up in my eyes again as I buried my face in his hair. "You will not," I sobbed, beating his back with one hand and desperately clinging to him with the other.

"Hope," he murmured soothingly while he stroked my spine.

"Promise me," I blubbered. I immediately realized when the words left my mouth that he'd refuse.

He let loose a forlorn sigh. "Hope, would you really ask me to continue living in misery for all of time? If you choose the other, and my children don't even want me anymore, how could you ask me to live and suffer and continue existing in such daily torture? I never meant for you to know. I didn't intend for this to impact your opinion. I'm not trying to force you. I don't want to feel like I'm forcing you. I don't want that hanging over my head for the rest of my existence—that wondering if you'd have chosen him if it wasn't for the guilt over my desire to die. I didn't want you to know!" he rambled while he kept trying to get me to meet his eyes.

I kept my face buried in his collarbone, letting his hair soak up my bloody tears. "Please," I begged him.

"My only Hope," he murmured, kissing the top of my head. The double entendre of that hit us both at the same time and he let loose a single sob before he regained his control. "I'm sorry. You know I didn't mean it like that."

"Please," I pleaded again. And I kept right on begging him while he tried to soothe me for over twenty minutes until we landed in our backyard.

Sandra was teaching Silver Panther in the garden. Rather, she had been until they heard us approach. By the time we landed, they'd already heard us coming for almost a minute and both watched us with open shock and confusion. I could feel the eyes and hear the minds of others who were watching us from windows, but I gave them no focus, really.

Deema was my entire focal point in that moment.

Sandra stepped toward us with hesitation. "What is happening?" she asked.

I was still sobbing into Deema's chest and clutching him tightly, whispering please.

"She read my mind and was upset by what she saw," he replied simply while he continued to rub the small of my back.

Silver Panther walked over to us, too. "What did she see?"

"He's going to kill himself if I don't choose him!" I wailed as I clutched at him tighter and ripped his purloined shirt even more.

"Now, that's not entirely accurate," he disagreed, pulling away just enough to try to meet my eyes.

When I wailed and clung to him again instead, he turned to focus on our daughters. I cried out again at that thought—our first and last daughters!

"I don't even know *how* to die unless I steal her Blade that I promised never to touch again," he began. "But actually…" He trailed off and turned his stare away from them, afraid to tell them and everyone else who was listening that he'd only do it if *they* all abandoned him, too.

"I know how to die," Sandra said as if it were nothing.

"No! No!" I sobbed. "Don't tell him!"

"She would tell me if she wanted me gone, if she didn't want me around anymore, either," he said softly while he peered down at me.

"That would never happen," Sandra whispered. She appeared beside us and laid a hand on his shoulder. "Even if Mama chooses the other, we'd not leave you again. I mean, we all talked about it yesterday. We kinda figured that if she left you, she'd be leaving all of us. I mean, if she leaves the tribe, they're part of the tribe, too," she said, gesturing to Silver Panther and the house.

"Brian said they wouldn't make us leave, but that they wouldn't argue with us if we wanted to go. So Aleks and I decided that maybe we'd do like a shared custody kinda thing—half of the time with you and half here. Or whatever." She shrugged. "But your kids aren't going to leave you just because your wife does. We *do* love you, you know." She eyeballed him like he was dim-witted.

"There, do you see?" he said soothingly, trying to catch my eyes again. "It all works out then. I said I'd only do it if you *and* all of our kids left me. *They* won't leave me."

That's when I finally peeked up at him. I caught the chagrin in his face before he fixed a comforting smile in its place to try to cover up his emphasis faux pas.

"So you don't have to feel guilty. You can make an honest choice now. Well, you know—eventually. I know you won't choose now."

"I can't choose now. I can't choose until after my people are saved," I said in a small, helpless voice. "We all have to live in this agony at least until then." A few sobs escaped my mouth before I was able to continue. "It is the way it has to be for us to win, for my people to live. We can save them all only if we can save them together."

"I—I—" Deema stammered angrily before he took a deep, shuddering breath.

Right as he was about to speak again, he sharply turned and glared at the house. But I already knew that it was Dmitrius he was glaring at—I could feel that he was near.

CHAPTER 49

I have something to say, if I may," Dmitrius said softly as he stepped out the backdoor.

"No one cares," Deema snapped.

"Hope might," Dmitrius replied in a way that could only be described as sympathetic. "I no longer wish to cause her pain, so I will give no objection to sharing her until the time comes that she must make her choice."

"What?" Deema, Sandra, and Silver Panther all chorused.

"I will no longer object to her staying with you, but I hope that she will not let you guilt her out of also spending some time with me. I have given this a lot of thought," Dmitrius replied in a serious tone.

But it was not only his words spoken aloud that soothed me. Inside of my mind, Dmitrius assured me that he'd never again protest about my children. He swore to never call them abominations because now he understood how much they meant to me. After seeing them through my perspective, he could not help but to also love them. They were, after all, half me—how could he not adore them for that very reason? It wasn't so much that he expressed this in words, but more of a burst of emotion that displayed his feelings down to the bare bones of the matter. Knowing his heart like I did, I had no choice but to forgive him for his misjudgment of them.

"You're insane," Deema snapped.

"Hush, now," I murmured as I snuggled against Deema, who still held me tightly. "Hear him out. Or do you wish to keep hurting me every minute of every day, breaking my heart with every look and touch?"

"I am her husband," he hissed at Dmitrius, as if I hadn't spoken. "We have children."

"And I have been her soulmate for millions of years. We have children, too—the entire world. You see, the two of us have lived so many times, in so many places, that it would be impossible for anyone on earth to not be descended from us at some point in history. Hope even said before that she was her own granddaughter," he retorted.

I giggled softly against Deema's chest. The relief I felt at the angel's proposal made me feel practically giddy. "Hear him out, lover," I whispered.

"Every time we show her that it hurts us, it hurts her. Because she loves us both and has very valid reasons for that love, our pain distresses her. She cannot help the way she feels. If she could stop loving one of us, she would, just so she did not have to hurt anymore. But for one, she is unable to do that right now. And for two, she would not know which one of us to choose even if she could do that, hence her inability to choose between us now."

Deema just glared at him.

"She cannot help the way she feels," Dmitrius said again. "Do you think she enjoys upsetting us? Dmitri, you have seen her pain over the heartache she causes us, her agony over needing to choose. Do you really think…" He trailed off as he studied us standing there for a moment. "No, of course you do not. I know you do not think that she hurts us out of malice. But good God, man, lose some of the bullheadedness. She has already gotten sick of that."

He sighed while he listened to Deema's mind. "I do not say and do the things I do for strategic maneuvers for her heart. I do what I do to make her happy. While it is true that I may be better suited to that because I am able to be inside of her mind and feel exactly how she feels about something...Well, that is how I am also able to know how much misery she is in over this whole situation. But come on, Dmitri—we need to help her save her people. And honestly, she could still choose you. Maybe someday vampires do expire. Maybe the limit is one or ten thousand years. We do not know because we do not mix with your kind." He almost managed not to sneer. "Or maybe someday far in the future, someone else does kill you. Maybe she knows that since you are not truly immortal, you will someday be gone from her always. And when that day comes, when she is ready, she will find me and we will love each other again. I am capable of waiting for her because she and I will both always exist. Some-day—eventually—you will no longer exist. Perhaps she will choose to banish me from her sight and mind until that day comes. But until that day, until she makes her choice, we need to be able to get along and work together. We cannot be fighting with each other and fighting over her when we need to be fighting to protect the tribe."

"Daddy, he does make sense," Silver Panther said in a begrudging tone after a moment.

Deema sighed. "Yes, I suppose he does." He met my eyes. His were filled with sorrow and pain. "So we'll share you after all," he whispered almost silently.

My cheeks flared and I stared at the ground. "I cannot help that I love you both. You are both wonderful in so many ways. I love you so much, Deema." I peered up and met his accusing expression. "You know I love you," I whispered intimately while I stroked his cheek.

I ran my hand down his neck and behind his head to

thread my fingers through his hair. Once I had a handful of his silken, glossy black tresses, I gripped it tighter and pulled him toward me. I kissed my husband passionately, not even caring who was watching. He kissed me back, but broke it off after a few moments.

"But you plan to still be with him, too? And you expect me to be okay with that?" Deema asked, his voice thick.

"I will not hold the same expectations of you both, since you're both different people. He will not be hateful if I display affection for you in front of him because he truly has come to peace with my choice should I choose you. But I can make no promises of what may happen when I go away with him."

Deema's arms tightened around me, but he turned his face away from mine.

"I will never touch him or show him affection in front of you because I know it hurts you. But baby, lover, husband…I do love him. I can't help but desire to show him affection and receive it from him. I'm sorry that it causes you misery, but I can at least abstain from doing it in front of you."

Deema sighed long and deep before he released me and took a step back. I felt like I was standing on a teetering precipice, about to plunge over the edge. I feared he'd choose that moment to leave me for good this time. He was right—it was sick. But I could not help the way that I felt. I could not love either one of them any less than I did.

"We will not have sex," Dmitrius said casually. "While it is nice, it is not needed. All I desire is to be able to hold her and kiss her, to let our wings press together," he said with a shrug, as if it were nothing.

Of course, none of the others would realize that pressing our wings together could be even more intimate than mere intercourse.

Deema sighed in relief. "Then I suppose I can agree to

that. I just don't want to have to see it or hear about it. I can handle it and forgive it."

I beamed and threw my arms around his neck. "Thank you, baby."

He hesitated for just a second before his arms slid around my waist and then he lifted me a few inches off the ground so he could kiss me without stooping over.

CHAPTER 50

H ope?" my brother called as he stepped out the back door. He had the leather over his eyes again, so he was back to being blind to both me and Dmitrius. "Hey, if you're out here, we need to have a chat." He obviously saw in his mind the awkward way Deema was standing and cleared his throat uncomfortably. "Uh, sorry if I'm interrupting, but it's kind of important."

I broke away from my husband and went toward my brother. "What's up?"

"We got a telegram."

"What?" I snorted in disbelief. "Who the fuck still sends telegrams?"

"The United States government still sends people telegrams. Like the one they sent our elders saying that we have six months to surrender our sovereignty, start paying them taxes, and hand over most of our land. Like, basically all of our livable land. They're not even trying to relocate us again. They're just kicking us out in the middle of the winter."

"So this is how it starts," I muttered. "War declared with a piece of paper. How bizarre."

"War is always declared with a piece of paper," was the only reply my brother could offer.

I sighed and walked over to the back porch so I could sit in my hammock. I sighed again when I settled into the mesh so that Brian would know where I was. He took the hint and sat on the wall in front of me.

"So, what's your plan?" he finally asked.

"We wait." I shrugged but quickly realized it was a useless gesture. "There's nothing else we can do. We will refuse and eventually they will come to attack us. Then we fight for our freedom. It's not like they can actually make us leave in February. They might really have to wait until June to fully invade. So, we still have time."

"Walter says—"

"I know what Walter says," I snapped. "And I know what he thinks, and I know what he knows. I also know a whole lot more," I said more calmly. "It would seem that all will be well, now that they've agreed to work together."

"It would seem," Dmitrius echoed with a hint of warning in his glance.

Yes, I knew that things were ever-changing. How many dozens of ways had I seen just the opening of the invasion? How many times had I watched the scene change as different decisions were made and different paths were taken?

He chuckled softly. "Exactly. There could still be outside interference that will affect the choices of those soldiers."

"We will continue to be vigilant," I assured him while I wondered what he meant.

"I meant the same as you do," he replied to my thoughts.

I began to pick the dirt out from under my fingernails. "You rarely do," I muttered.

He sighed. "Hope."

I just rolled my eyes at him. "So," I drawled, turning back to my older brother. "Don't worry. We're watching out." I gestured between Dmitrius and myself. Again, I realized he couldn't see either one of us. I rolled my eyes again at my own stupidity. "We'll handle whatever comes our way."

"And what should our people do? What about the shifters and the winged women who are all outside so much?" Silent Wolf wondered.

I was struck with a terrifying tidbit of information from one of my fellow angels. They knew and they'd keep watching us with their satellites until they invaded. "Oh, fuck," I said long and slow.

"What?" my brother demanded with a bit of panic in his voice.

"They've seen them flying. And shifting. The defense people got called when Google had some weird stuff showing up on their new map photos. Weird stuff like me. This was totally separate from the whole FBI crap, though if that had continued on, the DOD would've gotten involved. But now the DOD is after our tribe and our little patch of Colorado desert. They've been watching with their own stuff now and recently—Yeah, they've seen a lot of shapeshifters and women with wings. Though I guess really it doesn't matter if they continue practicing since we've already been discovered and marked for extermination. But—" I hesitated and thought about it some more. "Okay, so what if they all mostly try to shift inside or only on very overcast days? That way they're not really seeing it happen much anymore and they may think we've given up."

"What if they can see us right now? What if they can hear us through their technology?"

I considered that for a moment and a source revealed it. "They could if the satellites were aligned properly right now, but they're not. So I will say this once and no one will ever speak of it again. Ever!" I shouted as I leaned back and turned my head toward the open door and the super-hearing of most of the household. "We have a man on the inside, another true angel who remains in a wingless body, learning and influencing what he can. So when I say in the future that we have this handled, don't question it. And don't ever mention it ever again! Not even among yourselves, not even when inside of a building! I'm so serious, everyone. This is the only time it will be said *aloud!*" I stressed.

I heard a chorus of okay's from throughout the house and yard. I glanced over at Dmitrius and he began to speak inside of my head. Our friend on the inside was Victor, who was very soon going to be forced to take five weeks off work because he'd not taken any time off in so long. It would seem that he and his wife, Marci, were going to go hiking in Tibet. I smiled to myself, but Dmitrius knew that the smile was really for him.

"Yes," I murmured while I continued grinning. "Everything will be well. I'll have to go away for a while very soon." I cocked my head a bit and listened to shared knowledge. "In a week," I finally said. "In one week, I'll have to leave for five or six. I will check in daily to make sure that I don't need to return immediately. But they gave us six months—until the beginning of February. As things stand now, they still will not show up in force until the summer. I will be back before it is really winter."

"And I cannot go with you?" Deema wondered a bit sadly.

"I'm sorry, but I must travel through the Nothingness," I said. I raised my eyebrow a bit and moved my eyes to the sky as a signal that they were watching us again. I glanced back at him and made sure he understood before I continued. "It would kill you should I take you through it. But it's okay. I just have to go see a man about a bird."

Silver Panther ran toward me. "I'll be fully grown by

then," she whispered. "I might even be flying by the time you come back," she said while she climbed into the hammock with me and snuggled up against my side.

"I bet you will be," I agreed. I put my arm around her and held her close. "And I am sorry, but I need this bird. Very rare, you know. Almost extinct in Peru. It's not like I won't be back—I will. Just stay with the others and learn what you need to learn."

She frowned up at me. "Okay." She was a bit confused by my misdirection until I briefly explained inside of her mind.

"How will you check in on us without revealing your secret?" Brian asked me casually.

"I can block you or anyone else from seeing me when I watch them," I said with raised eyebrows. "How about this? If you need me, have someone put tape over your leather. If I see you are marked, I'll head back and contact you on the way."

"That's genius," Dmitrius said.

I muttered a sigh before I stood up and turned for the house. I went inside and found Walter in the den, watching TV by himself.

"Give me your cellphone," I said abruptly, holding out my hand.

"W—why?" he stammered as he removed it from his pocket.

I just wiggled my fingers impatiently. He hesitantly handed me his phone. I checked his recent calls and saw lots of incoming calls that had been rejected. None had been answered for a long time. No outgoing calls had been placed.

"Why even keep it turned on?" I grumbled.

"Habit, I guess," he said, somewhat confused.

I opened the back and took out the battery before I removed the sim card and crumbled it to dust. "I have my photos and music backed up on my laptop," he informed me quietly. I crushed the entire phone between my hands and burned the remains to ash using my powers.

"I've had a vision," I whispered to him. "You cannot stop it. They will come for you. You must be strong. I am sorry."

CHAPTER 51

He stared at me with his mouth gaped open. "Who?"
"I don't know. They didn't seem to know you. But I will not be here. I'm taking the others with me." I peeped in on Victor. They were monitoring us live. Even inside the house, they could distinguish our whispers. I managed to restrain the shiver of horror building inside of me. "But I've seen others coming, like you'd planned to come before."

He smiled up at me. "Before you won me to your side."

I couldn't help but smile back. "Yes, but there isn't time for that this time. They'll come too soon," I replied. I laid my hand on his shoulder. "You must be strong."

"When?" His voice was even smaller than before once he finally caught on to why he would need to be strong.

"It is not yet decided." I paused and looked away from him. "They—they think that they know, but I think someone else has yet to have their say. I think they may try to wait for me to come back. Or maybe they will catch me before I leave."

I gasped when Victor finally latched on to my train of thought. Back in their offices, Victor told his bosses that he'd been right, and they'd missed something important in a window between satellites and, because of that, they should come immediately.

"But no matter what they decide, I can stay ahead of them," I gasped breathlessly.

"Do you see?" I heard Victor say, persuading them. "We must go soon. Before my forced vacation."

"Fine," his boss growled. "We'll go in five days."

I turned to Walter. "You must be strong. You cannot run from them."

"But you can?" he nearly sobbed.

I could not stop myself before I scoffed at him. "And just who the fuck are you? What are you compared to me? Do you honestly think I should just sit here idly and let some government agency snatch me up so that I can't protect my people? No," I said with a sneer. "I will not be here, no matter how many times they change their minds. They will never catch me."

"And if they move against you full force now instead of next year?"

"Then war is declared and I will stay so that I can crush them all with a glance." My voice was as cold and hard as steel.

"And if I don't wish to die under their torture?"

"Then I can kill you right now. Or right before they arrive and I depart."

"I wanted to fight with you," he muttered forlornly.

"You are fighting with me," I said, gently touching his shoulder again. "You fight with us by not revealing our numbers or any of what you've seen."

"And what if I am weak?" His voice was full of hopelessness.

"Then be weak by taking your own life in order to protect our secrets," I hissed as my hand tightened painfully on his shoulder. I could feel the bones wanting to snap so I quickly released him before they did. He fell to the floor, sobbing, and I walked out of the room without turning back.

On my way back to the yard, I informed my brother mentally that they could hear us even if we spoke in whispers inside the house. We must keep all of the important information protected that we could. Therefore, we needed to keep as much strategy as we could telepathic.

'I can't find you,' he thought back at me. *'How am I supposed to talk to you if I can't even find you? We can only do this now because you allow it.'*

I walked over to him and removed the leather from his eyes. He blinked and squinted at the sunlight, but I turned his back to it and made him face me. I held his chin and stared up into his eyes. *'It is no different than sending a beacon for when I couldn't find my way home. If you call for me, I can hear it. That does not mean you have access, it means that I have access.'*

"I'm sick of seeing that on your face. I understand why you wear it, but you will not wear it while I'm here. You cannot see me and I'm sick of my expressions being useless. Body language is most of a conversation. I'm sick of it," I snapped to cover my actions, though my words were true enough.

"Okay, Hope," he nodded when I released him. *'Most everyone either is able to or can be taught to speak with their minds. I'll work with the others all that I can.'*

I gave him a nod in return before I turned to Dmitrius. "Sit," I ordered, pointing to the ground. He flopped down between rows of green bean trellises, stretched his legs out in front of him, and reclined back on his palms. His wings were awkwardly trying to find a convenient way to lay. The angel gave me an uncomfortable smile.

"I know." I sat down across from him and mirrored his posture. "But you know I don't have weeks to waste with a knowledge exchange of wings. I just want to talk, so you keep those things away from me," I warned him.

We sat across from each other and remained silent and still for several minutes while we exchanged and discovered information at breakneck speed. Victor had kindly mapped out in his head a series of routes to thickly forested areas that would be blind spots to the satellites. I sighed internally. I could actually get the other women away so they weren't hauled off. What a relief.

The DOD cared nothing of our shifters. They had plenty of their own who were very compliant. There was no use in trying to weed out and brainwash ours. Yet Victor had been allowed in on this particular project only because it was in his file that he had experience with shapeshifters. None of us could quite figure out the reasoning behind that.

While we knew that they'd been watching and knew we had angels, we didn't know how many they'd verified the identities for. Even though there were many people working on the Desert Mine Mission, they were keeping them divided into fairly strict factions. Victor was in on some of the observation, but only because of his experience with shifters. He'd tried, but had been unable to get the group studying the angels to reveal their secrets.

It frustrated us all that different parts of the government were run more competently. The group in the FBI who'd been studying our paranormalness had had no experience with such things. These DOD guys, on the other hand, had been *tested* for their abilities. Everyone there was someone who'd ranked highly in their ability to block others from entering their minds. But Victor *should* be able to enter the minds of mere mortal souls, except that without his wings being formed, his own abilities were limited.

We all three let loose a collective sigh. Luckily, there was a brief delay so it was not noticed by the others watching the video screen.

"They're just sitting there," Victor grumbled. "They said they were going to talk and they've hardly said anything. Is this what you guys do all day? Watch these people sit there and stare at each other?"

"Sometimes," one of the other guys said with a smirk. "Sometimes they argue, sometimes they screw." He shrugged and Victor gawked at him as if he was demented.

Victor knew all of their big plans, so now that we wanted to know them, we did as well. It would be complicated to get everyone to do what we needed them to do. But we could do it. We knew we had to make it through the next year before we could leave.

If I left.

I opened my eyes and glared at Dmitrius. He seemed abashed and then he looked away. "Please," he implored, holding his hand out to me when I began to stand. "Ignore my idle thought. I didn't mean to hurt you. Please," he begged me. I hesitated. "We must finish our talk. I'm sorry I let that slip through."

"Fine," I huffed. I sat back down and stretched out my feet to his. '*Just keep the cockiness to yourself until we get to actually be alone.*'

Again, he appeared almost ashamed when he turned his face away from me and closed his eyes.

CHAPTER 52

Four nights later, just after midnight on September first, I entered the minds of all of the winged women on the reservation. Some were still awake and others I had to wake. '*It is time for you to go hide. Stay there for one week. You may return after seven days, unless one of our tribe contacts you mentally to tell you otherwise,*' I said to them all.

Over the previous nights, I'd met personally with each winged woman and had lengthy silent conversations with all of them. I gave them tips on how to fly better and make their strength last for the long journeys they'd all be embarking on soon. I also showed each woman her route and let her know where she could rest and for how long. I gave them watches with alarms on them and showed them how to use them. Of course, we didn't meet in the open. I went into each of their houses by traveling through the Void. I also never said a single word aloud to them, nor them to me. It was perfect.

Victor had tried his best to get more details, but they'd only tell him his part of things. He was supposed to try to spot signs of our men being shifters. Again, we were confused by the choices of his superiors.

Shifters looked just like normal people so there were no signs to be spotted.

I cried when I sent my daughters away. Silver Panther's shiny grey wings had grown large enough that she'd flown for the first time earlier that day. But I did at least let them all go together.

Most of the other women had left in pairs.

By the time they could spy on us again via satellite an hour later, Dmitrius and I were the only angels they'd seen since they'd decided to come to the reservation. I went out to my backyard once they could see us and met Dmitrius when he exited the Void with his back to the rising sun.

"We have one day until they arrive," he said aloud for their benefit.

"I know." I sighed. "I can feel them watching us now."

"I know." He smiled and walked toward me. "Where is your husband?"

"He left with the other vampires last night."

The angel reached out and took my hand, turning to face their vantage point with me. I squeezed his hand and we held our wings away from each other. "I won't leave your side," he whispered while he used his telekinesis to caress the opposite side of my face.

"I know." I turned and embraced him, stretching out my wings behind me so that they'd be out of range for an accidental connection to his wings. "But you know it's only because I allow you to stay."

He was a bit startled by my sudden closeness, but quickly recovered and returned my embrace. "I'm so glad you didn't send me away," he whispered in my ear.

I smiled while we held each other, our minds connected and in sync. Everything we'd said aloud for the last four days had been strategic. He smiled, too, as we thought over our plan for what would happen the following day.

"I like him, you know," Silent Wolf said softly when he

came out of the backdoor. "He doesn't anger me like the vampire."

"I know." I sighed and Dmitrius gave me a little squeeze. "But I've yet to make my choice," I said past the lump that rose in my throat. "Can we please not discuss this now?"

"Yeah, sorry," my brother whispered. He stretched out in the hammock.

"I wonder how and why they're watching us when they should be on their way to us," I mused convincingly. Of course, I already knew that they were watching us in a mobile unit on their way to us. But the fools coming to attack us had no idea that we could see them even more clearly than they could see us.

"Do you think they are using mobile equipment to watch us, and that was why there was such a long pause? It felt like we weren't being watched for several hours earlier." Dmitrius was just as good at our little ploy as I was.

"A satellite went out," my brother said from the hammock. "It's the only thing that makes sense given the pattern of when we feel watched and when we don't."

"Yes," I agreed. "Or maybe a few went out. It seems like before this morning, we haven't had more than an hour or so of not being watched."

"And maybe they didn't lose any," Dmitrius interjected. "Maybe it's just the way the orbits are."

"We'll know when they get here and we can read their minds," Brian asserted with confidence.

"Like it'll matter then," I said with a snort.

"Good point," he agreed with a grin. "But what *will* happen when they get here?" he wondered.

"That entirely depends on the choices they make," I replied before I turned my face into Dmitrius' chest.

We all fell silent then and finished our plans for the next day via our telepathy.

CHAPTER 53

When the first cargo truck filled with soldiers pulled onto the Navajo reservation, the people there tried to stop them. The man driving stopped just long enough to yell that they were passing through and didn't want any trouble with the Navajos. They were allowed to pass, along with the nineteen others that followed behind.

When the caravan of canvas-draped trucks rumbled over our borders, I would let the two columns of ten trucks each go no farther. Dmitrius and I appeared in the middle of the road and caused the engines to explode.

The driver of the vehicle closest to us jumped out with a rifle in his hands. Before he could even get it half-way aimed, I sent it into the Void. I did the same to the rest of the guns of the drivers that chose to get out with their weapons in their hands. It was far easier than I'd thought it would be. When I was partially connected to the Void like that, time seemed to slow down or even come close to standing still. Dmitrius reminded me that time didn't exist in the Void. Once I'd spotted all of the guns and sent them into the Nothingness, time snapped back to a normal speed.

It took the soldiers a minute to gather themselves before

they also started pouring out of the backs of the truck beds. Dmitrius and I worked together to cause their guns to vanish. While everyone bumbled around in confusion for the moment, I scanned the vehicles to ensure that they contained no life before I sent the empty ones into the Void as well.

Some of the soldiers from the rear of the column hadn't gotten out yet. I scanned their minds and realized that the last six vehicles in the caravan were full of the scientists. That many scientists meant a lot of experimentation on my people.

I was instantly enraged.

So was Victor. He'd thought only the one he was in had scientists in it.

Now that I was there with them all, he could enter some of their minds with me as a proxy. Their purpose there was not only to try to gather some winged women, but also to gather shifters. While they had no desire to try to tame the Hopi men, they did want to experiment on them and run tests on their DNA. There was absolutely no concern for the lives of Native Americans to these people. We were nothing more than animals to the wretched bastards behind all of this. I hated them.

Every time someone pulled a sidearm, Dmitrius would send it into the Void. An officer kept yelling at them, but they were all ignoring him and panicking. While the solders tried to get their shit together, I managed to single out each remaining truck and send them into the Void, while leaving the living creatures inside of the vehicles here in this world. They all fell to the ground in terrified confusion.

Victor was among them. His closely cut white hair and emerald green eyes were almost shocking to see after so many years. '*Ah, my dear friend.*' With my telekinesis, I gave him a hug since I knew it'd not be that day that I got to give him a real embrace. Oh, and Marci…Yes, I'd get to see Marcello soon, too. How I'd missed her.

I turned slightly to the mass of soldiers and froze them where they stood—or panicked, as it were. Dmitrius and I calmly walked through them, knowing they'd not move an inch until I allowed it.

When we reached the man in charge of this little field trip, I held him up in the air by his throat. Without using my hands. "What gives you the right?" I demanded.

He'd actually not expected that. He didn't know how to answer, not that he could have if he'd wanted to. I held him up in the air for another minute, until he was about to pass out, and then I set him back on the ground.

He stumbled backward and gulped for air while he bent over and grasped his throat. His answer was starting to form in his mind, but he'd not clarified it yet. Something about curiosity.

I grabbed him by his hair to stand him up straight. "Haven't you ever heard?" I hissed in his face. "Curiosity killed the cat."

"But perseverance brought him back," he gasped.

I released him in disgust and turned slightly to examine the others who stood by, many terrified but calm. It was a mild shock to see more people than I'd expected, but I kept my surprise to myself.

"What do you think I am? Some creature for your dissection? I can assure you that I am not." I sighed and looked away from them in disgust.

Many of them thought that the wings were just some odd mutation of the shapeshifter genes. They wanted DNA from all of the winged women and DNA from any shifters related to them.

"You people are perverse. And perversely curious about things that have nothing to do with you and could in no way be of any use to you. So why even bother with it?"

I wondered while I inspected them more closely. It finally struck me—when I tried to peek into each individual mind—they were demons.

CHAPTER 54

Not all of them were demons incarnated, but several of them were. Nine, actually, and they were among the strongest encouragers of our dissection. I almost shivered and Victor nearly jumped in shock. They didn't have all of our powers and they couldn't connect to our minds, but we couldn't read theirs, either.

They knew what they were and what they were doing. They knew who I was. I could see it in the way that they appraised me and Dmitrius. I quickly searched their features for signs of familiarity and found none.

Memories of the menacing green eyes with blue flecks flashed through my mind. I studied their eye colors and saw none of them were the eyes which I'd dreamed of when I was still mortal.

They also avoided staring right into my eyes so that I couldn't see deep into theirs yet. But yes, they knew all about themselves. Otherwise, their thoughts would have been just as clear as the humans' thoughts were.

Inside of our minds, I apologized to Dmitrius and Victor for failing to take into account the fact that demons and their choices were a blind spot for me. They forgave me without question.

"You *will* come with us, Hope," one of them said after a moment of my appraisal.

I looked him right in the eyes and knew then who he was. "Peartix," I gasped.

"Pete," he said with a cocky smirk.

"Go fuck yourself," I said breathlessly, but with conviction, my fists clenched at my sides.

He chuckled and took a step toward me. "Now, now."

I growled and stopped him in his tracks.

"Hear me out," he said soothingly. He easily accepted his frozen feet and held out his open palms to me in a gesture of peace.

"Demon," I spat at him.

"Weakling," one of the others muttered under his breath. I met his eyes and also knew him right away.

"Larmont," I growled.

"His name is Larry," a shrill voice chirped from the rear of the group. "I'm Suzi."

"Suzarmi," I gasped. The last anyone knew, she had not incarnated in over 20,000 years.

She smirked at me when she saw my brief flash of shock. "I've got something for you, bitch," she said so softly that only Dmitrius and I could hear her. She opened her mind just enough for us to see a flash of an Immutable Blade.

I barked out a laugh and I pushed two images into their traitorous minds. The first was when Dmitrius had slashed my cheeks open. He blushed with shame, turning his face away. The second was when Deema had buried the Blade in my forehead.

"Do I appear to be scarred to you?" I snapped.

"Shut up, all of you!" The demand came from the mortal soul who I'd accosted. "What the hell is going on here? Why is she answering your thoughts? Shield your minds, morons!"

"I answer their words," I shouted back at him. "The words they speak so softly that you can't hear them because they wish for you to not know that they know me. That I know them." I met the eyes of the others and whispered their names. "Pontier, Onrai, Poulierre, Saulierre, Boltuer, Tchorgom. I'll kill you all."

"Terry, Henry, Lynn, Sal, Bob, and Tom," Suzi corrected me with a smirk.

I lunged at her. "You're first, bitch," I hissed.

She flinched in fear, and I flashed her a cruel grin.

"Righteous, my ass," she grumbled, nervously brushing dust from her pant legs.

"Easy, love," Dmitrius whispered, touching my shoulder softly. "Suza," he said with a nod toward her. "Are you in charge of these Others?"

"Suzi," she corrected, smiling seductively. "And yes, you know I would be."

"I'm in charge," the officer barked. "You're nothing here, Suzi. A glorified gopher."

"Shut up," I grumbled. I sealed his lips with my telekinesis. "And you—cut the shit," I snarled at Suza when she batted her eyes at Dmitrius again.

Victor stood apart from the rest, his mouth gaping open while he watched the demons. "Impossible," he muttered. "Suza, Tchor, Saul, Onrai, Ponti, Poli, Boltuer, Larmont, Peartix. All this time you knew and you worked to subvert me?"

"Of course," Suza said while sneered at him. "What else would we do but try to ruin your party?"

I latched onto Marcello's mind and called her to us. We needed all the help we could get. She was at home, preparing a salad for lunch. She felt me and saw what I saw, then scanned Victor and Dmitrius. Marci dropped her bowl on the floor and her salad scattered.

She'd not yet claimed her immortal body and thus

could not travel through the Void on her own. In fact, if she did travel through the Void, she'd be forced to shed her mortal body and take on her angelic form. She dithered for only a second before she and Victor came to the same decision at the same time. I was to come get her and Dmitrius was to take Vic to the mountain in Tibet.

My angelic lover was instantly at Victor's side. When Dmitrius took him into his arms, Vic met Suza's eyes and told her to rot in Hell before they slipped into the Void.

Suza peered at me and smirked in victory. "Go ahead and run away. It's all you cowards are good at—running from fights, from confrontation. Can't even stand up for yourselves," she said while she sneered at me.

"I fight every day," I replied in a cool, even tone. "And regrouping isn't running. Gathering others isn't running—it's leveling the playing field. You play your games in your powerless, mortal body. I'll be back for you, Suzarmi. You and all your little troublemakers."

She glared at me viciously as she whipped out a Blade. I was momentarily stunned when she threw it at my heart. She would've hit me, too, if I hadn't been spending so much time focusing on my telekinesis and its use with my own Immutable Blade. I stopped the Blade within an arm's reach of my chest. I snatched her Blade from the air with my hand and the sheath from her back with my mind. The other eight all reached to draw their Blades from their backs.

"Thanks bunches," I said before I blew her a kiss and escaped into the Void, one Immutable Blade richer.

CHAPTER 55

How was I to know?" Victor erupted as he spread his wings for the first time in decades. He stretched and flexed them, as if relishing in the feel of them while simultaneously hating himself for not seeing the truth sooner.

"You could not," Marci comforted him while she stretched her wings in a similar manner.

"I agree," Dmitrius chimed in as I handed him our new Immutable Blade. "They look nothing like they've chosen to in the past," he continued. "They are not at all like their former bodies before the Fall."

"Exactly," I agreed. "I didn't even recognize them until they spoke, and I met their eyes. Actually, I didn't know who they were until they wanted me to know," I realized.

"We must return," Dmitrius asserted.

We all agreed and joined hands before we jolted through the Void and back to my people's reservation.

Since the invaders were on foot, they had not made it far. Without weapons, they were of little threat to the few houses they passed on the outskirts of town.

"We're not leaving without you," Suza screeched at me after we all exited the Void.

"Victor? Marci? What the fuck?" his boss exclaimed, taking in their wings.

"Yeah, Mike. I quit. I'm joining Hope to defend her people. Half your staff are demons. I doubt they'll let you live to tell this tale," Victor replied to the shocked mortal. "Now shut up and stay out of this," he added gently.

"Always the tender heart," Suza sneered when he froze her in her tracks. We all froze the rest of the group as well.

"It doesn't matter," Saul said with a leering grin.

"We'll not leave here empty handed, even if we must leave here dead," Tchor said with a wicked smile. He let me have a peek at his mind and I saw a helicopter landing in my backyard.

I immediately checked in on my brother and saw him locking himself inside the hidden room along with our nephew. '*We're safe,*' he thought once he felt me in his mind. '*Only Walter is left running loose in the house.*'

Good. I grinned back at Suza and I pinned all of the demons' arms to their sides.

"I don't know what you're so happy about, cunt," she chirped. "We're getting you, even if we have to kill you."

I couldn't help it. I barked a laugh at her, startling some of the bitch off her face. "Are you really this stupid, Suzarmi? On our first encounter, you reveal who you are. Then, time after time, you tell me your plans." I shook my head and began to slowly pace. "You give up your exceptionally rare Blade in our first almost-fight. Just—Wow! I mean, how the hell did you all even *get* Immutable Blades? Did you get the last ones in Hell? How did you even get them into this plane of existence? You can't travel the Void in these mortal forms."

When I made another turn and had my back to her, I realized the truth of it. They'd been hidden in *this* world, right here on Earth, for tens of thousands of years. Back when the Blades were still being forged, they'd probably hidden some all over the world in hard to reach mountain caves.

"Ah." I turned back and paced toward her again. "It doesn't matter, I suppose. What does matter is that they're all mine now." Without any hesitation, I used my telekinesis to rip the sheaths from her eight companions' backs and belts.

Suza roared in outrage, and I flung the weapons into the empty hands of my companions. They each had two Immutable Blades and I had four. I nearly shivered at the thought of having four. It was absolutely unheard of, just as having two was a ridiculous notion.

"Micha'el would lose his mind," I said, chuckling softly, as I secured the last one to the small of my back.

"Perhaps we should call you Micha'el," Marcello said while she also laughed.

I grinned over at her before I turned my attention back to Suza. "I don't care if you take Sarkovski. You're actually doing me a favor by killing him."

Not that she'd be able to read it in me, but I knew that I was lying. Something had changed and the future had shifted again. Another angel employed by the government was going to help Walter create a plausible cover story about being lost in the desert so that he'd have a chance at returning to his normal life. I hoped it worked out for him in the end. He didn't deserve to die just for wanting to help us, despite his inability to actually do so. I'd realized that being white should not preclude him from caring about us, and if he'd been a Native American, I'd have never tried to turn him away to begin with.

She glanced down at her watch before she grinned again. "They touched down in your yard fifteen minutes ago. We have the only ones with telekinetic powers occupied *here*." Her smile grew more sinister. "We have your children by now," she said darkly.

I laughed at her. "I doubt that."

"Why? Because they fight?" She barked out a laugh. "I

bet they are not quite so impenetrable. At least, not like you are. I bet they *can* be tranquilized and by now they have been."

I broke her gaze. "I sent them away with the others," I said. Not being capable of truly loving any offspring she'd ever had, she took my look of weakness to mean that I was lying. She couldn't comprehend that I was merely upset over being away from them.

She sneered at me again. "Nice try, but I know you're lying. You sent the other women away several nights ago because we haven't seen them in days. We saw your daughters less than thirty-six hours ago."

"Yes," Dmitrius said with raised eyebrows. "Right before you had a few satellites explode and you lost sight of us for hours. That was the last time you saw her daughters."

"But we've heard them," Pontier objected in an almost nervous tone.

"We played tapes of their voices. Conversations we'd prerecorded during other times of your blindness," Dmitrius said matter-of-factly.

"Bullshit," Suza spat.

"How did you know we'd lost satellites? We heard you discussing it the other day like you didn't know..." Boltuer trailed off when he realized the answer to his own question.

"Because they blew them up," Poulierre grumbled after she came to the same conclusion.

"But they were fighting with each other when they exploded," Pontier objected.

"It was another cover," Saulierre said in a defeated tone. "They've been playing us ever since they knew they were being watched."

"At least I got to watch you fuck again," Tchorgom said in a lusty tone before he licked his lips and made a kissy face at me a few times. "How I'd missed seeing you in action."

I'd had enough and didn't want to hear another word come out of his degenerate mouth. I detested that soul—that demon—immensely. He used to be a Watcher before the Fall. Now he was a creeper. In most of his lives, he was some kind of sexual deviant.

I casually raised my hand and made a small horizontal gesture with my index finger. His perverted smile only had time to halfway turn to shock before his head fell from his body and he was dead. Blood spurted from his headless corpse and it toppled to the ground. A collective gasp came from the mortal men and women standing frozen in the road with us.

"You should have made him suffer," Marcello whispered while she incinerated his carcass.

"Oh, I'm sure I'll get to kill him again someday," I replied with a small smile.

All of the mortal souls were staring at us in absolute shock. A few had actually wet themselves and that made me feel bad. While the demons were taking a moment to realize just how badly they'd failed, I took the opportunity to try to comfort the poor humans.

'I'm sorry that things have gone so far off track from what you'd expected. I know you all must fear me even more now than you had before, but I will not harm you if your intent to harm me has changed. But these whom I know—They will die before your eyes.'

"Never liked most of them anyway," Mike grumbled.

I was unable to resist giving him a small smile before I turned back to Suza.

"Wait," she begged once I met her eyes.

"Why? So you can have another chance to move on me? So you can try to plan it better? Not likely, bitch."

I started the fires under them slowly. At first, they

didn't even realize that the soles of their boots were melting into pools on the pavement. They all just watched me, waiting for me to continue speaking. Then they did realize that their feet were hot. But, since we still kept them frozen with our powers, they could not lift their feet.

The tiny blue flames caught the laces of their boots before the leather really caught. By the time the tops of their socks caught fire, they were already screaming in pain and begging for mercy.

"Oh, but I thought I'd make you feel at home—like the fiery pits of Hell," I said innocently in reply to their pleas.

When the legs of their pants caught, the fire raced up their clothes and over their flesh like they'd been soaked in kerosene.

When Suza's hair caught fire, she stared right into my eyes and opened her mind to me for just a second before she purposely inhaled the flames and dropped dead. As her soulless body burned on the ground, I stood there stunned at the information she'd revealed to me.

CHAPTER 56

I mechanically turned to Dmitrius, my mouth gaping open. I was speechless. Then again, I didn't have to speak. He knew exactly how I felt by being connected to my mind.

"Baby," he said in a soft tone that said he could not be faulted for what she'd shown me. Oh, but he could be faulted. "No," he said in the same tone. "Hope, my one and only love. How could I—"

"Exactly," I cut him off in a choked voice. "How could you?" I turned away from him and the bloody tears spilled over onto my cheeks. I slipped into the Void to run away from him.

I writhed in agony as I dove through the Void. My soulmate had bedded a demon. I couldn't believe he'd done that to me. I pulled myself out of the Void in Australia and collapsed underneath a eucalyptus tree, sobbing into the crook of my arm. It took only a few moments before Dmitrius appeared beside me and crouched down.

"My love," he said tearfully.

"Go away," I blubbered. I pulled away from his hand that was reaching for my shoulder.

"Please," he begged.

I slipped back into the Void and reappeared in the safe room in my house.

"Hope!" Brian whispered in shock. "What are you doing here? They're still searching the house!"

Dmitrius stepped out of the Void at my side again. I glared at him before I cast my brother an apologetic look and went back into the Void.

I exited in Siberia, Brazil, Uruguay, Egypt, Japan, Iceland, India, and even Antarctica. He was always just a few seconds behind me. He also knew I was refusing to be inside of his mind.

"Why won't you go away?" I snapped at him when I finally exited the Void in my practice valley.

"Is that an order?" he asked me, tears of his own wetting his cheeks.

The thought of never seeing him again stopped me cold. I could not be with him right then, but I could not say the words in our language that would banish him.

The only time he'd ever purposely chosen another, which we'd both known was, in effect, cheating, I'd forgiven him by saying, "It's not like she was a demon." But she was. He'd bedded Suza in a life where he'd allowed himself to be born with some of his knowledge. And now that I knew the key to that lock on his mind—Suza—I could see it all.

"But you can also see how sorry I am, how much it has tormented me over the millennia," he said in answer to my thoughts.

"Had you told me 40,000 years ago when it happened, we'd have been long past it by now," I whispered into the wind. "But, instead, you hid what you'd done." I loosed a quick, disbelieving sigh. "And now it comes to light, in these days when a choice must be made." I glanced at him over my shoulder, bloody tears still flowing from my eyes and dripping from my chin.

Dmitrius fell to his knees and he begged me, "Please."

"I even said—" I began, turning my face away and staring off in the distance.

"I know," he sobbed into his hands. "You gave me an opening without even realizing it, and I could not be brave enough to take it. I used a demon to compartmentalize my mind from you and all of the others of our kind."

"It is the only way to keep a secret," I said aloud as I remembered that truth.

He took to his feet again and strode forward. "But now you know. Now you have the key and you can see anything inside of me," he said desperately. "Please don't run," he cried when I cast a look at him over my shoulder. I could see in his mind that he read my expression as being a mixture of flighty, pensive, and pained.

He reached for my shoulder and I jerked away. "Don't touch me," I sobbed.

He stayed where he was and let his hand drop while I checked in on the invaders again.

The helicopters were leaving. They had Walter, along with a collection of samples they'd taken from my house. They had every hairbrush and toothbrush, and a number of feathers they'd found around the house. I sent my sight and influence into the helicopter that contained DNA of my family. When I found the giant box, I couldn't help but smile just a little as I carefully incinerated the contents to a small pile of ash. I made sure to quickly extinguish the fire so that there would be no smell of smoke to alert them of their loss.

I peeked in on Brian and found him exiting the safe room through a bookshelf. They were fine, so I skipped right out of the vision. I checked on Victor and Marcello. They were still working on calming the humans who were terrified of them and the events that had transpired.

While I was occupied, Dmitrius crept up beside me. I could feel him and was fully aware of his proximity, but I chose to ignore him while I watched Marci try to soothe a sobbing woman who shrank from the angel's touch.

Dmitrius brushed his wing against mine for just a second when he walked past me and turned to stand in front of me. I shuddered at the sudden flash of intense emotion that rushed through me during that brief connection. I automatically pulled away from Marcello's mind when Dmitrius's flooded into mine. His love and his sorrow were just so engulfing.

"My love," he whispered, his fingertips brushing down my cheek. Unable to help myself, I leaned into his hand and my eyes slid closed in contentment. His intense love for me was still reverberating throughout my mind and body. He took advantage of the opportunity to dart his wings forward and back again, making another quick connection to my own. I moaned and my knees felt a bit less stable than they always did. I melted into his hands as he pulled my face to his and kissed me. My arms slid around his waist while he continued to beat his wings forward and back against mine.

We were one, but we were not lost to time. It was a brilliant idea, really, but I knew he couldn't keep up the concentration to do it for very long. Soon, he'd forget to pull his wings back and we'd be trapped in our ecstasy for days or weeks before I remembered that I was mad at him and pulled away. By then I'd be burning with thirst and attack him again.

I stretched my wings out behind myself while I reached up behind him so that I could press the bases of his wings together. I was glad that it worked and made it so that he had trouble reaching mine with his.

"Please," I whispered against his lips. "Stop. We do not have time for this right now. I must protect my tribe."

'Can you ever forgive me?' he pleaded inside of my mind while he kissed me with fervor.

I sobbed once before my arms tightened around him and our kiss deepened. I would eventually. Someday, it would not cause me pain to think of this betrayal that was already 40,000 years old. Then again, the betrayal had, in a way, lasted for all that time, too. His answering sob almost made me feel guilty for the thought. Almost…

His arms tightened around me when the idea that I should pull away began to form in my mind. "Please," he begged. He managed to beat his wings against mine one more time.

A fresh sob broke in my chest. I turned my face from his and loosened my grip on him. I did not—could not—drop my arms yet, though. "We need to help Vic and Marci. This is not their fight." But once the words were out of my mouth, I knew that wasn't true. The truth came from where it always did recently—the minds of the millions of other angels.

My sorrow and anguish was brought to a sudden halt by the shock of the knowledge to which I now had access. My tears stopped flowing, and I leaned back sharply as I unwound my arms from my soulmate. I grabbed him by the shoulders and gave him a little shake to catch his attention. But he was already staring at me in shock, listening to the bigger view of things right along with me.

It *was* their fight. It was everyone's fight.

This wasn't just the collapse of one government. It was the collapse of all.

This wasn't just a war between men with a few angels as protectors. It was a war between Heaven and Hell.

Those nine were not the only demons who had their hands in this. It would end up going much further before we had any peace.

"We need to wrap this up," he whispered.

"Yes," I breathed. "I forgive you, but know that it will continue to hurt. We—" I turned to the northeast, where

Marci and Vic were still with the humans. "We've got bigger fish to fry. Things more important than some demon trying to subvert us. I do love you," I murmured before I kissed his soft lips.

"I love you, too," he replied, giving me a gentle squeeze. "Thank you."

"Come on, let's go." I released him and he caught my hand before we skimmed the Void to go help the others.

"It's going to be a long year," Marci muttered when we appeared beside her.

"I know," Dmitrius agreed as he began to make a plan for how to deal with these frightened people.

Victor used his telekinesis to slap my soulmate. Marci mirrored him at the same moment so that Dmitrius's head didn't turn. They both agreed—Shame on him. But there wasn't really time for them to properly scold him.

He agreed that now was not the time for this. These people were stranded with no vehicles, no food or water, no communication with their superiors, and they would not let us help them. If we'd let them, they'd have run away. But then they would have died in the desert, and we couldn't allow that. They were just hysterical, though some appeared to be slipping into shock rather than madness.

EPILOGUE

When Deema and our kids returned home a week later, I was in an emotional funk. My time alone with Dmitrius had been wonderful. I also knew that Deema could not have helped near as much as my angel had. I felt guilty for being so happy that it was the angel and not the vampire who had stood beside me.

But I'd also missed Deema considerably. I felt like I had countless things to tell him about what had happened and what he'd missed. I ran right into his arms when they landed in the backyard and squeezed him in a tight hug.

"I'm so sorry," Deema whispered when he returned my embrace.

"For what?"

"I promised you before that I'd be here when they invaded. I wasn't."

I shrugged halfheartedly. "Doesn't really matter. *You* couldn't have done anything to help this time."

I felt him wince at my slight inflection. Without saying anything to anyone, I gripped him tightly and pushed off into the air. We soon landed in my valley for a bit of privacy.

"I'm sorry that all I do is hurt you. You don't have to leave next time. When they come again, everyone stays," I told him seriously while I studied his eyes.

"And everyone fights," he said with a hard smile and clenched fists.

"Yes," I said softly before I glanced away. "Everyone fights. The shifters, the mortal winged women, and our kids."

He tried to soothe me and pulled my head against his chest. "It'll be okay."

"You don't know that," I breathed. A single bloody tear made a path down my cheek.

He leaned back just a bit. "And do you?"

"No," I whispered. I turned my head away from him so he wouldn't see the tear. "I know nothing. The demons have pretty much nullified my ability to see the future."

He sputtered in shock for a second before I got him to listen to me again. I spent over a day explaining to him all that had happened and the ramifications we'd thought of so far.

Things were not looking pretty and they were about to get a whole lot uglier.

About the Author

Janelle Samara lives in Kansas City, Missouri, with her husband. When she's not busy writing, her favorite pastimes include devouring classic books on her tablet, growing organic vegetables, and creating new recipes for her family. When she needs to get out of the house, she has many interests, ranging from watching ballet to fishing with her brothers.

www.ingramcontent.com/pod-product-compliance
Lightning Source LLC
Chambersburg PA
CBHW070535260626
47161CB00002B/399